cvlg

The
INNKEEPER'S
Bride

Center Point
Large Print

Also by Kathleen Fuller and available from
Center Point Large Print:

A Love Made New
A Reluctant Bride
An Unbroken Heart
The Farmers' Bride
The Promise of a Letter
The Teacher's Bride
Words from the Heart
Written in Love

The INNKEEPER'S *Bride*

Amish Brides of Birch Creek

Kathleen Fuller

CENTER POINT LARGE PRINT
THORNDIKE, MAINE

This Center Point Large Print edition
is published in the year 2020 by arrangement with
Zondervan.

The text of this Large Print edition is unabridged.
In other aspects, this book may vary
from the original edition.
Printed in the United States of America
on permanent paper.
Set in 16-point Times New Roman type.

ISBN: 978-1-64358-530-7

The Library of Congress has cataloged this record
under Library of Congress Control Number: 2019954769

To James. I love you.

Glossary

ab im kopp: crazy, crazy in the head
bruder: brother
bu: boy
daed: father
danki: thank you
Dietsch: Amish language
dochder: daughter
familye: family
frau: woman, Mrs.
geh: go
grossmammi/grossmutter: grandmother
grosskinner: grandchildren
grossvatter: grandfather
gut: good
gute nacht: good night
haus: house
kaffee: coffee
kapp: white hat worn by Amish women
kinner: children
maedel: girl/young woman
mamm: mom
mann: Amish man
mei: my
mutter: mother
nee: no
nix: nothing

schee: pretty/handsome
seltsam: weird
sohn: son
vatter: father
ya: yes
yer/yers: your/yours
yerself: yourself

Chapter 1

Selah Ropp leaned against a sheltering oak tree in the backyard of the Detweiler place and took a sip of hot chocolate. As she watched adults and children mingling in celebration of Martha and Seth Yoder's marriage, laughter filled the crisp November air, and a group of young adults had just started a rousing game of volleyball nearby. The wedding ceremony had been lovely and touching, and everyone's happiness was contagious. *Almost.*

She clung to the Styrofoam cup as if the hot chocolate was the one thing keeping her nerves at bay. Conflicting emotions weren't exactly new to her, but she was getting better at managing them. At least she hoped she was.

"Selah!"

She looked up to see Martha heading toward her with a grin of wedded bliss. When she reached Selah, she hugged her. "I'm so glad you're here," she said.

"I wouldn't miss *yer* wedding for anything." She gave her a smile—a genuine one. When Martha had asked her to be her maid of honor, she hadn't hesitated to say yes. She was the only real friend Selah had made in Birch Creek when she moved here the first time, almost two years ago, but not

9

because the community wasn't friendly. Her lack of friends was entirely her fault.

"I'm not just talking about the wedding." Martha squeezed her hand. "I'm glad you decided to move back." Her smile dimmed a little, and concern entered her blue eyes. "Are you?"

She nodded, although she wasn't being completely honest. Doubts had plagued her ever since she'd made her decision to return. But today wasn't about her feelings. "I'm thrilled for you and Seth."

"We're blessed with happiness." Martha beamed again. "I want you to be happy, too, Selah."

So do I.

"Are you going to play volleyball?"

Selah glanced at the game. She recognized all the players—Seth's brother Ira Yoder, barrel-chested and well over six feet tall, standing next to a stout, tomboyish-looking girl named Nina Stoll. Selah's sister-in-law, Ruby, was playing, too, but not Christian. Her brother was a disaster when it came to athletics. Of course numerous Bontrager men were on both teams, their ages varying from early teens to early twenties. The Bontrager family had so many members they could form two volleyball teams by themselves.

She shook her head. "Not this time."

Martha nodded, and Selah knew her friend wouldn't push her to join the group. "I better *geh* see to Seth."

Seth seemed fine talking to Andrew Beiler and Sol Troyer by the barn, but Selah wasn't going to point that out. She smiled again as Martha hurried to her husband's side.

She stayed by the grand oak tree, an outsider looking in. She closed her eyes for a few moments, pushing aside her gray thoughts, reminding herself that she needed to focus on the positive— Martha's happiness, the beautiful fall day, the start of a new life after she'd made so many mistakes. When she opened her eyes, to her surprise Cevilla Schlabach was standing directly in front of her.

"Thought you'd fallen asleep there for a moment." The bold octogenarian, blunt as ever, tapped her cane on the soft grass.

Selah shook her head. "Just thinking, that's all."

Cevilla moved to stand next to her. "How are you settling in with *yer bruder* and sister-in-law?"

"*Gut*." This time she was being honest. She'd lived with Christian when they first moved here from New York, after he'd accepted the teaching job at the Birch Creek school. More than a little tension had been between them, and again, that was her fault. But their relationship was different now. She was different. "I've been busy helping Martha with the wedding."

"Ah, weddings. I've been to *mei* fair share of them over the years. Never a bride, though. Come to think of it, I haven't been a bridesmaid too often, either."

"Does that bother you?"

"The bridesmaid stuff? *Nee.* I don't let things like that get to me."

"I mean . . ." She didn't know Cevilla that well, and she wasn't sure if she should ask such a personal question. But Cevilla was exactly the right person to talk to about this.

"Mean what?"

"Does it bother you that you're single?"

An odd look passed over Cevilla's face for a second, but then she shook her head. "Absolutely not. Singleness has its advantages, you know. You're responsible for only *yerself*, and you don't have to ask someone else their opinion before you make a decision. I enjoy *mei* privacy, and I was never too keen on little *kinner*. I like them after they grow up."

"Then you don't feel like you've missed out on anything?"

Cevilla tilted her head and looked at her. "The Lord is all I need. He always has been. So *nee*, I don't feel like I've missed out on anything."

But Selah caught Cevilla's gaze shifting to Richard, her friend and neighbor, who was seated at a table with Martha's and Seth's parents, engaged in what looked like lively conversation. She knew even less about Richard, except that he and Cevilla were special friends. Selah wouldn't pry into Cevilla's business about that.

She felt Cevilla's hand on hers and then met

the woman's gaze. Deep wrinkles etched her face, but her pale-blue eyes were bright and clear. "Life never goes like we plan. God usually has something better in store for us even if we don't know we needed or wanted it." She patted Selah's hand. "Focus on that instead of regrets."

An unexpected lump formed in Selah's throat. Cevilla smiled, and then she hobbled toward Richard. She was right, of course. Her counselor back home in New York, Anne, had been drilling basically the same concept into Selah during their therapy sessions. Some days she believed it, other days she didn't.

She brought the Styrofoam cup to her lips. *Here's to conflicting emotions.*

Whack! Something had slammed into the side of her head, knocking her off balance. Hot chocolate splashed all over her hands and down the front of her navy-blue coat.

"Oh *nee*!"

She shook out her hand as Levi Stoll sprinted toward her. He pushed up his silver-rimmed glasses, his eyes filled with concern. "Are you okay?" he asked, peering at her. "Ira doesn't know his own strength when it comes to hitting a volleyball."

"Sorry!" Ira waved at her from the other side of the net.

"I'm all right." She held the cup out in front of her. Fortunately her skin had been cold and the chocolate lukewarm, so she didn't get burned. Her head throbbed in the spot where the volleyball hit, though. "But I might have a bit of a headache later on."

"I'll run and get some ice—"

"That's okay." She didn't want him making a fuss and drawing attention to her. "*Mei* head's pretty hard."

He chuckled a little, and then he said, "It won't take but a minute to get an ice pack."

"I'm fine." She brushed at her coat, which wasn't too wet.

He bent down and picked up the ball, tucking it under his arm. "Selah, right?" At her nod, he said, "I don't think we've formerly met. I'm—"

"Levi Stoll." She'd seen him at church last Sunday, two days after she arrived from New York. Ruby had pointed out all the people who'd moved to Birch Creek while Selah was away. She'd seen quite a few new faces.

His brow shot up. "I'm impressed you remembered."

"I'm pretty *gut* with names." She switched the cup to her other hand.

"Here." Levi reached into his pocket and pulled out a handkerchief. As he handed it to her, he said, "Want to join in?" He tilted his head toward the volleyball net, where the players were now milling around.

Oddly enough, she was suddenly tempted. Then

14

her nerves got the best of her. Only a few people in Birch Creek knew about her past, and only three were privy to her diagnosis—clinical depression. The thought of that was enough to change her mind. She didn't want to put herself out there. "Not today."

"Maybe next time." He jogged backward. "You're missing a *gut* game, though." He tossed the ball into the air, caught it, and then spun around and hurried back to the other players.

She dabbed at her coat with Levi's handkerchief and then put it in her pocket before taking in a deep breath to calm her mind. Over the past year and a half, she'd learned to turn to God when she was confused and anxious, and she needed him right now. *I know I haven't done much listening in the past, Lord, but I'm listening now.*

After his encounter with Selah, Levi struggled to focus on the rest of the volleyball game. He kept looking over his shoulder to check on her, and in the process he, too, got smacked with the volleyball—twice. The second impact smarted a little, which reminded him of her getting hit with the ball. He peeked over his shoulder again in time to see her walk away. She'd insisted she was fine, but something in her eyes had told him she wasn't—at least not completely. He had no idea why he'd picked up on that. Or maybe he was reading too much into what he'd seen.

"Levi!" Nina hollered. "Look up!"

He did, just in time to see the ball zoom toward him. He quickly spiked the ball over the net. He might not be as tall as Ira Yoder or as strong as Zeb and Zeke Bontrager, but he could jump like a frog, and his aim was true. Devon, Zeb and Zeke's brother, dove for the ball and missed.

"That's the game." Nina jumped up and down but then stopped herself, smoothing out her skirt. His sister had changed for the better since they'd moved here almost a year ago. Levi guessed it had to do with her platonic relationship with Ira—if that's what it was. The two of them insisted they were only friends, but Levi suspected something more was between them. So did his grandmother, even though they hadn't talked about it. *Grossmutter* always assumed any male within a five-mile radius was a possible suitor for her granddaughter. Nina wasn't her only target, though. She'd kept a hawk's eye out for potential spouses for him for years, and that hadn't changed when they arrived in Birch Creek.

When they first moved here, she'd tried to set him up with Martha and Nina with Seth. Then there was the matchmaking scheme Cevilla had come up with to get Martha and Seth together. That hadn't worked, but Martha and Seth fell for each other anyway—on their own. Thinking about all those shenanigans made his head swim. Hopefully both women had realized they should keep their noses out of other people's romantic business. His grandmother had said as much, but Levi didn't hold much hope that she had learned her lesson. He'd yet to meet anyone as stubborn as Delilah Stoll.

That gave him pause. Would Selah be in *Grossmutter*'s crosshairs? If so, he needed to nip that idea in the bud.

"Ready for another game?" he asked. But the other players were dispersing, the men predictably heading toward the food table. "Guess not," he mumbled, a little disappointed. He and his family had spent the past year transforming the large English house they'd bought into a small inn and building a house behind it for them to live in. In two weeks they would open for business, but right now he appreciated the respite from work the Yoder wedding provided. He hadn't spent much time at social events, something he'd always enjoyed. He was usually so tired by Sunday that he had only enough energy for church.

Although a big, delicious meal had been served after the wedding ceremony, Levi could use a snack. He was making his way to the refreshment table, which was full of cookies, cakes, homemade pretzels, chocolate candy, and other goodies, when he heard his grandmother call his name. He pushed up his glasses and turned around to see her bustling toward him. Delilah Stoll never simply walked. She was a whirlwind, and now was no exception. He looked longingly at a tray of chocolate chip cookies, but then he went to meet her.

"Wasn't the wedding wonderful?" *Grossmammi* looked up at him, smiling so wide her plump, rosy cheeks touched the bottom edge of her glasses.

Uh-oh. He recognized the gleam in her eyes. "*Nee*," he said, his voice firm.

Her brown eyes widened with fake innocence. "Levi Stoll, how can you say such a thing?"

"The wedding was just fine. Whatever tom-fooleries you're up to are not."

"Tomfooleries?" She put her plump hand over her heart. "I have *nee* idea what you're talking about."

"Then you haven't met Selah yet?" Maybe he had misinterpreted that gleam. Maybe she was just that enamored with Seth and Martha's wedding, which was a typical ceremony in his opinion. He'd been to more than a few.

"Of course I have." The gleam intensified. "Isn't she a lovely *maedel*? Her *bruder* is the schoolteacher, you know."

"*Ya*, I know." His grandmother was hung up on family connections. Seth's father, Freemont, was the bishop, and that was one reason she'd been keen on Nina and Seth getting together. She still held out hope since Ira was Seth's brother.

"Intelligence is a *gut* trait to have, Levi."

"I'm all set, then, since I'm the smartest *gross-sohn* you have."

"You're *mei* only *grosssohn*." She gave him a light pat on the arm and then smiled. "But I mean it's a *gut* trait in a future *frau*—"

"I'm not interested."

"Why not? I was already married by *yer* age, and so was *yer vatter*. The lack of interest you and Nina have in getting married is baffling. Don't you want a *frau* and a *familye*?"

"Possibly."

"Possibly?" Her eyes widened again, looking like stupefied saucers behind her glasses.

"I think *Daed*'s calling me," he said, slipping past her.

"I don't hear him—"

"See you later," Levi called out. He hurried away before his grandmother selected his wedding date. Maybe he should tell her why he was opposed to her constant pressure to get married—besides the annoyance factor. He believed being single wasn't the worst fate in the world. He could be satisfied being single for the rest of his life. He was sure of that.

Then there was the unusual lack of available females in Birch Creek—as in zero, since the only young single woman had been Nina. And he wasn't going to go after the first single woman who moved to the community, namely, Selah, just because she wasn't taken. If he were to marry, it would be to the right woman. He would make his own decision, and his grandmother and everyone else would have to stay out of it.

But even if he explained all that to his grandmother, and he wasn't eager to do that, he doubted she'd listen. When Delilah Stoll made up her mind, it was set. Better to just dodge her attempts than to try to convince her to give up the goal altogether.

With quick steps, he walked to the front yard, giving him enough separation from his grandmother. Then he saw Selah walking down the driveway. Was she leaving? Christian and Ruby were still here, and it was only midafternoon. Plus, she was Martha's maid of honor, so he figured she'd be one of the last to leave. Curious, he jogged toward her, catching up to her as she stepped onto the asphalt road. "Heading home already?"

She stopped and turned, her expression guarded. "*Ya.*"

"Why?" A better question would be why he was being so nosy.

Her eyes narrowed. "Because I'm ready to *geh.*"

Her tone was testy, and he didn't blame her. He held up his hands. "Sorry. I didn't mean to bother you."

"You're not bothering me." She glanced down. "I was just surprised anyone noticed I was missing."

"I'm sure Martha will."

"She knows I'm leaving."

"I hope you're not leaving because of *yer* headache."

A flash of surprise crossed her features. "Oh, *nee. Mei* head is fine."

"*Gut.*" He paused, the silence growing awkward between them. "Well, I'll let you be on *yer* way."

She nodded and then left.

He watched her for a moment before returning to the reception. He had to admit she was pretty. Very pretty. Dark-brown hair, blue eyes, soft-looking skin. But he'd seen pretty girls before. Not one who was so aloof, though. It was as if Selah had a three-foot invisible fence around her, and if someone got too close, they'd get shocked. For some reason, that both bothered and intrigued him.

Levi shook his head. Intrigue didn't equal interest. Still, as he headed back to the refreshment table, he couldn't help but turn around and check on her one more time.

"I've been thinking about hosting a sister gathering this spring." Cevilla Schlabach placed a piece of golden french toast on Richard Johnson's plate and then set the platter on the table in her tiny but comfortable kitchen.

Richard lifted one gray eyebrow. "You don't have any sisters."

She handed him the syrup. "I have my sisters

here in the community. We're not related by blood, but we are sisters in Christ."

"And what would you do during this gathering?"

"Quilting, crocheting, knitting. Needlepointers are welcome too. I'm all about inclusivity."

"Is *needlepointers* a word?" He flipped open the lid of the syrup bottle.

"It is now." She sat down across from him.

"What about stamp collectors? Are they invited?"

She peered at him over her glasses. "If they're female, then *ya*. Yes." She was careful to speak only English with Richard, but occasionally she slipped into *Dietsch*.

"Doesn't sound all that inclusive to me."

"Are you saying your feelings are hurt?" Her mouth twitched.

"Stamp collecting is a solitary endeavor anyway, so no. I'm not." He smiled and winked before pouring syrup over his toast. Sugar-free, of course. During their eighteen months together as *friends,* she'd been mindful of his dietary needs, and according to his last checkup, he had excellent laboratory numbers. He'd moved here from California, but he still insisted on seeing his doctor in LA. Those visits also allowed him to spend time with his daughter, Sharon, and granddaughter, Meghan. Meghan had been out to visit only once since she'd accompanied Richard when he showed up on Cevilla's doorstep after decades of their being apart.

Little had she known that day that her future, which she had always thought was set in concrete in her dotage, would change forever.

He set the syrup down on the table. "Shall we pray?"

Cevilla bowed her head for silent prayer, and as usual, not only did she thank God for the food and ask him to bless it, but she prayed for Meghan and Sharon and a good dose of patience. Lately she'd needed patience more than ever. To the rest of the community—except for her nephew, Noah, and his wife, Ivy—she and Richard were just friends. But there was more between them than that. Respect, understanding, and yes, romantic love.

But roadblocks were in the way, not the least of which that if they were to marry, Richard would have to join the Amish church. But he hadn't decided about that yet. He would also be leaving his family behind in California—for good except for visits. She knew he talked to Meghan as much as possible. The two were very close. But they hadn't talked recently, because she was so busy trying to get her interior design business off the ground.

Then there was his daughter, Sharon, Meghan's mother, whom he rarely talked about. Cevilla had the impression that she didn't approve of his moving to Birch Creek, and she hadn't come to visit him since he'd left LA. One thing Cevilla did know—the woman refused to talk to her.

She'd called her more than once, but she always got voice mail, and Sharon never returned her messages.

All she could do was put the situation in God's hands. *Yer will be done.*

She opened her eyes, and then she picked up a tiny dish with a bit of powdered sugar in it and sprinkled it over her toast.

"I think your idea of a gathering is a good one." Richard took a sip of orange juice. "What made you think of it?"

"In Iowa, we used to get together all the time for quilting bees. I didn't care for quilting, so I always took my crochet. I enjoyed the company. But when I moved here, social gatherings were few and far between. That had taken some getting used to. Actually I'm not sure I was ever really used to it."

"From my understanding of the Amish, socializing is extremely important."

"It is."

"Then why wasn't it here? Because of the bishop?"

Early on she'd told him about Emmanuel Troyer, the bishop who started the Birch Creek community more than twenty years ago. Emmanuel had been a greedy man, and not until he left had Cevilla realized how much of a pall he'd cast over Birch Creek. But even though she hadn't understood why, the Lord had led her here years ago, and

24

she'd obeyed. Birch Creek, for all its past and present faults, was her home, and she couldn't imagine living anywhere else.

"I'm not sure it was only because of Emmanuel," she said, picking up her fork. "The community never felt truly cohesive until Freemont became the bishop. When Emmanuel left, several families moved away too. Those of us who stayed have grown closer."

He nodded and took a bite of his french toast. After he swallowed, he said, "I've always admired the closeness of the Amish communities. Back in Los Angeles and in other large cities in general, a lot of people are around, but one can still feel isolated." He gave Cevilla a warm smile. "Remember how close we all were in Arnold City?"

She nodded, thinking back to the small Pennsylvania city where she and Richard had spent their formative years. "You could always count on your neighbor, whether he was next door or three streets over."

"The milkman still delivered milk, televisions were rare, and we had a parade for every holiday." He sighed. "I miss that."

"Well, we don't do parades here," she said softly. "But when there's a need, you can count on anyone in Birch Creek to lend a hand."

"I know."

Her heart skipped. Was he trying to tell her something else? Had he *finally* decided? He'd moved to Birch Creek from California more than a year ago, and he was practically a member of the community already. All he needed to do was get baptized. That was no small thing, but they were both in their eighties, and time was a precious commodity. She could practically hear it ticking away as she held her breath while he held her gaze. Then he dipped another piece of toast into the puddled syrup on his plate without saying anything else.

Her breath rushed out like a popped balloon. *Patience, remember? I asked for patience. It's not exactly* mei *virtue.* But despite her prayers, she wished the man would stop dragging his feet. "Wasn't that a lovely wedding last week?" she said, hoping to draw him into a conversation that was well past due.

"Um-hum." He finished his french toast and then picked up the copy of the local paper he'd brought with him this morning.

Okay, that didn't work. She tried a different tack. "Have you talked to Sharon and Meghan recently?"

Richard nodded. "Meghan's doing well. Sharon . . . well, she's Sharon." He unfolded the paper.

"What does that mean?"

He glanced up at her before looking over the front page. "My daughter is a bit stubborn." He put the newspaper in front of his face.

Cevilla lightly tapped her finger on the table.

She had half a mind to call the woman and ask her what her problem was—if she would even answer her phone. But Richard wouldn't like that. If only he were more willing to talk about what had happened between them. He talked to her about everything else—his late wife, Nancy, his flourishing businesses in California, Meghan, the past . . . Very little about the future, though. And even though she wanted to force him to open up about both Sharon and his thoughts on their future, she couldn't bring herself to do that. She let out a long sigh.

He pulled down a corner of the paper and peered at her. "You all right?"

"Dandy," she said, forcing a smile. "Everything's dandy."

Richard grinned and went back to reading the paper. *Conversation closed.*

The next morning, Cevilla dressed for church and waited for Noah and Ivy to pick her up in their buggy. While she enjoyed having company on the way to church, she missed driving her own horse and buggy. That part of her independence had been hard to give up.

Richard had told her last night that he was attending the Mennonite church in Barton again. When Noah and Ivy arrived and she stepped onto the front porch, she glanced at the house he'd built next door when he moved to Birch Creek. She frowned. His car was gone.

27

A short while later they arrived at the Chupp farm, where the service was being held, and she entered their expansive barn. She pushed Richard out of her mind and settled in for worship, glancing around like she usually did before the service started. Couples and children were everywhere, and several young, single men sat next to one another. Most of them were from the Bontrager family. Newly married Seth, along with his brothers, Ira and Judah, sat behind them.

Selah came in behind her brother, Christian, and sister-in-law, Ruby. Cevilla thought about her conversation with Selah at Martha's wedding. She hadn't been completely truthful with the young woman, a fact that had pricked her conscience. Yes, God was all she needed, she did live a contented life, and any regrets she had she'd taken to the Lord. But it did bother her that she was single, something she hadn't felt until she'd fallen in love with Richard.

Bother. There she was again, thinking about him. She turned her focus to the front of the barn and waited for the singing to start. Once the service was in full swing, her every thought and feeling was turned toward the Lord.

Following the service, Cevilla had spent some time visiting with friends before Noah and Ivy approached her. She noticed Noah's pale complexion, which alarmed her. "Are you all right?" she asked when he stopped in front of her.

He nodded at the same time Ivy shook her head. "*Nee*, he's not. He hasn't been feeling too well this morning," she said. "But he insisted on coming to church."

"I'm fine," he said, but his normally strong voice lacked its usual punch.

"We need to *geh* straight home," Ivy said to Cevilla.

"Is it the Meniere's?" she asked, turning to Noah.

"*Ya*," he said, admitting the truth quietly.

Her heart went out to her nephew. His disease affected his hearing enough that he had to wear hearing aids, and despite the medication he was on, he sometimes still had bouts of vertigo and nausea. The illness had also taken away his ability to be an auctioneer, a profession he'd loved. But that hadn't stopped him from having another career, one he shared with Ivy. Their antiques store was thriving in Barton.

Ivy reached for his hand and gave it a quick squeeze, and then she looked at Cevilla. "I'm sorry we're not staying for the meal."

"That's fine." She waved her hand. "I'm a little tired myself. And if I wanted to stay, I wouldn't have a problem finding a ride."

"We'll get the buggy," Ivy said.

A short while later, with Ivy driving the buggy, she and Noah dropped Cevilla off at home. She didn't invite them inside, as she might have if Noah was feeling like himself. She knew he would try to sleep off his symptoms once home. Come to think of it, a nap sounded nice right now. She bid her family good-bye and then glanced at the empty space in Richard's driveway where he usually parked his car. He must still be at the Mennonite church. What—or *who*—drew him there? She banged the end of her cane on the porch before going inside.

She tamped down the unexpected spike of jealousy. She'd never been a jealous woman. Then again, she'd never had reason to be.

"Poppycock!" she exclaimed to the empty house. Then she removed her coat and black bonnet and placed them on pegs near the front door. "Jealousy doesn't become you, Cevilla Schlabach." There was no point in dwelling on what she didn't know, and it wasn't Richard's fault she was short on patience. She loved him, and she knew he loved her. The rest would sort out itself.

She decided to take that nap. If Richard came by after church, fine. If not, then *fine*. She didn't have to be around him twenty-four hours a day—even though she wanted to.

Chapter 2

Isn't it nice to come home to a delicious meal?"
Selah glanced at Ruby, who was prodding Christian's arm as they sat down at the table. She had spent today, like she'd spent the last two weeks since the wedding, making sure the house was spotless and meals were prepared and ready on time for her brother and sister-in-law. When Selah and Christian had lived together, Selah's motivation to clean house and cook meals had been almost nonexistent. Looking back, she realized how unfair she'd been to Christian, who had been putting in extra hours to establish himself as an excellent teacher. She'd given him a small amount of support and a large amount of trouble.

Christian arched his brow at Selah, which he often did when he was considering an answer. "*Yer* cooking has been more than adequate."

"Is that all you have to say?" Ruby frowned at Christian.

But Selah knew her brother well, and in his unique way, he'd given her a compliment. "*Danki,*" she said, smiling.

Ruby turned to her. "I can't tell you how much we appreciate what you do around here. School has been so hectic"—she looked at Christian again—"because someone keeps changing his mind about the Christmas program."

Christian looked at her coolly. "*Yer* ideas, unlike Selah's culinary skills, are *inadequate*."

"That's not what you said when I first presented them."

"That's because I was half asleep. Three a.m. is not an appropriate time to present *yer* Christmas play proposal."

Selah dipped her spoon in the bowl of chicken noodle soup and ignored their bickering. She didn't mind it. She realized soon after she'd moved in that they enjoyed arguing with each other. She thought it was strange, but then again, Christian was strange, and Ruby was odd in her own way. They were a perfect couple.

But even though she didn't mind their squabbles, she still wanted to move out. Being the third wheel was getting old, and while she put all her effort into cleaning and cooking, she wanted an income. Trouble was, she hadn't been able to find a job, and she was getting restless—not to mention a little anxious.

She had used the shanty phone yesterday to call Anne, who asked her why she hadn't found a new counselor yet. That was another issue. Her parents had paid for her therapy with Anne, but she didn't want to depend on them this time. She also didn't want to ask Christian for the money, even though she knew he would give it to her without question. Until she had a job, she wouldn't have a therapist. "I don't know why I can't keep calling you," she'd said to Anne.

"I thought you said you wanted to start a new life."

"I do."

"How is that possible if you're still clinging to parts of the old one?"

Anne had a point, but that hadn't settled Selah's anxiety.

"Enough."

Ruby's tone, which now had a bit of a sharp edge to it, brought Selah out of her thoughts. She looked up to see Christian's contrite expression.

"I'm sure Selah doesn't want to listen to this." Ruby looked at her. "I'm sorry."

"Me too," Christian said, his tone meek.

Selah almost laughed. Christian, meek? He was a humble man, but with his high intelligence, insistence on using complicated English vocabulary, and overall quirkiness, he sometimes came across as condescending. Obviously Ruby knew when to bring him down to earth.

"How was *yer* day?" Ruby took a sip of her iced tea.

Boring. "*Gut.*" She picked up the basket of rolls she'd baked this afternoon. The tops were golden, and even she'd been impressed with how they turned out. "Roll?"

"*Danki*." Ruby took one and then put the basket back on the table.

"Is that all?" Christian asked.

She looked at her brother and saw the doubt in his eyes. Ever since that day she'd almost made a mistake that would have ruined her life, he was attuned to her needs. That hadn't been the case when they were growing up. "*Ya*," she said, her voice firm. "It was fine."

"You said it was *gut*."

"Fine, *gut*, same thing."

"But they're not." He lifted his spoon. "Fine indicates something is acceptable."

"Like *mei* cooking?" She rolled her eyes.

"While *gut* means something is pleasing. Satisfactory. You, Selah, do not seem satisfied."

"Christian," Ruby said, putting her hand on his arm.

"It's okay, Ruby. He's right. I'm not exactly satisfied."

"Is it something we've done?" Ruby's eyes filled with worry. "Something Christian said?"

"I'm not the only one who misspeaks," Christian said.

Ruby ignored him. "If we can do something to make things better for you, please tell us."

Selah smiled. Ruby was so sweet. "It's *nix* you or Christian have done or said."

"I think you're overworked." Christian stirred his soup.

"How can I be overworked if I don't have a job?"

"You've been working hard here," Ruby said, nodding at Christian. "I've never been in a cleaner *haus*."

"Ruby is correct. Perhaps you should find a job, Selah."

She sat back in her chair. "I've been trying. I check the want ads in the paper every day. There's *nix* I'm qualified to do. Do you know if anyone is hiring around here?"

"*Nee*, I don't." Ruby drummed her fingers against the table and then looked at Christian. "Do you?"

"I suggest you check at Carolyn Yoder's bakery. Conceivably she could be hiring, considering it's the Christmas season."

"Would you want to work in a bakery?" Ruby asked her.

"I'd work anywhere. I really want a job. I'll stop there tomorrow morning." She sipped her soup again. "*Danki* for the idea, Christian."

"You are welcome."

Later, when Selah started to clear the table, Ruby stopped her. "I'll clean the kitchen tonight. You can *geh* relax in the living room."

"I'll do it," Selah said.

"You will not." Ruby crossed her arms and lifted her chin.

"There's *nee* use in arguing," Christian said,

moving to stand beside his wife. "Her obstinacy has *nee* match."

"That's right." Ruby tilted her head toward him. "What's obstinacy?"

"Stubbornness."

Selah chuckled and started for the living room. But before she left, she saw Christian put his arm around Ruby's shoulders, and she leaned against him. She was seeing the softer side of her brother she hadn't even known existed. He had learned how to love and how to be a good husband. He was satisfied.

If there was hope for him, there was hope for her. Right, Lord?

She went into the living room and sat down on the couch. For some reason Levi Stoll came to mind. She'd thought about him once before since Martha's wedding, and she knew she'd been rude to him before leaving the Detweilers'. True, she'd been ready to go home, but she'd also been reminded of the troubles Martha had with the single men in the community before she and Seth dated. She didn't know Levi, and she didn't want to give him any ideas. Still, she could have been nicer about it. Once again, she'd made a mistake.

Remembering what both Cevilla and Anne had said about regrets, she stopped stewing in her guilt over Levi and pulled out a real estate catalog from under the couch cushions. She'd seen the catalog on a rack by the front door of Schrock's Grocery when she'd shopped there earlier that week. The catalog was free, and it listed all the houses for sale and rent, along with available apartments in the area, including Barton. She had no intention of moving out of Birch Creek, but the three houses she saw for sale, all formerly owned by English people, were out of her price range—which was zero until she got a job and saved some money.

"Selah?"

She looked up and saw Christian walking into the room. She tossed the catalog on the floor by the couch and put her hands in her lap. She hadn't expected him to come in here. Usually he was grading papers or working on lesson plans at the kitchen table after supper.

"May I talk to you?" He sat down on the chair near the couch.

"Sure."

He was sitting straight, his posture always faultless. But the tip of his foot was tapping against the wood floor. The sound was almost silent, but she noticed it. Her brother had something on his mind.

After a few minutes, he reached down and picked up the catalog. "I'm curious about this."

"That?" Selah said, trying to feign innocence and failing spectacularly.

"*Ya.* This. I saw it poking out of the couch

37

cushions yesterday. I thought it was part of the newspaper. Is it *yers*?"

"Of course it is, Christian." She sounded snappy, but they both knew who it belonged to.

"Are you considering moving again?"

To her surprise, she caught a glimpse of hurt in his eyes. Still, she nodded. "As soon as I'm able to."

"I see." He paused. He and Ruby were rarely at a loss for words. Clearly he was bothered by her decision.

She leaned forward and looked at him. "Christian, I appreciate you and Ruby letting me live here, but I need a place of *mei* own."

"Are you unhappy living with us?" He frowned. "I know you stated the contrary, but I want you to tell me the truth."

"This is not about you and Ruby. It's about me." She glanced down at the floor, which she had scrubbed yesterday until it gleamed. "I made so many mistakes—"

"And you've learned from them."

"But they follow me. In here." She tapped her temple. "This used to be our *haus*, Christian, when we first moved here. Now it's *yers* and Ruby's. I need a new life. And like Anne said, how can I have one if I keep hanging on to the past?"

Christian nodded. "I understand. But I don't like the idea of you living alone."

"Cevilla Schlabach has been living alone for years."

"*Nee* one in their right mind would tangle with her." For the first time Christian cracked a smile. "Then again, they wouldn't tangle with you, either."

Selah reached over and grabbed Christian's hand. They had grown up with parents who'd been distant, and physical affection had been rare. But at that moment, she wanted to reassure him. "I'll be fine. And I'm not going anywhere soon. I don't even have a job yet."

"Thus the urgency."

"That, and . . ." She took in a breath. "I have to get a new therapist. Plus, there's medication to pay for. I have three months' worth, but it will run out in January."

"Ruby and I can help you with that—"

"But I don't want you to."

He let go of her hand. "Selah, if there's one thing living in Birch Creek has taught me, it's that you don't have to do anything alone. The contradiction of our parents, who were unable for whatever reason to fully embrace the Amish concept of community, isn't something we need to continue. If you need help, ask us."

"I will." Her voice trembled. It was a wonderful feeling to feel so cared for. But that didn't change her mind. "I have to do this, Christian. At least, I have to try."

"I understand." He handed her the catalog. "Just know that Ruby and I will always be here for you." He rose from the chair and went back into the kitchen.

Selah sat back against the couch, feeling true optimism for the first time since she'd returned to Birch Creek. She had the support of her brother, and she knew Ruby would agree with him. She opened the catalog. She might not be able to afford anything in it, but she could dream about the day she could.

The next morning, Selah walked to Yoder's Bakery, her hands shoved into her coat pockets, her lungs tingling as she breathed in the brisk air. The distance was long enough for a buggy drive, but she didn't mind the walk. She'd learned that exercise helped when she was out of sorts.

Half an hour after she left the house, the delicious scents of fresh bread, sweet rolls, cinnamon, and cloves warmed her as she stepped inside the bakery. Carolyn, the owner, stood behind the counter. Other than being introduced to her at church, Selah hadn't had any interaction with her. Ruby, always eager to provide information, had explained that Carolyn was Freemont's sister, and she'd moved back to Birch Creek after Selah left.

Ruby had also made a point to mention that Carolyn had recently married for the first time, which surprised Selah. Carolyn and her husband, Atlee, had to be at least in their late forties, judging by the gray in Atlee's beard and the silver that streaked Carolyn's dark hair.

Mary Yoder, who was the bishop's wife and Carolyn's sister-in-law, stood behind the counter too. Both women were wearing light-blue dresses, white aprons, and white *kapps*. They were also dark haired and nearly the same height, which made them look like biological sisters. Selah took a deep breath. The bakery had just opened for the day, and so far no customers were in the store. If she was going to ask about a job, the time was now.

"Hello, Selah." Mary smiled. "How are you today?"

"Fine," she said, returning the smile, hoping she looked friendly. But not too friendly. She dialed back her grin as her anxiety ramped up. She didn't want to ruin this opportunity by appearing *seltsam*.

"What can we do for you?" Carolyn asked. Her smile resembled the bishop's, kind and welcoming.

Selah started to put her hands on the counter, but then she thrust them behind her back. She had never directly asked for a job before, and she wasn't sure how to start. "I, uh, wondered if you had any job openings."

"Oh, I'm sorry," Carolyn said. "Atlee's niece Mattie is here helping us. She's been a lifesaver since I lost *mei* last two employees." Her brow creased. "I'm not sure about hiring the English anymore. Not that they don't work hard, but I've had trouble keeping them here."

"They've always left for *gut* reasons, though," Mary added. "A new job, a marriage, moving to a different state."

"Oh, *ya*. And the women have been wonderful to work with. That's what's so disappointing. I don't want to hire anyone unless they plan to stick around."

"I'll be here," Selah said. *For a while, at least.* She wasn't sure what she was going to do if she couldn't find employment. She didn't want to put her plan on hold because she had to spend months trying to find a job.

Carolyn looked at Selah. "I wish I could help you. We're in the middle of our Christmas rush, so if it gets busier, I might have some work available. But I don't want that to keep you from looking for something more permanent."

"I understand." She took a step back from the counter, disappointed.

"Would you like to try a donut?" Mary gestured to a glass display pedestal on the counter. "Made them fresh this morning."

"Um . . . ," Carolyn said.

Mary looked at her. "What?"

"*Nix.*" Carolyn bit her lip, a spark of humor in her eyes.

At Selah's confused look, Mary explained, "I've been working for years to find the right donut recipe."

"*Years,*" Carolyn repeated.

Mary shot her a pointed look. "I think I finally got it this time." She lifted the glass lid and selected a plump, glazed donut. "Here," she said, holding it out to Selah.

"*Danki.*" Noticing both Mary's and Carolyn's expectant expressions, she bit into the sweet dough. It was soft and chewy with just the right amount of sugary glaze. After she swallowed the delicious bite, she said, "Very *gut.*"

"Really?" Carolyn looked surprised.

"*Ya.*" Selah took another bite. Maybe it wasn't a good idea for her to work in a bakery. She had a sweet tooth, and she wasn't sure she could resist the temptation.

"I told you," Mary said, grinning in triumph. She picked up one of the donut holes from the center of the plate and handed it to Carolyn.

She popped it into her mouth, and her eyes widened. "Wow." Carolyn stared at the display of donuts, and then she gaped at Mary. "You actually did it."

Mary beamed. "Best donut you ever tasted?"

Carolyn frowned slightly. "I wouldn't *geh* that far—"

"You should take some to Atlee." Mary reached under the counter and pulled out a flat piece of gray-and-white cardboard. With quick movements, she transformed it into a box and started placing donuts inside. "Selah, would you like another one?"

She shook her head. "I'm tempted, but I just had breakfast before I came over here. *Danki* anyway."

Mary closed the box lid and handed it to Carolyn. "Spread the word. I've finally figured out how to make the elusive donut."

Carolyn chuckled. "I'll start with Atlee. He can take this to Sol's when he goes to work. He should be leaving soon. Be right back."

Grinning, Mary turned to Selah. "Would you like to meet Mattie? She's near *yer* age and working in the kitchen right now. She's from Fredericktown, where Atlee and the Bontragers used to live. I can ask her to take a break for a few minutes. I'm sure she needs one by now."

Selah hesitated. She didn't want to pull Mattie from her work. But that wasn't the real reason she didn't answer right away. Something was still holding her back from getting involved with the community. She would have to interact with people if—no, when—she got a job, but otherwise she wasn't ready to make friends.

Two English women entered the bakery, saving her from having to answer. "Excuse me, Selah." Mary went to greet them, and from the familiar way they were talking, it was obvious they were regular customers.

44

Selah decided to go home, but she couldn't resist looking at the displays of baked goods first. Maybe she should take home a treat for Christian and Ruby. Thanksgiving was next week, and they both loved pie—a dessert Selah hadn't quite mastered yet. Her crusts were always soggy.

She checked out the pies and selected one pumpkin and one apple. The bell above the door rang again, but Selah didn't look to see who had come inside. Instead, she took in a display of fresh fruitcakes. She picked one up and examined it. How could a baked good look so delicious and taste so awful?

"You like those?"

She almost dropped the fruitcake at the sound of Levi's voice. She turned to see him standing nearby and then returned the fruitcake to the display. "Not particularly."

He walked over and picked up the loaf. "I don't like them, either. They always look so tasty, though. Then I try a piece and . . ." He wrinkled his nose and set the loaf back down. "I'd rather eat shoe leather."

She couldn't help but smile as she stepped away from him and the display, but then she immediately questioned what she was doing. He was just being friendly, and here she was giving him the cold shoulder again.

If it bothered him, he didn't let on. "*Mei grossmutter* ordered something from here." He peered around the display at the counter, where Mary was checking out the English customers. "I guess I'll wait until Mary's free." He turned to her. "Everything looks *gut*. What are you partial to?"

There was no reason for her to continue to be rude to him. "This is *mei* first time here. I haven't tried anything except the donuts, which are really *gut*." As she spoke, she noticed a display of candies used to decorate the tops of cookies and cakes. She picked up one of the packages.

"You like red hots?" Levi asked.

"We always called them cinnamon dots." She set the bag back down, memories of Christmases past washing over her. "I used to decorate Christmas cookies with them when I was little. *Mei mamm* would get on me for eating the dots instead of putting them on the cookies." She smiled at the memory. She hadn't baked Christmas cookies in a long time, mostly because she grew so apathetic about everything as her depression took hold. Now the idea of decorating cookies appealed to her. Maybe Ruby would like to do that with her this Saturday.

After the English customers left, Levi said, "I guess I'd better find those orange twists. *Gross-mutter* will be waiting, and one thing you don't do is keep her waiting." He smiled at her again and pushed up his silver-rimmed glasses. "I'll see you around."

Selah watched as he went to the counter. He

really was friendly. She should apologize to him for being rude at the wedding, but she decided it was better to let that go. He didn't seem to hold it against her, thank goodness.

Mary said something to him and disappeared in the back, presumably to get the twists for him. As Selah waited for him to check out, she perused the rest of the bakery. Every spare inch was decorated for Christmas, and it was all festive and beautiful.

After Levi left, Selah took her pies to the counter. "You'll enjoy those," Mary said, using a small pad to write down the prices. "Carolyn bakes the best pies in Birch Creek. Probably in the whole county." She added up the amount. As Selah pulled her wallet out of her purse, Mary said, "Wait a minute." She hurried to the candy table and picked up a container of cinnamon dots. "From Levi," she said, and then she added it to the other items in Selah's bag.

Selah frowned. "What?"

"He bought these for you and told me to tell you Merry Christmas."

Stunned, she said, "But . . . why would he do that?"

"I don't know." Mary had a twinkle in her eye. "He is a nice young *mann*, though. Friendliest one I've ever met. His whole *familye* is agreeable— even Delilah, although she's got a bit of vinegar in her."

Selah looked at the bag, confused. She wasn't sure she should even accept them.

"Selah," Mary said, her tone gentle. "We've come to know the Stolls since they've moved here. I'm sure Levi didn't mean anything other than a friendly gesture." She moved the bag toward her. "Take them and enjoy."

"Okay." She handed Mary the money, tempted to pay for the dots herself. But they were already purchased. After Mary handed her the receipt, Selah said good-bye and walked home, pondering Mary's words. She was probably reading too much into the gesture, which wasn't a surprise. *It's not like I haven't done that before.*

When she arrived at the house, Selah set the pies on the kitchen counter and then glanced at the package of cinnamon dots. They did look delicious. She couldn't resist opening the lid and tasting some. The flavor was sweet and spicy at the same time, and the candies were fresh. A small part of her had to admit she was glad Levi had bought them for her.

But what if he expected something in return? Wasn't that the way all men were?

She tied the bag back up and put it in the back of the pantry, unable to eat another piece. Levi might be friendly, but she would have to keep her distance. She didn't trust her judgment—and she wondered if she ever would.

Chapter 3

Levi thought about Selah on the way back to the inn in his buggy. He had no idea why he had started a conversation with her, much less bought the candies. He'd done both on the spur of the moment. Something about her intrigued him, and he couldn't put his finger on what that was. He'd noticed it at church, but there it was easy to set his thoughts about her aside and focus on worship. When he saw her again at the bakery, though, he couldn't stop himself from approaching her. That bothered him. A lot.

He'd always been eager to reach out to others. That wasn't anything new. Like making sure the person who got picked last for games didn't feel bad. Or going around after church and greeting everyone, especially visitors. When his family bought the house to establish an inn, *Daed* pointed out that Levi's friendliness would be an asset. "You've never met a stranger," he'd said.

Selah wasn't exactly a stranger, but she felt like one to him. He'd noticed again that she was aloof when he first asked her about the fruitcakes. After talking for a little while, she seemed to relax, but not much. He got the sense that she was feeling lost, and that also bothered him.

Levi frowned as he pulled into the driveway. He had other things to think about than Selah Ropp. He parked the buggy in the barn, unhitched his horse, Rusty, and then took the box of orange twists inside the inn. He put the box on the kitchen table and paused when he heard a pounding sound. Was it coming from the roof? "Oh, *nee*," he said, groaning.

He went outside and looked up. His father was perched on the incline of the roof, replacing the few shingles that had blown off in the storm they'd had the night before.

"I told you I was going to do that," Levi hollered.

Daed lifted his head, his hammer poised over a shingle. "It will only take me a minute."

"Fixing things around here is *mei* job." He gestured to the roof. "You don't need to be crawling around like that anymore."

"Levi, I'm perfectly capable of repairing a few shingles. Besides, I get tired of being in the office all day. Fresh air does a *mann gut*, you know." He pointed his hammer at the inn. "If you're looking for something to do, the toilet in room four still isn't flushing right."

He knew better than to argue further with his father. *Daed* was easygoing, but he had his stubborn moments too. "I'll take a look at it."

Plumbing was the worst of the jobs at the inn, and the last thing he wanted to do was deal with a toilet. But everything had to be in working order when they opened in a week. They should have opened before Thanksgiving, but the inspector who was supposed to give them the final go ahead had rescheduled. Hopefully there wouldn't be any more delays.

He went inside the mudroom at the back of the inn and opened the cabinet where he kept all his tools. He pulled out his tool belt and fastened it around his waist as he headed for the lobby. When he got there, he saw his grandmother dusting the custom-made coffee table in front of the woodstove. "Why did you let *Daed* get up on the roof?" he asked her.

"You think I can tell him anything?" She pointed the feather duster at Levi. "I had to come in here, he's making me so nervous."

"Where's Nina?"

She attacked the coffee table again as if it had a foot of dust covering it. "She went to Ira's. Probably for the same reason. She should be back soon." She banged the duster on the table. "He just got over spraining his wrist last week." She sighed and looked at Levi. "I don't know where he gets his mule-headedness."

"Me either." Levi hid a grin as he headed up the staircase. When they remodeled the old English four-bedroom house into an inn, they'd added three small bathrooms to the top bedrooms. Each one had a shower, a toilet, and a pedestal sink.

51

Everything had worked well except for the toilet in room four. This would be the third time he tried to fix it.

When he opened the bedroom door, he heard Nina screaming his name at the bottom of the stairs.

"Levi! *Daed*'s fallen off the roof!"

Panic made his blood run cold. He ran downstairs, his tool belt smacking against his hips, and dashed outside to their house. His father was lying on the ground, *Grossmutter* kneeling next to him. Levi crouched on the other side. *Daed*'s face was contorted with pain, his left leg twisted in a way that made Levi's stomach churn.

"Loren, can you hear me?" *Grossmutter* said, holding his hand.

"*Ya*," he said. "I'm not . . . unconscious."

But his pallid face told Levi his father was close to passing out. Nina arrived, out of breath. "I called nine-one-one," she said, gasping. "They should be here any minute."

"I told you not to *geh* on that roof." *Grossmutter*'s voice trembled. "Why didn't you listen to me?"

Daed closed his eyes and nodded. "I . . . should have."

Levi felt Nina's hand on his shoulder, and he reached up and squeezed it. "He'll be okay." Levi saw the fear in her eyes. "Once we get him to the hospital, they'll take *gut* care of him."

But Nina didn't respond as she held Levi's hand tight.

He remained calm, believing what he'd told Nina. Panicking and worrying wouldn't help the situation. "You'll be all right, *Daed*," he said as his father's eyes remained closed. "Everything will be fine." *Lord, please let it be.*

A few hours later, Levi sat in the surgery waiting room with Nina and *Grossmutter*. Nina had the presence of mind to call a taxi right after she called nine-one-one, and when the ambulance arrived, the taxi was right behind it. Fortunately the ER wasn't busy, and not long after they arrived, *Daed* was taken into surgery. "He's lucky he only broke a leg," one of the ER nurses had said. "He could have died from that fall." Levi didn't know anything about being a nurse, but the family could have done without that information.

"*Kaffee*?" Nina held out a cup to him. "Black, two sugars."

He nodded as he took it, taking a sip even though it was after five o'clock and he usually cut off his coffee consumption by noon. He'd never been in a hospital before, and he was surprised at how slow treatment worked here. His father had been in surgery for more than three hours. But he didn't care how long it took if it meant *Daed* would be okay.

"*Grossmutter* wants to talk to us."

He turned to her. "Is she okay?"

"She seems to be." Nina half-smiled. "She's the strongest woman I know, that's for sure."

Nodding in agreement, he accompanied his sister to the back corner of the waiting room where there were chairs and some privacy. Nina sat down and pulled her navy-blue sweater closer around her, even though the waiting room was comfortable and warm. He sat next to her, and they were both opposite their grandmother, who had on what Levi called her no-nonsense expression—eyes sharp, mouth pressed thin, shoulders held back.

"We need to discuss the future," she said, her tone also no-nonsense.

"*Grossmutter*, he's going to be all right," Levi said. "He's not on death's door."

"I realize that. I'm talking about the immediate future. We're opening the inn in a week."

"You're not thinking of opening without *Daed*, are you?" Nina said, balking. "That's not fair to him."

"Nina, we have to be practical." *Grossmammi* pushed up her glasses, which was as much a habit for her as it was for Levi. "I know *yer daed* would want us to be." She turned to Levi. "You'll have to be the manager until Loren gets back on his feet."

"Me?" Levi almost spilled his coffee. "I don't know anything about management."

"You're a smart *bu*. You'll learn." She looked at Nina. "And you'll have to take care of *yer vatter* until he heals. I'll still prepare breakfast and snacks for our guests."

"What about cleaning?"

"Thankfully we don't have to worry about that yet since we're not open." She shook her head. "I never thought I would look at the inspector's delay as a blessing, but it was. Levi, you'll have to hire a maid right away. I know Loren wanted to wait awhile, see how many guests we have, but this changes everything."

He was about to point out that he didn't know how to hire anyone either, but he kept his mouth shut. This wasn't the time to complain or doubt his abilities. His family needed him to step up and manage the inn, and that was what he was going to do. "I can put an ad in the paper."

"That's a *gut* start."

Levi turned around and glanced at the electronic board above the courtesy desk. They'd been given a number and a doctor's name so they could follow the progress of his father's surgery. "*Daed*'s in recovery," Levi said, getting up.

"Then the doctor should be out soon to talk to us." *Grossmutter* rose. "We need to lean on one another more than ever. I know *yer vatter* will be fine." She paused, her bottom lip quivering once. "But it will take time for him to recover. You don't bounce back from surgery as quickly at his age."

Both Levi and Nina nodded. "You can count on us," Levi said.

Grossmutter touched his arm. "I know I can. *Yer vatter* knows it too."

Jackson Talbot took a huge bite out of a strawberry jelly donut and stared at the computer screen. He chewed slowly as he tried to figure out what his father had done to the hotel's website. This was the third time in a month the site had gone down, all because Dad couldn't leave well enough alone.

At least he had Jackson's correct email now. Last year, before he'd moved to Barton, neither his father nor the head desk clerk, Lois, had known what to do when the hotel network faltered. When Jackson didn't respond, they thought he was ignoring them. At least a dozen angry emails from his father were floating out in cyberspace somewhere.

They had a good reason to contact Jackson. He had a degree in computer science, and he'd minored in web design. It wasn't as though he didn't know what he was doing. The employees at the Stay Inn clearly didn't, though.

He glanced at the jelly donut and then set it down on the plate next to the keyboard. Maybe he didn't know what he was doing either since he'd thoughtlessly eaten one of the messiest foods known to man beside a five-thousand-dollar computer.

He slid from the stool and picked up the plate

before taking it to the front desk and laying it beneath the counter. "I'll be back," he told Lois. She'd worked at the hotel for more than ten years, enduring three owners. But according to her, Trevor Talbot was the most challenging. Jackson hadn't been surprised to hear that.

Before Jackson could go to the restroom and wash off his sticky hand, the glass front doors slid open and his father stormed inside. Uh-oh. From the enraged look on his father's face, Jackson assumed something was really wrong. On second thought, his father was probably just overreacting again.

Dad glanced around the lobby, which was still being renovated by the slowest construction crew Jackson had ever encountered. At least they'd finally installed the carpet, a dull gray-and-black-striped pattern that was supposedly chic but looked like it belonged in a dive bar from the early eighties. His father glanced around the lobby, and when he saw it was empty, he spewed a curse and slammed a newspaper on the front desk. "Do you believe this?"

Lois calmly peered at the paper through her bright-pink reading glasses. "Teenager loses his pants in bathroom sneak attack gone wrong." She cracked a half-smile. "Serves him right."

"Not that." He shoved the paper at Jackson and pointed to a tiny ad in the right-hand corner of the paper. "This."

Jackson licked the powdered sugar off his fingers and looked at the ad. It said Stoll Inn was opening in a week. Oh, so Birch Creek finally got an inn. He wasn't surprised. The small Amish town had been booming for the past several years. Jackson had grown up in Chardon, but after his parents divorced, he'd spent his summers with his father in Barton. After high school he'd attended Cleveland State, and then after graduation he'd bounced around the Cleveland area before moving to Barton two months ago. He'd never paid much mind to local news, but on his visits here he'd heard about the secretive Amish community that had suddenly become welcoming and was now experiencing rapid growth. No one knew many details—or at least not enough of them to make anyone he was acquainted with pay any attention.

He pushed the paper back at his dad. "I don't see what you're flipping out about."

"You don't?" His father sneered. "You don't have a shred of business sense, do you? Competition." Dad tapped at the Amish ad. "The last thing we need is competition."

"Competition isn't a bad thing," Jackson said. "Besides, you've had the monopoly on the hospitality business in this area only because Stay Inn has been the only hotel. This was bound to happen sometime."

Dad grabbed the newspaper and crumpled it

in his hand. "This isn't the same as some hotel popping up down the road. This is an Amish inn. People are crazy for anything Amish these days. You think they're going to think twice about staying here when they find out there's an Amish inn less than thirty minutes away? And Stoll Inn? The name's too close to Stay Inn."

Stoll Inn sure is a better name. Jackson had always thought Stay Inn was corny. "I think there's enough business to go around."

"Really?" Dad spread his arms wide. "Do you see all the guests here? How we're turning away people because we have no vacancies?"

"You've been in perpetual construction for over a year. That's why you don't have many guests."

"I'm investing in this property," Dad said in a low voice that carried a warning—Jackson was close to saying the wrong thing. He tugged at the neck of his expensive polo shirt. "By the time it's done, we'll have people dying to stay here."

Jackson hoped so for his father's sake. He was sinking a lot of money into this hotel, which he'd inherited from a distant aunt and uncle along with a sizable amount of cash. But Dad had always been loose with his money, owning and losing several businesses over the years. Jackson wondered if this construction company was dragging out the renovations for a reason other than ineptitude.

Lois disappeared into the office and then came

out with a cup of water and a roll of antacids. "Take these, Trevor," she said, handing them to Dad. "You're going to give yourself an ulcer, carrying on this way."

At that point one of the construction guys walked into the lobby, Sheetrock dust covering his jeans. "Mr. Talbot, we got a problem."

"Problems, problems," Dad muttered, tossing the rumpled paper on the counter. "Always problems." He and the construction worker disappeared down the first-floor hallway.

"Don't worry about him," Lois said, patting Jackson's hand, the numerous and colorful plastic bangles circling her wrist clacking together. She was in her early sixties but dressed like she was still living in the disco era. "He'll settle down."

Jackson knew Lois was right. His father had always had a short fuse, and it was getting shorter as Dad was getting older, which was one reason Jackson had cut his summer visits short the past five years. The last summer he'd visited here, right before his senior year, he'd left after three days. Technically he didn't have to keep visiting his father in the summers since he was an adult, but he had felt some loyalty to the man— and he still did. That loyalty had been tested when Jackson spent Thanksgiving Day alone in their apartment, eating a microwave pizza and watching football. Not too big of a deal since it wasn't his first Thanksgiving alone, but it would have been nice if his father had at least been there.

But loyalty wasn't the reason he moved here. Desperation was. "I'm not worried," he said.

"Oh really." Lois clucked her tongue. "For some reason I'm not buying what you're selling."

He leaned his hip against the counter. "Well, I am a little worried about the website. He needs to stop making these so-called upgrades. He's made six since I took this job. They're unnecessary, and his computer is swarming with viruses."

"You know your father," she said, taking off her readers. They swung on a beaded chain around her neck. "He's always tinkering with things. Looking for ways to improve."

"Or he doesn't trust me." Jackson knew it was the latter. "Do you think a little Amish bed and breakfast is going to cause us problems?"

Lois shook her head. "I'm with you. Competition is good for business. Part of the reason this construction is taking so long is that your father isn't staying on top of it. He's too busy spending his time on vacations with that . . . that . . ."

"Ashley?"

"Yeah. That Ashley." Lois sniffed. "He's far too old for her. And why does a young thing like that want to hang around your father?"

"His bank account?"

Lois sighed, patting the back of her auburn hair, which was coiled into a loose bun on top of her head. "She's so transparent." The phone rang, and as Lois went to answer it, Jackson picked up the balled-up newspaper.

He unfolded it and looked again at the ad. The opening was in a week. Being in the hospitality business wasn't easy—even he knew that. It took time to build up clientele, and money was always an issue, except apparently for Dad. This was his second time renovating the hotel, this time with Ashley's advice. "It's too dull and old looking," she'd whined, her nasal voice scraping against Jackson's nerves like a rusty nail on an old cheese grater. He didn't care for Ashley at all. She was hot, all right—in a plastic, shallow way that made him wonder if she'd ever had a deep thought in her life. Definitely not his type. He wouldn't have guessed she was his father's type, either.

Jackson set aside his thoughts about Ashley and his father's worries about the inn. Lois was right—the hotel would be much more successful if his father would stop tinkering with everything, including Ashley, and focus on building clientele and relationships. But between his inheritance and the lack of competition, he hadn't been too worried about not filling the rooms every night. Until now.

Maybe this was a wake-up call for him to get back on track. Jackson hoped so. At twenty-three, he should be out on his own, following his dream of having his own IT and web design business, not putting out fires his old man was making during a midlife crisis.

Jackson glanced at the ad again. "Good luck to them," he said, and then he dropped the paper into the trash.

Chapter 4

Selah halted in front of the Stoll home, hesitant to knock on the door. She was carrying a basket of food she'd made for the family after hearing about Loren's accident a few days ago. He'd spent three days in the hospital, and during that time several families had not only taken meals to the Stolls but helped with chores and anything else they needed.

She had volunteered to bring a meal today. Not only was it ingrained in her to help others when a crisis happened—which she'd lost sight of when she was in the throes of her illness—but in counseling she'd learned that focusing on others instead of herself was also therapeutic, not to mention biblical. Her focus lately had been solely on herself, and maybe that was the problem. Hopefully, helping the Stolls would break the ice when it came to involving herself in the community. She'd cooked for over two hours last night, and from the weight of the basket she carried, she might have made a bit too much.

Despite her decision to help, her stomach twisted a little. What if Levi answered the door? She had washed and pressed his handkerchief, even though he told her to keep it. She didn't want to be in his debt, and she'd even brought money to repay him for the cinnamon candies.

Stop being foolish and knock on the door. She couldn't continue to be wary of Levi—or of any young man. But once she settled things with him, she would feel a lot better. She knocked on the door, and after a minute, Delilah answered.

"Hello, Selah." She smiled despite the weariness in her eyes. "Come in, come in."

"This is for you," Selah said, holding up the basket as she walked inside. She glanced around the tidy living room. Loren was sitting in a chair near the woodstove, his leg propped up on an ottoman, crutches by his side.

"Hi, Selah. Excuse me if I don't get up." His smile, like Delilah's, was kind, but his voice was raspy with exhaustion. Selah had never had surgery, but from what she'd heard about Loren's compound fracture, she wasn't surprised he was tired and possibly woozy.

"You're very kind." Delilah took the basket. "Oh my, it's heavy."

"I made a few things. More than a few, actually." She put her hands behind her back. "I hope you like them."

"I'm sure we will," Loren said. He leaned back against the chair and closed his eyes.

"Nina will bring you some soup in a minute, just as soon as she's back from Schrock's," Delilah said to him.

Loren nodded. "That's fine."

Delilah gestured toward the kitchen. "Join me for some tea," she said. "I just made a pot of peppermint."

She had taken the baby step of voluntarily coming over here, but she hadn't anticipated staying any longer than it took to drop off the basket. "I should probably get back home—"

"Surely you can spare a few minutes?" Delilah peered at her over her glasses.

Selah wasn't about to say no. "Of course. May I carry that for you?"

"*Nee*, I can handle it."

Selah followed Delilah into the kitchen, where the older woman set the basket on the counter and then pulled two white mugs from a cupboard. "Do you like sugar or honey in *yer* tea?"

"Plain is fine."

"That's how I like mine."

Selah took off her coat and laid it over the back of an empty chair before sitting down.

Delilah poured tea into the mugs and then brought them to the table. She set one down in front of Selah. "We've been so thankful for everyone who's helped us out since Loren's accident," she said, sitting down in the chair nearest Selah. "It's made this unfortunate incident much easier to bear."

"I'm glad." Selah blew on the tea and then took a sip, enjoying the strong mint flavor. "How is he feeling?"

"Tired, as you can see. He's still on pain medication. He didn't want to take it, but he found out the hard way what happens when he doesn't." She set down her tea and looked at Selah. "I want to talk to you about something, if I may."

Selah steeled herself. Had this woman somehow found out about her past? Martha had assured her that she never told anyone why Selah left Birch Creek, not even Seth, and of course Christian and Ruby would never betray her confidence. She relaxed, feeling irrational again. Why did she always jump to the worst conclusion? "What would you like to talk about?"

"We're in a bit of a pickle right now." Delilah explained that because Nina was tending to Loren, she had to give up her job cleaning the inn, at least for the time being. "We've been trying to hire someone, but we haven't had any luck." Her eyes locked with Selah's. "Would you like the job? As I said, we need someone now because of Loren's accident. But we've always planned to hire additional staff when the inn starts being full most of the time, so this position can quickly become permanent."

Selah's mouth dropped open. That was the last thing she'd expected Delilah to say.

"I heard you've been looking for employment." Delilah picked up her mug and took a sip. "I believe Carolyn Yoder mentioned it. Or Mary. I can't remember, honestly. But if you still are, and you'd like the job, it's *yers*."

"I . . . I don't know what to say."

"I don't mean to pressure you, dear. But we are due to open this weekend."

She wanted time to think about it, but she also recognized that they would need time to train her.

"If you can't take the job, we'll have to find someone else. But so far, no one has answered the ad we put in the paper."

Selah had stopped reading the want ads this week, not wanting to be discouraged. Delilah stared at her, expecting a response. What am I waiting for? This is an answer to prayer. Besides, how could she turn down the Stolls when they needed her? And Delilah had assured her the position could become permanent. "*Ya*," she said. "I'll take the job."

"Wonderful." Delilah set down her mug and clasped her hands together. Then she popped up from her chair. "You'll need to fill out some paperwork. Loren is a stickler for that. Levi's over in the office at the inn, and he can give you the forms." She went to Selah and practically lifted her out of her seat, and then she grabbed her coat and thrust it at her. "You can start tomorrow."

"O-okay," she said, dazed as she put on her coat. As soon as her arms were in her sleeves, Delilah ushered her to the small mudroom off the kitchen and directed her to go through the back door of the inn.

"The office is off the lobby." Delilah opened the door. A blast of cold air hit them, but her grin stayed in place. "*Danki*, Selah. I think this is going to work out . . . for all of us." She quickly closed the door as soon as Selah had stepped outside.

Selah stood in the cold, her coat still half on, wondering what had just happened. Then it hit her. She finally had a job. She smiled and glanced up at the cloudy sky. Thank you, Lord.

After she shooed Selah to the inn, Delilah went back into the kitchen and sat down at the table. She picked up her tea, satisfied. She was often surprised by God's timing, and this was no exception. When she saw Selah standing on their front doorstep with the heavy basket of food in her hands, it hit her that the young woman was the answer to several prayers. First, they did need a maid, and no one had answered the ad. Now they wouldn't have to scramble to find someone at the very last minute before they opened.

Selah Ropp was also another answer to Delilah's prayers, her private ones. She had promised to stay out of Levi's and Nina's love lives and had fully intended to keep that promise. But that was before Selah moved back to town. She belonged to a responsible family—her brother and sister-in-law were teachers and had the trust of the community with their most precious possession, their children. Quality relatives were of the utmost importance. She knew firsthand how life could be when family wasn't what it was supposed to be.

Selah's family was a good sign, but Delilah had fully made up her mind to intervene when she caught Levi looking at Selah during the last church service. Her grandson had always ignored female attention, and she had never noticed him paying attention to a particular girl before. Seeing him gazing at Selah had lit a lightbulb in her head. She had to jump at the chance to nudge Levi in the right direction. Of course, any woman would be happy to date her grandson. That was a given. The best way to make sure that happened? Put them in each other's proximity.

She grinned again, the stress of the past few days finally starting to fade. Seeing Loren in so much pain as he lay on the ground after falling from the roof had taken a few years off her life. But he would mend. The doctor had assured her of that. Even more important, the Lord had too. Nina was taking excellent care of him, and now that they had someone to clean the inn and the inspector was finally coming on Thursday to certify them, they could open for business this weekend.

Delilah looked up as Nina came into the kitchen carrying three bags of groceries. They hadn't needed much from the store since the community had brought them plenty of food, but they'd been running out of some toiletries. In addition, Delilah had wanted a few special items for Christmas baking.

Nina set the bags on the counter. "Who brought the basket?"

"Oh, I can't believe I forgot about that." Delilah jumped up. When she opened the basket's lid, she saw an array of food—a breakfast casserole, cabbage rolls, buttered noodles, bread, a chocolate cake, a thermos—most probably filled with soup—rolls, and a jar of pepper jelly. Selah was right. She had made too much. But what a thoughtful *maedel*.

"What are you grinning about?" Nina asked, taking jars of molasses and honey out of one of the bags.

"Oh *nix*." She picked up the jar of pepper jelly. How did Selah know Levi loved pepper jelly? Yes, getting the two of them together would be as easy as shoofly pie. "*Nix* at all."

Levi sat at his father's desk and rubbed the back of his neck, which had been aching since yesterday. He stared at the pile of receipts and the ledger book in front of him. He'd never paid attention to paperwork other than to file a couple of permits with the city of Barton during the inn renovations, but his father was a stickler for documentation. What he wasn't so particular about was telling the family exactly how in debt they were.

Nearly all the renovations on the inn had cost overruns. Levi had known about the broken sump pump and cracked septic tank, but his father had assured him they had the funds to pay for the repairs. Yet when he looked at the ledger book, he saw that wasn't the case. His father was making only small payments on the bills, which meant they were also paying more and more interest.

He sat back in the creaky office chair. The chair was brand-new but sounded like it had been hidden in a shed for ten years.

Soon the hospital bills would come in, and they would be high. Levi could do nothing about them until the inn opened and they had guests booked, but yesterday, in a hospitality magazine, he'd read that the winter season was the worst time for tourism—unless one was operating a ski lodge or something similar. All the red in the ledger made his stomach queasy. No wonder his father had been quieter than usual lately. This also explained the bottle of antacids he'd found in the top desk drawer. He was tempted to take one himself. If *Daed* hadn't had the accident, Levi would still be unaware that they owed so much money.

He took off his glasses and rubbed his eyes. They couldn't afford any more problems before they opened this weekend.

"Levi?"

Was that Selah's voice? No, he had to be hearing things.

"Is anyone there?"

That definitely sounded like her. What was she doing here? He pushed back from the desk and stepped out of the office. Selah was standing before the front counter, looking a little stunned. He had to admit he was a little stunned to see her. "Hi," he said, shutting the office door behind him.

"*Yer grossmutter* sent me over." Selah glanced at the wood counter and then back at him. "She offered me the cleaning job."

Levi stilled. "She did?"

"*Ya*. I accepted, and she said you would have some paperwork for me to fill out."

He was still trying to grasp the fact that his grandmother had hired Selah. Why had she done that after telling him he had to do the hiring? Was it because she didn't trust him to hire someone himself? Or did she have something else in mind? His stomach churned. She'd better not have—

"It's okay, *ya*?" she said. "That I took the job?"

"Oh. Of course." He blinked, trying to bring her into focus. "Uh, let me find that paperwork." He turned and opened the office door. Selah would have to fill out a job application. He knew that much. What else was he supposed to give her? "Just a second," he called out, opening a cabinet drawer and riffling through it. "I'm not sure where *Daed* keeps the papers."

73

"Okay."

She sounded as unsure as he felt, which added more pressure for him to hurry and get the paperwork so she wouldn't have to wait any longer. Had *Grossmutter* pressured her to take the job? Just the idea of it stuck in his craw. His grandmother could be difficult to refuse at times. Most of the time, actually. The last thing he wanted was for Selah—or any other employee— to work at the inn reluctantly.

Finally he found the folder labeled Employee Forms. He pulled it out and took out the papers he thought Selah would need, and then he shoved the folder back into the drawer and slammed it closed, catching the tip of his thumb. "Ow," he yelped.

"Are you okay?"

"Fine." He put his thumb to his mouth, and then he rushed out to the lobby. "Here," he said, giving her the papers and grabbing a pen out of the jar next to the guest book. "Just, uh, fill these out."

"*Danki.*" She skimmed through the four pages. "Mind if I sit at one of the tables?"

"Be *mei* guest." He inwardly groaned at the awkward hospitality pun as he walked to the table. His gut churned as he imagined what his grandmother had said to Selah to get her to take the job. "I'll be back," he said, unable to take the uncertainty. He raced from the inn to the house and burst into the kitchen.

"Why did you hire Selah?"

Grossmutter turned to him, her eyes wide with innocence. Fake innocence, he was sure. "You didn't let her leave before she finished the paperwork, did you?"

"Forget the paperwork." He went to her as she put a jar of pepper jelly on the table. "Don't you trust me to do the hiring?"

"Of course I do." The smug look on her face disappeared.

"Then why did you hire her?"

His grandmother took a step back, looking uncharacteristically unsure. "I thought she would be a *gut* fit."

"For the inn?" He ground his back teeth. "Or for me?"

"Of course for the inn." She averted her eyes for a second.

That was enough to tell him she had ulterior motives. "I don't believe this. I told you I'm not interested in Selah!"

"Excuse me."

Levi and *Grossmutter* both whirled around. Selah stood in the doorway of the kitchen. "I'm sorry for the intrusion, but I had a question about the form." She started to back away. "I'll wait for you back at the inn." She looked at Levi, her face impassive. Before he could stop her, she disappeared. Had she heard what he said? Good grief, he hoped not. While it was the truth, it still sounded hurtful.

"Now look what you've done," *Grossmutter* said.

"Me?"

"*Geh* after her and apologize." She crossed her arms over her chest. "And next time, make sure you do a better job of explaining the forms."

He would have argued with her, except she was right. He did owe Selah an apology. Levi rushed back to the inn, where Selah was still working at a table in the lobby. Thank goodness she hadn't decided to leave right then and there. Maybe she hadn't heard him after all.

"I figured it out." Selah gathered the papers and handed them to him, her expression inscrutable.

An awkward silence filled the room as he gave the paperwork a once-over, as if he were reading it, but the words swam in front of him. "Everything looks, uh, in order." Levi lifted his gaze.

Her eyes resembled steel. "What time do I report for work?"

"Seven a.m."

With a nod she said, "See you then. And please tell *yer grossmutter danki* for the opportunity." She turned and left through the inn's front door.

Levi leaned against the counter and let out a deep breath. Then he dropped off the forms in the office before going back to the house, where he found his grandmother cleaning the front of the kitchen stove.

"Did you set everything straight?" *Grossmutter* dried her hands on her apron. "Or did she turn down the job?"

"She'll be here in the morning."

Nina came into the kitchen, saving him from having to tell his grandmother that he didn't apologize. "Was that Selah I saw leaving?"

Grossmutter nodded. "She's our new maid, starting tomorrow."

"That's great." Nina grinned. "Martha said she was looking for a job." She looked at Levi. "*Gut* idea to hire her."

"It wasn't *mei* idea," Levi muttered. What was he going to say to Selah tomorrow? Should he bring up what happened? Leave it alone? Avoid her?

"*Daed* wants to talk to you," Nina said. "He says it's important."

Levi got up from the table, the sickening lump still in his stomach. He never wanted to offend anyone, but for some reason, knowing he might have hurt Selah made him feel worse than usual. He went into the living room, not wanting to keep his father waiting. He was glad to see *Daed* looking more lucid than he had since he'd come home from the hospital.

"Have a seat," *Daed* said, motioning to the couch next to him.

Levi complied, pushing Selah out of his mind. "How's the leg?"

"Painful. But it will heal." He paused. "I suppose you've been in the office."

"*Ya.*"

"Mutter explained what you three have worked out to manage while I'm incapacitated." He frowned. "I didn't want you to know about the bills, *sohn*."

"Why not? I could have helped. Gotten a second job or something."

"You were already working so much around here and had put in so much time and effort that I couldn't ask you to do more because of *mei* mismanagement." He fumbled with one of the suspenders that had slipped off his shoulder. Levi pulled it up for him. "Besides, I'm confident that once we open, we'll catch up on those bills."

Levi had always known where he got his endless optimism, but it was hard to feel optimistic about anything right now. Hopefully they would have caught up on their debt soon after guests started arriving. But now they'd have the hospital bills too. He just wasn't going to point that out now.

"So there's *nee* need to worry." *Daed* gave him a weak smile. "Remember that verse in James? 'But let him ask in faith, nothing wavering. For he that wavereth is like a wave of the sea driven with the wind and tossed.' We might be feeling tossed lately, but that will change. I have faith that it will."

"I do too." Hearing the Scripture verse bolstered him a little, which happened whenever he remembered God's promises. They didn't need to waver over a temporary setback. After all, life was full of them.

He dug deep and found hope. When he went back to the office in the inn, the sight of the ledger didn't turn his stomach. Then he glanced at Selah's forms. Noticing her slightly messy handwriting made him smile a little. He still felt crummy about what happened in the kitchen at the house, but if she'd heard what he said, he'd figure out how to make it up to her. Maybe he and his grandmother were wrong. Maybe Selah hadn't heard him. *Dear Lord, I hope not.*

I'm not interested in Selah!

Selah pushed a small red potato against the slice of chuck roast on her plate. She gripped her fork as Levi's words reverberated in her mind, just as they had all afternoon. He wasn't interested in her, and he couldn't have been firmer about that.

On the way home from the inn, she'd tried to stem her embarrassment with the realization that she didn't have anything to worry about when it came to Levi—either when working at the inn or running into him anywhere else. But knowing that fact didn't help much. Although she wasn't interested in him either, it didn't help to hear him reject her so plainly—and loudly. She also felt silly for thinking his friendliness might have meant something. Like Mary Yoder said, he was a nice man. Her ego had just taken a well-deserved hit for making any other assumption.

"Selah?"

She glanced up to see Ruby looking at her with concern. "*Ya*?"

"You haven't touched *yer* food. Are you feeling all right?"

Selah nodded and cut the small potato in half. "I'm fine." She tamped down her hurt feelings and forced a smile. "I got a job."

"You did?" Ruby grinned. "I'm so happy for you. Where?"

"Stoll Inn." She explained how she got the job, leaving out the part about Levi not liking her. Or being interested in her. Whatever.

"Imagine that." Ruby turned to Christian. "Isn't that wonderful news?"

Christian meticulously spread a small pat of butter on his roll. "Indeed. Excellent news. When do you start?"

"Tomorrow morning." She cut the half of a potato in half again and then took a bite. It was cold, but she swallowed it despite the nerves rioting in her stomach. By the time the meal was finished, she had managed to eat only a few bites, but she whisked away her plate before Ruby or Christian could notice.

As she prepared for bed later that night, she

80

remembered Levi's handkerchief and the money for the cinnamon dots. In all the fuss over the job, she had forgotten to give them to him. She'd make sure she did tomorrow. As she brushed out her hair, she reminded herself that this was just a job, and she would do it to the best of her ability. It didn't matter what Levi did or didn't think of her. She would be an ideal employee, making sure she stayed out of the Stoll family's way. She had other things to focus on anyway. She had already started a budget and a plan for how she was going to afford a house. She needed to keep that goal at the forefront, not Levi Stoll's or anyone else's opinion of her.

This time she managed a genuine smile. *Thank you, Lord. You truly do provide.*

"I might have made a terrible mistake."

Cevilla handed Delilah a bowl of sugar-free candies. When the woman declined to take one, she returned the dish to the coffee table and leaned back in her rocking chair. She'd been surprised when Delilah showed up right before suppertime. Usually Richard was here by now, but he said he had a meeting to attend. He didn't elaborate, but she knew it wasn't his stamp club meeting. What other meeting would he be going to? *One at the Mennonite church?* She pressed her lips together.

"Cevilla? Did you hear me?" Delilah sniffed.

"I'm going through a crisis, and you're over there daydreaming."

Cevilla blinked. "I'm sorry. You said you made a mistake."

"I *might* have made a mistake. I've been under a lot of stress lately. I blame that for *mei* lapse in judgment."

"Of course." Cevilla held in a chuckle, knowing Delilah wasn't in a humorous mood. She really did look distraught, which was unusual for her. She and Delilah weren't exactly friends, but they were the only two women in their age bracket in Birch Creek, so they visited each other from time to time. "Tell me what happened."

After Delilah explained everything from Loren's fall to hiring Selah at the inn, Cevilla said, "It sounds like everything is all right now. Loren's going to be okay, and you have a maid."

"I should have known you wouldn't under-stand." She sniffed again. "You've never had *kinner*."

Cevilla's eyes narrowed. "That might be, but I consider all these young people *mei* adopted *kinner*. I care very much for them."

"I'm sorry." Delilah stared at her lap. "That was uncalled for."

"That's okay." And it was, for the most part. She was used to people making offhand comments about her being single and childless, but they'd rarely used those comments as weapons like

Delilah just had. Usually they bounced off her, but right now she was feeling more raw than usual.

"I didn't tell you the worst part." Delilah explained how she'd seen an opportunity for matchmaking when Selah showed up at her door. "It was so perfect. She and Levi would be working together, and naturally they would fall in love with each other."

"Uh-oh."

"But Levi is having none of it. And then Selah overheard him yelling at me that he wasn't interested in her."

"Oh dear." Cevilla leaned forward. "I see why you're so upset now."

"Levi hasn't talked to me since. Not that I blame him." She smoothed the skirt of her plum-colored dress. "I wouldn't blame Selah if she didn't show up tomorrow, either."

"I don't think Selah would be that petty."

Delilah nodded. "Neither do I. I still think she and *mei grosssohn* would make a wonderful pair."

"Like him and Martha? Like Nina and Seth?"

"I was new to the community." Delilah lifted her chin. "And there's still a chance for Nina and Ira, you know."

Cevilla blew out a breath. Had she been this persistent when she'd been in her matchmaking prime? *I'm sure I was.* "Perhaps it would be best to let *yer grosskinner* find their own spouses, Delilah."

"I considered that option, but then I realized if I leave them to their own devices, they'll never get married." Her bottom lip jutted out slightly.

"That's not the worst thing in the world."

Delilah looked at her. "I wasn't insinuating that it is. Besides, you have Richard now." Her expression turned soft. "How blessed you are in *yer* old age."

Nodding, Cevilla stood, using her cane for balance. She opened the door of the woodstove and put a small log inside. For years the Yoder boys had taken turns cutting wood for her for winter, and Judah had brought over the latest batch. They always made sure the pieces were light enough for her to lift.

"You have *nix* else to say?" Delilah asked.

"About what?" Cevilla sat down.

"About you and Richard." Delilah shook her head. "You've been out of sorts since I got here. Is something wrong between the two of you?"

She paused, unsure whether she should confide in Delilah. So far she knew the woman wasn't prone to gossip, only misguided intentions. Even then it was clear she loved her family dearly. Since she had confided in Cevilla, Cevilla should do so in return. "We're . . . okay."

"Just okay."

"*Ya*. I'm concerned about how his *familye* is reacting to our relationship. His *dochder* seems upset about it."

"Have you talked to her?"

"I've tried. Her phone always goes to voice mail." Cevilla scowled. "And she never returns *mei* calls, but Richard says she's just a very busy woman."

"Sounds like an excuse."

"I thought so too. But there's not much I can do about it. The ball is in Richard's court, so to speak. Just like it's in Levi's and Nina's courts. You have to let them figure out things for themselves."

"Then why were you so insistent on playing matchmaker with *yer* nephew? And with Martha and Seth?"

Delilah didn't even know about another couple, Lucy and Shane. But they lived in Iowa, and Cevilla wasn't going to admit to another episode of meddling, which had turned out well only because of God's will, not her machinations. "Because I was a nosy old biddy, that's why. But I'm retired from the matchmaking business now. I mean it this time. I suggest you do the same unless you want to drive a wedge between you and *yer grosskinner*."

"*Nee*," she said, sounding horrified. "I hadn't thought about it like that."

A knock sounded on the front door, and Richard walked in. "Pardon me," he said. "I didn't realize you had company, Cevilla."

"I'm a surprise guest." Delilah popped up from

the couch and picked up her coat. "I'll see myself out." She turned to Cevilla and said, "*Danki.*"

Cevilla nodded and stood. When Delilah was gone, Richard asked, "What was that all about?"

"Girl talk." Cevilla couldn't help but smile.

"Which means none of my business." He returned her smile, his eyes filled with warmth. "Is it too late for supper?"

She couldn't resist him when he looked at her like that. "No," she said. "It's never too late."

Chapter 5

The next morning Selah wondered what she had gotten herself into.

"*Nee, nee.* That's not the proper way to clean a sink," Delilah said, shaking her head.

Selah turned toward her, bewildered. Delilah had insisted on training her the moment she'd arrived at the inn. She looked at the sink, which seemed fine to her. How many times had she cleaned a sink? Too many to count. "What did I do wrong?"

"Always wipe counterclockwise." She took the rag from Selah. "Like this."

She watched as Delilah wiped the sink with quick, efficient, and counterclockwise movements. Talk about being picky. Selah didn't think it mattered which way she wiped the sink as long as it was clean. But Delilah was her new boss, and Selah would do it her way.

"Now try it again."

Selah recleaned the sink according to Delilah's specifications. She even found a spot Delilah had missed but said nothing and cleaned it off. She took a step back while Delilah inspected her work. It did look better than it had the first time she'd cleaned it.

"Perfect." She turned to Selah and gave her a

small smile. "I think you'll work out fine."

Selah remained under Delilah's tutelage for the rest of the day, learning how to clean each room until it shone. The guest rooms were decorated simply but with typical Amish touches—quilts, a calendar on the wall, a bouquet of artificial flowers on the windowsill, a few books and a Bible in a small bookcase across from the bed. Each room also had a small bathroom with a pedestal sink, a cabinet above the toilet, and a shower. The only thing different between the four rooms was the paint color—a delicate blue, a butter yellow, a soft rose, and a pale sage green. Each room was peaceful and inviting. Selah imagined the inn would have plenty of business when it opened.

After cleaning the rooms, she was instructed on the proper way to mop the wood floors, which were brand-new but had an artificial patina to make them look old. Then they spent the rest of the afternoon in the prep kitchen, where breakfast would be assembled each morning. The bulk of the food preparation would be done by Delilah in the larger kitchen in the house. "As soon as we start having guests, you'll be serving breakfast until Nina can. That means coming at six in the morning, not seven," Delilah said, and then she proceeded to show her how to put together the meals and serve them.

Selah hadn't known that would be in her job

description. She'd served plenty of meals, and she didn't mind getting to the inn that early. But she was glad the task would be temporary. She didn't want to make a mistake that would put a damper on the guests' experience.

Delilah showed her how to clean the kitchen, and even though all the appliances were already clean, Selah cleaned them again. "The kitchen must be spotless and efficient at all times," Delilah stated. "You never know when an inspector might drop by unannounced."

Selah gave a counter a final wipe and then glanced at the clock. Four thirty. Her first day was nearly over, and she was exhausted. She was confident she could handle working for Delilah Stoll. It wouldn't be easy, but she was determined to work hard and prove they hadn't made a mistake by hiring her.

They were walking out of the kitchen when Levi burst out of the office. Delilah had kept her so busy that she hadn't seen him all day—for some reason he hadn't joined them for lunch—but she'd had his handkerchief and the money for the candy in the pocket of her apron, ready to give them to him.

"*Gut* news!" he exclaimed. "We have our first reservation!" He pulled out a ledger from behind the counter.

Delilah rushed over to him. "Who is it? When are they coming? How long are they staying?"

"One guest, a Mr. Talbot. Staying for two days." Levi grinned. "He'll be here on Friday."

"But we're not opening until Saturday," Delilah said.

"I made an exception." He looked at his grandmother, his expression suddenly and uncharacteristically stern. Just as uncharacteristically, Delilah nodded and didn't say another word.

Selah was happy for them. Now that she had seen almost every nook and cranny of the inn, she realized how much work and financial investment had gone into creating the beautiful property, and she found herself also wanting it to succeed.

"Wait," Delilah said, frowning. "Is the inspector still coming tomorrow?"

"He is. I confirmed with him again. After that, we'll be open for business."

"If everything checks out," Delilah mumbled.

"It will. I spent the day going over everything, including the plumbing. Three times." He smirked, and then his smiled widened. "Where's *yer* faith, *Grossmammi*?"

She glanced up at him, her smile returning. "God's will," she said.

"God's will."

Selah leaned against the kitchen doorjamb. Levi had to be the most optimistic person she'd ever met. Except for the moment in the kitchen yesterday, when he was upset with his grandmother, it was as if nothing bothered him.

She was a little envious of that. While she was learning how to see life on the brighter side, Levi's optimism was natural.

"Selah," Delilah called. "Come here."

Selah went to her while Levi wrote down the reservation in the ledger. She glanced at his handwriting, which unlike hers, was neat and easy to read.

"We still have so much to do," Delilah said. She started ticking off tasks on her fingers. "I need to show you the laundry, and how to clean the quilts properly . . . I defy anyone to say Stoll Inn isn't as clean as freshly fallen snow."

"They wouldn't dare," Levi said, looking at Selah with the beginnings of a grin.

"Then we have to make sure everything is stocked, from bathrooms to firewood to—"

"*Grossmutter*," Levi said, his voice gentle, "we have time to get everything done."

Delilah nodded, looking calmer. Then her eyes widened. "Nina was supposed to get Christmas decorations." She gestured to the tidy lobby. "We can't have a guest here without decorations."

"Actually we could—"

"Did she get them, Levi?"

He shook his head. "Not unless she's hiding them in her room."

"I guess she could *geh* shopping tomorrow. I can tend to Loren."

Selah watched the back-and-forth between

Delilah and Levi. Although he was much calmer than his grandmother was, for the first time she noticed tiny lines of strain on Levi's face. "I can pick them up," she said, surprising herself by volunteering. "I just finished decorating Christian and Ruby's *haus* the other day." She couldn't bring herself to call it her house, even though she would be living there for a while yet. "I know exactly where we can get some *schee* decorations in Barton. Just tell me what you need."

"Oh, that's wonderful, Selah," Delilah said. "Levi will give you the money in the morning, and then you can help me tackle our remaining tasks in the afternoon."

"I'll just *geh* with her," Levi said.

"You will?" Both Selah and Delilah looked at him.

"*Ya.* I need to stop by the bank in Barton. The inspector isn't coming until after lunch, and we can knock out two birds with one stone."

"I never liked that expression," Delilah said, her brow pinching.

"You know what I mean." He turned to Selah. "As long as it's all right with you."

Selah nodded, but she was confused. She wouldn't say no to him since he was her boss and this was her first day of work, but she was stunned that he was willing to ride with her after what he'd said to Delilah yesterday. He was a confusing man.

"Are you sure?"

To Selah's surprise, Delilah's words were directed to her. She looked genuinely concerned for some reason. "*Ya*. I'm sure."

Her expression relaxed. "Then it's settled. *Danki*, Selah, and I'll see you tomorrow at seven sharp. I'll arrange to have a taxi pick up both of you at nine." She left the lobby.

Selah turned to see Levi looking at her. He didn't say anything, and neither did she. She realized this would be the perfect time to return his handkerchief and money, so she started to reach into her pocket.

"How did you survive *yer* first day?"

Surprised by the question, she said, "Fine. Although *yer grossmutter* is particular about how she wants things done."

"Nitpicky is what we call it." He stuffed his hands into his pants pockets. "She can be a tyrant sometimes, among other things. But she's harmless." He met Selah's gaze, his eyes serious. "I, uh, want to talk to you about—"

"I almost forgot." Delilah barged back into the lobby. "Before you *geh*, Selah, stop by the kitchen to get *yer* basket. I put a few treats in there for you and Christian and Ruby to enjoy."

Selah smiled, pleasantly surprised. "*Danki*, Delilah. You didn't have to do that."

With a bright grin, the "tyrant" bustled out of the lobby again.

Levi glanced at the wood-carved clock on the wall above the woodstove, and Selah followed his gaze. The clock was simple but well made. "It's quitting time for you," he said. "I'll fill out *yer* time card." He hesitated. "Do you need a ride home?"

"I don't mind walking."

"It's pretty cold out. I can give you a ride."

She shook her head. "*Danki* just the same. I'll see you tomorrow." She left the lobby to don her coat, bonnet, and scarf in the mudroom, and then she went to the house to get the basket. On her way home she peeked inside and saw a plate of Christmas sugar cookies and a loaf of bread wrapped in a tea towel. Both smelled yummy.

She was halfway home when she remembered the handkerchief and money. Not again! She would definitely give them to Levi tomorrow. She snuggled inside her coat against the winter chill and let out a long breath. It had been a long day but a satisfying one. She wasn't concerned about Delilah too much despite the woman's pickiness—or nitpickiness—and her sometimes contradictory nature. The cookies and bread were a nice treat, something she hadn't expected from her. Levi must have gotten his thoughtfulness from her.

Levi. He had started to say something before Delilah interrupted him. If it was important, she was sure he would tell her tomorrow when they went to Barton. She let out another breath. She and Levi would spend at least a couple of hours together. The ride in the car, the shopping, the ride back . . . Her nerves tightened. Then she settled down. He was her boss. Nothing else. She would be business friendly, polite but distant. That would be easy to do, especially with no other expectations between them. What a relief.

After Selah left, Levi questioned his impulsive decision to join her on a trip to Barton. He'd been stunned when she volunteered to shop for the Christmas decorations. It was outside the scope of her job for one thing, but he was grateful she said she would do it. And for some inexplicable reason, he didn't want her to go to Barton alone.

Not that he didn't think she was capable. Clearly she was. But it didn't feel right for her to take care of a task that should have already been done. At least his grandmother and Nina had thought about decorations. Decorating the inn for Christmas hadn't even crossed his mind.

He locked the front door of the inn and turned out the lights. Birch Creek was safe for the most part, but there'd been an incident of vandalism at Yoder's Bakery last year. The perpetrators had been teenagers, but he wasn't taking any chances. He also locked the back door before dashing through the cold to the house.

Grossmutter was at the stove finishing supper

preparations as Nina came into the room, *Daed* hobbling beside her.

"Loren," *Grossmutter* snapped. "What are you doing up?"

"I can't sit in that chair any longer." He gave her a weary smile. "I'm joining you all for supper tonight."

Levi went to the mudroom and took a folding chair from against the wall. They kept a few there for when extra company showed up. He opened it and set it down at the end of the table where his father usually sat. Nina helped *Daed* settle into his regular chair and prop up his leg on the extra one.

Grossmutter banged a wooden spoon against the pot where she'd been stirring navy bean soup. They had soup at least three times a week during the winter months, and none of the family ever got tired of it. "You should be resting, Loren."

"I have been." His face was a little pale, but a spark shone in his eyes. Levi didn't blame him for wanting to get out of the living room to eat with them. If he were in his father's shoes, he would be bored out of his mind too.

Nina helped set the table while Levi sat down next to *Daed*. "Are you sure you're comfortable?" he asked.

"*Ya.*" His father squirmed a little. "I'm *gut*. I'm also ready to eat." He patted his flat stomach. "It's been awhile since I've had a real appetite."

When the table was set and everyone had taken their places, they said grace. Then *Daed* picked up his spoon and said, "How's the new hire working out?"

Levi opened his mouth to answer, but *Grossmammi* beat him to it. "She'll do," she said, putting several heaping ladles of soup into her bowl. She added a warm biscuit smothered in butter. If there was one thing his grandmother enjoyed, it was food.

"C'mon, you can give her more credit than that." Levi turned to his father. "I think she's going to work out fine. If she was able to handle her"—he pointed at his grandmother with his thumb—"she can do anything."

Nina snorted and took a sip of her iced tea. "That's a miracle."

"I beg *yer* pardon." Delilah looked offended. "And snorting is very unladylike."

Nina rolled her eyes. "I'm sorry." She sat up straight and lifted her little finger as she picked up her fork. "Is this better?"

Levi and his dad chuckled, but *Grossmammi* just rolled her eyes. She took a bite out of her biscuit and chewed furiously. He was glad to see Nina in a good mood, which was a big change from her attitude when they first moved to Birch Creek. She'd been homesick for Wisconsin and unsure about the family's grand adventure in opening the inn. At the time he had been worried about her, but after she made friends with Martha and then Ira, she settled in.

He smiled. It was good to see his family somewhat back to normal.

"Glad to hear Selah can hold her own." *Daed* dipped his spoon into the bean soup.

"She's also *schee*," Nina commented. "Don't you think so, Levi?"

Since they'd been teenagers, Nina and Levi had made it a game to tease each other about possible love interests, which was harmless since neither one of them had ever had one. But he wasn't in the mood for teasing, especially about Selah. He also couldn't disagree with Nina's assessment, but if he agreed out loud, Nina would never leave him alone. "She's . . . cute." Oh no, why had he said that? He might as well have said she was the prettiest girl in the county. She might just be.

His sister, father, and grandmother all looked at him.

"Cute?" Nina said, her eyes wide. "Did I hear you correctly? You've never said that about a *maedel* before."

He picked up a roll, and for a split second he thought about throwing it at her.

She continued to gape at him. "You've never said anything about any *maedel*, other than you're not interested."

He cringed, his words from yesterday coming back to haunt him. *I'm not interested in Selah.* If she had heard him say that about her, she hadn't mentioned it today. That didn't assuage his guilt, though.

Daed remained quiet, as he usually did when dinner conversation turned to teasing about non-existent relationships. Inwardly groaning, Levi looked at his grandmother, expecting that sly look she always got when she was thinking about pairing him up with someone. But she kept her head down and stayed silent like his father. Strange.

"So you do think she's *schee*," Nina said, persisting.

"I never said she was *schee*," Levi said, insistent. *I thought it, but I never said it.*

"You might as well have," Nina added.

"Good grief." He set down his fork, more than annoyed. He turned to *Daed*. "We're all set for the inspector tomorrow afternoon."

"He's changing the subject," Nina said in a loud whisper.

Grossmutter looked strangely confused. "I noticed that too."

"I'm talking about business." Levi scowled. "It's not like that isn't a relevant topic around here."

"Like I said, changing the subject." Nina grinned at him. "You do like her, Levi."

"I never said that, either."

"Then you're attracted to her?" *Grossmammi* pointed her fork at him, no longer looking confused but thoroughly interested.

"I'm not attracted to her!" He squeezed the roll in his hand. Fortunately he hadn't buttered it yet.

"Sounds like you might be interested, though," *Daed* said.

His entire family had gone *ab im kopp*. That was the only explanation. He pushed away from the table. "I'm going to do the chores."

"But you didn't finish *yer* supper," *Grossmammi* called out.

"I'm not hungry anymore." In the mudroom, he snatched his coat and woolen hat off their pegs, and then he stormed outside. Flakes of snow floated down, but he barely noticed them. He yanked open the barn door and barged inside. Taking a deep breath, he paused. He was sweating under his coat, and he stripped it off. Normally family teasing didn't bother him, and he'd always skillfully deflected it before. Not tonight. Tonight he was angry, and he had no idea why.

He plopped onto a hay bale and calmed down. He shouldn't let this get to him. He'd made it clear how he felt about Selah the other day, and that hadn't changed. Sure, he admired her for stepping up and helping with the decorations, and if *Grossmutter* was pleased with her work, then she was doing an excellent job as a maid. He was grateful for that too.

And so what if he thought she was pretty? And a little intriguing? That didn't mean anything. He had other things to focus on, like the inspection and the inn's opening. Hopefully they would get more reservations for this weekend and the inn would be full. With all that pressing on him, he didn't have the time or inclination to deal with teasing, no matter how good-natured—or in this case, immature.

Levi stood to give his horse his feed and a quick brushing. If his family wanted to childishly tease him about Selah again, he would ignore them. They were wasting their breath anyway.

Chapter 6

The next morning, Cevilla sipped her tea as Richard poured cream into his coffee. He'd joined her for breakfast, as was his habit every morning since he'd moved next door. Their routine was always the same. They had breakfast before seven, lunch at eleven, and supper at six. In between he read while she crocheted, and he helped her with light cleaning around the house. Then there was the obligatory nap—he on the couch, she in her chair—in the afternoon, and after supper he went back to his place. Normally she liked routine, but this morning the sameness of their days annoyed her.

Last night after Delilah left, they'd had a wonderful evening. But Richard still refrained from speaking about his daughter and joining the church. It appeared that today would go the same way. She set her teacup down with a clank. "Are you always this slow?"

Richard stopped stirring his coffee and looked surprised. "You're not exactly Speedy Gonzales yourself."

"Who?"

"Remember the cartoon? The mouse who moved so fast?"

"Oh." It had been so long since she'd watched

cartoons or any other kind of TV that she had drawn a blank.

"'The Fastest Mouse in All of Mexico.'" He chuckled. "Classic."

"That's not what I'm talking about."

He looked at her, lifting one gray eyebrow. "I don't understand."

She was tired of this roller coaster. She was used to being independent and not having to wait on someone else to make up their mind. Maybe that was the best way for her to live. God had known she was too impatient for a spouse. But that didn't sit well with her, either.

"Never mind," she said, grabbing her teacup and taking a long drink, ignoring the burn in her mouth.

"I'm not playing this game again."

Her gaze darted to him. "What game?"

"The one where you're clearly so bothered by something to make a comment about it, only to give me radio silence after." He rubbed his brow. "You're frustrating, you know that?"

His unexpected words hurt. "So are you." She crossed her arms. If he wanted a fight, she would give him one.

"Are you going to tell me what's wrong?"

She had been considering it, but now that he'd insulted her, she wasn't going to reveal anything. She uncrossed her arms and picked up her teacup, taking a leisurely sip this time.

"I see." He pushed away from the table, grabbed his cane, and stood.

"Where are you going?" she asked, shocked that he was taking his leave when they hadn't even started eating.

"Away from here." He turned and walked out of the kitchen.

By the time she'd scrambled to her feet and grabbed her own cane, the front door had slammed shut. For a slow man, he could move quickly when he wanted to.

She sank down on the chair, her frustration replaced with regret. Oh, why had she let her foolish pride get the best of her? She and Richard rarely argued, but they were both aware of the tension between them, which she knew was mostly her fault. He wasn't wrong about her being cagey with her thoughts. That was uncharacteristic of her, but she had vowed not to put undue pressure on him. Still, he wasn't exactly being forthright, either.

"Humph." She crossed her arms again. If he wanted to be this way, let him. In fact, let him go back to California. She ignored the stab of pain in her heart. *I need only you, Lord. Only you.*

She waited for the peace and encouragement that often came when she reaffirmed her devotion to the Lord. And it was there, mixed in with guilt and yearning that never seemed too far from her emotions. She loved Richard more than she ever thought possible. *But how long is he going to string me along?*

Or maybe he was satisfied with their relationship as it was. Maybe he didn't want anything more, like she did. Maybe when he told her he loved her, it wasn't as a potential husband to a potential wife, like she had wanted or hoped it would be. It was as a friend. A companion. Someone to pass the time with. She glowered. If that was the case, he should have gotten a dog.

Rarely was Cevilla confused, but she was now.

She needed to talk to someone about this. But who? Her grandniece Ivy? Other than Noah, she was Cevilla's only family relation. Or maybe she should seek out someone older than Ivy—like Ivy's mother, Mary Yoder, or Naomi Detweiler. They'd both had long, solid marriages that had weathered some difficult times.

"Or should I get a man's perspective?" she said out loud, tapping her finger against her chin. The more she thought about that, the more she thought it was a good idea. She also knew just the man she wanted to talk to.

"I want you to check into that Amish hotel."

Jackson looked up from his freshly poured bowl of fruity loops. He and his father were at the kitchen table having breakfast together, a rarity. Although Dad lived in a nice apartment complex near the hotel, he wasn't there that often, mostly staying over at Ashley's or going on trips with her. As for Jackson, he'd been spending more and more time at the hotel, working on his business. He frowned, disgusted. He never thought he'd be the mature one out of the two of them. "It's an inn, Dad. Not a hotel."

"Whatever." His father waved a dismissive hand.

Jackson squinted at him. "Did you wax your eyebrows?"

Dad ran a finger over the thin line of graying hair above his eye. "Ashley says it makes me look younger."

"More like ridiculous," Jackson mumbled before shoving a spoonful of cereal into his mouth. He frowned. "These things taste weird," he said with his mouth full.

"They're organic and unsweetened."

Jackson choked down the cereal. It seemed that Ashley, who subsisted mostly on carrots and kale, had infiltrated the kitchen too. He shoved the bowl away. What was the point of eating fruity loops if they weren't full of sugar and preservatives?

"I want you to check into that Amish *inn*," Dad repeated. "For a day or two, and then report back to me."

"Report what?"

Dad leaned forward. "Their weaknesses."

"Huh?"

"Don't play dumb." His father took a sip of

orange juice. "There has to be something there we can exploit."

The milk seemed to turn sour in Jackson's stomach. "I'm not playing dumb. I'm sincerely baffled that you would involve me in something like this." *And appalled.*

"Your future is at stake too."

"How? You have enough money to buy a street full of hotels, with plenty left over."

"That's not the point." Dad sat back in his chair. "It's not only about money. It's dominance. Being the top dog." He clenched his fist. "Crushing your competitor."

"I thought it was about integrity and customer service."

"Not if you want to succeed."

This was one reason he'd been eager to go away to school. Even when his father didn't have money, he was still consumed with being number one, even if it meant leaving a wake of damage in his path. The money just gave him more opportunity. "Keep me out of your schemes."

His father scowled. "Here I am giving you a roof over your head and food to eat—"

"Questionable food," he muttered.

"And you would refuse me this one small request. Not that I'm surprised. You've always been an ungrateful son."

Jackson took a deep breath and counted to ten, something he'd learned to do a long time ago

when dealing with his father. "I'm not ungrateful," he said, keeping his tone even. "What
you're asking me to do is wrong."

"You have to get a stronger spine if you're
going to have your own business, Jackson. That's
what I bought that fancy education for."

"One year," Jackson said, reminding him. "You
paid for one year. I took out loans for the rest."
Which was why he'd ended up back here. He
couldn't afford to go into any more debt.

"So you're just going to forget all the money I
spent raising you? All the time I invested?"

Jackson searched his father's expression, which
didn't match his words at all. He was emotionless,
as if he was talking about the weather instead of
using manipulation. But that was how he was—
at first, anyway. Jackson knew if he didn't give
in, his father would fly into a rage. *Let him.* He
wasn't going to be guilted into doing something
that violated his core beliefs.

"Maybe you should go live with your mother.
Let her take care of you for a while."

He rolled his eyes. "I'm not a child."

"You're not independent either, are you?"

The point hit home. He couldn't live with his
mother, who had moved to Nevada with her
boyfriend, Fred, right after Jackson had graduated
high school. Jackson had visited her a couple
of times, but she was so wrapped up in her own
life, the same way his father was, that he stopped

spending what little money he had on airfare to go see her. At least his father could afford to let him live here and pay him a wage. His mother couldn't do that. Jackson wasn't sure she would even if she could.

Dad stood up from the table and looked down at him. "I knew you were going to refuse," he said. "That's why I made a reservation for myself."

Jackson clutched his spoon. "You what?"

"This weekend I'll be staying at the Stoll Inn. I'll get the information I'm looking for, one way or another." He grabbed his keys off the kitchen bar and strolled out of the apartment.

Jackson scrubbed his hand over his face. Now what was he supposed to do? Without a doubt his father would go through with his plan. When Dad set his mind to do something, good or bad, he always saw it through, and he was determined to bring the Amish owners down.

He fell back into his chair and massaged his temples, his conscience kicking into high gear. After a few minutes, he grabbed his phone off the kitchen table and called his father.

Dad answered right away. "Yeah?"

"I'll do it." Jackson squeezed his eyes shut and then opened them again. "Cancel the reservation. I'll set up another one for the near future."

"You don't think I'd agree to that, do you? I know you'll never make a reservation on your own. That's why I made this one for you."

He could practically see his father smiling in triumph. "I don't understand."

"The reservation I made isn't in my name. It's in yours. I knew you'd eventually see things my way, son. Oh, and clean the kitchen before you leave. Ashley says you're a slob." *Click.*

Jackson clenched his teeth. His father had manipulated him again. *Like he always does.* He banged his fist on the table. *Guess it didn't matter that I might have had plans this weekend.* That wouldn't have stopped his father, either. Jackson's plans were never a consideration. Dad was only focused on one thing—getting his way. And as usual when it came to Jackson lately, he'd gotten it.

On Thursday morning Selah walked to work again. The air temperature was a little colder than it had been yesterday, and at breakfast Christian had mentioned there was a possibility of snow this weekend. There wasn't enough time for Delilah to train her on the inn's laundry procedure before the taxi arrived to take her and Levi to Barton, so she went outside and swept the porch and steps, first placing her purse on the two-person swing at the end of the porch. When she finished, she sat down on the swing, breathing in the crisp air and looking at the trees. They'd lost the last of their fall leaves, so the landscape was stark. But it was also tranquil.

Since she'd returned to Birch Creek, she hadn't

taken any time to sit in silence. She was always doing something—cooking or cleaning for Ruby and Christian or searching real estate ads. When she took walks, she took them with purpose—either walking to her new job or trying to exercise her worries away. Last night she'd been so tired from work that she'd fallen asleep without saying her nighttime prayers. This was the first moment she'd had to just sit in the stillness that was calming her mind. She closed her eyes, letting the peace wash over her—

"Selah."

She jumped, her eyes flying open. Her hand went to her chest.

Levi winced. "Sorry. I didn't mean to scare you. I didn't realize you were asleep."

"I wasn't." She popped up from the swing so quickly that the seat banged into the back of her knees. "I was just sitting for a minute." She grabbed the broom leaning against the porch railing and began to sweep again.

"It's okay to take a break once in a while." He took the broom from her. Then he smiled and looked out at the parking lot. "I've come out here a few times myself to enjoy the peaceful mornings."

"You weren't on the clock," she said.

His smile faded. "I'm always on the clock." He turned to her. "The taxi should be here any minute."

She reached for the broom. "That's enough time to finish the porch."

Levi held the broom out of her reach. "The porch looks fine. Like I said, you can take a break. Even two or three, if you want."

"I don't think Delilah would like that."

"She's not really a tyrant, Selah. Okay, sometimes she can be, but she doesn't want you to work *yer* fingers down to nubs." His expression turned stern, but there was a gleam in his eyes. "We're also legally obligated to give you breaks and a lunch, and you're obligated to take them."

She couldn't help but smile a little. Despite his father's broken leg and the inn's upcoming opening, he seemed relaxed and lighthearted, which was having an even more calming effect on her. "I understand." She picked up her purse and opened it. "I have something to give you."

"Oh?" His brow lifted.

Selah took out the handkerchief and two one-dollar bills and then handed them to him. "I washed the handkerchief," she said. "*Danki* for letting me borrow it. I'm sorry it took me so long to return it to you."

He frowned as he looked at the items in his hand. "I said you could keep it." He glanced up at her. "What are the two dollars for?"

"The cinnamon candies. *Danki* for those too."

His frown deepened. "I didn't expect you to pay me back."

"I want to." She gripped the handle of her purse. His disturbed expression bothered her. He seemed almost offended.

A silver four-door car pulled into the driveway. Levi turned around. "Taxi's here." He stuffed the handkerchief and money into his pocket and went down the porch steps.

Selah let out a sigh. She didn't have that small debt hanging over her anymore. But why didn't she feel relieved?

"Front or back?" he said in a curt tone when she met him at the car.

"Back."

He held the door open for her but didn't say anything. Maybe he really was upset because she gave him back the handkerchief and money. But why would he be?

"Where do you want to go in Barton?" the dour driver asked, her gray hair tightly wrapped into a small bun at the nape of her neck, her pale lips wrinkled around the edges.

"The craft store. Noelle's something," she said as Levi got into the passenger seat. "I can't remember the exact name. I've only been there once."

"I know where it is." She threw the car in reverse, and they were on their way.

Selah stayed quiet as Levi tried to engage the driver in the smallest of small talk, but the woman wasn't having any of it. Finally he gave up. At least one person was immune to his charms. The rest of the ride to Barton was completely silent.

The driver, who, Levi managed to find out, was named Marge, pulled up in front of Noelle's. "Be back in an hour. Unless you need longer than that."

"Could you make it an hour and a half? I need to stop by the bank down the street. You can just pick us up there." He told her the name of the bank, and she nodded. Levi shut the passenger door, and before Selah could fully open hers, he opened it.

When the driver took off, Selah turned to go into the store, but Levi stopped her. "We have some extra time," he said. "Before we do anything else, we need to talk."

Levi led Selah to the parking lot on the side of the store. It was empty except for two cars, and he was thankful for a little privacy. He shoved his hands into his coat pockets. When he felt the handkerchief, his irritation started all over again.

"Is something wrong?" she asked.

He was about to speak, but the worried look in her pretty blue eyes caught him off guard. He hadn't meant to scare her. He just knew they couldn't spend the rest of the morning together without setting things straight. "Not exactly."

"Did I do something?"

The vulnerability in her voice made him want to reach out to her, to reassure her that she didn't need to worry. *"Nee.* You haven't. I just want to clear things up between us."

A strong, cold wind kicked up, and she shivered. He needed to hurry this along. It wasn't fair to make her stand out in the cold while he tried to find the right words—and tried not to stare at her red cheeks so he wouldn't be tempted to warm them with the palms of his hands.

He froze. Where did *that* thought come from?

"Whatever I did, I promise not to do it again." The words came out in a flurry. "I really need this job, Levi. Please don't fire me."

Her statement brought him out of his stupor. "Fire you? This has *nix* to do with the job. Don't worry, *yer* job is safe."

She let out a deep breath.

"We need to talk about us." That was the wrong thing to say. Panicked, he added, "I mean, there's *nee* us, of course."

"Because you're not interested."

His stomach seemed to sink to his knees. As he feared, she had heard what he said in the kitchen that day. "I can explain that. *Mei grossmammi* is an annoying romantic when it comes to Nina and me. She tries to fix us up with every single person she meets. I wanted to set the record straight with her before she started meddling. That's all."

Selah glanced at the ground and then up at him again. She huddled further into her coat. "That makes sense," she said.

He blew out a breath. "I'm glad you understand. She can be manipulative sometimes. I wanted to spare you—I mean both of us—her shenanigans."

She nodded, looking a little less tense. "I appreciate that."

"And as far as the handkerchief and money go, you didn't have to do that. I have plenty of handkerchiefs, and the candy . . ." How was he supposed to explain the candy when he didn't fully understand why he'd bought it for her? "Early Christmas present," he said. Not the best explanation, but that was all he could come up with.

"Oh. That was very nice of you."

"I'm a nice guy." He grinned. "At least I try to be."

She smiled and looked at him from beneath her lashes. "I don't think you have to try too hard."

Her compliment warmed him so much that he barely felt the cold. But she was still shivering, and he couldn't let that go on. "Let's get inside and get you warm."

They headed for Noelle's front door. "You're not cold?" she asked. "It's freezing out here."

Levi just smiled. *Nee. I'm not cold at all.*

Chapter 7

Every bit of Noelle's store was filled with Christmas decorations, some for sale, some for show. The scents of cinnamon and pine filled the air, and Selah breathed it in. But she had to force herself to focus on the task at hand—purchasing Christmas decorations for the inn. She was finding that difficult after her talk with Levi. She'd been afraid he was going to fire her, although she had no idea what she could have possibly done wrong yesterday. She hadn't meant to beg him for her job, but she'd been so anxious that the words just flew out of her mouth. Thankfully he reassured her, but then he shocked her when he alluded to what he'd said the day she'd been hired.

Now that she knew the real reason behind his words, the sting she'd felt was gone. His explanation made sense. She knew from Martha how Cevilla had meddled when it came to her and Seth. They had fallen in love on their own, which had proven Cevilla right that they belonged together, but that still didn't make Martha appreciate Cevilla's intrusion. Selah wouldn't want that for herself, either. She was grateful Levi had nipped that idea right away.

She considered apologizing to him about returning the handkerchief, but she stopped herself. Sometimes she overthought a situation, and this was probably one of those times. She felt more at ease around him now, and he seemed relaxed as they walked through the store. There was no need to give an apology and make things between them weird again.

The decorations and crafts Noelle, the store's English owner, had stocked seemed more rustic and in line with Amish décor than typical English glitter and sparkle, so they had plenty of options to choose from.

"If you can make the inn smell like this place, I'll make you employee of the month," Levi said as they walked down an aisle filled with scented pine cones and boughs, as well as cinnamon sticks.

Selah grinned. "I'll see what I can do."

They spent almost an hour choosing decorations. Rather, Selah chose the decorations while Levi tried to be interested, at least in the beginning. When she heard him sigh for the fifth time, she turned to him. "I think I can take care of the rest of this. You don't have to keep shopping with me."

He picked up a cranberry-scented candle. "And miss out on all this excitement?"

She took the candle from him and set it back down. "I'll put you out of *yer* misery."

He looked relieved. "I'll be in the hardware store next door."

When he dashed off, she chuckled. Apparently shopping at a hardware store wasn't as much of a hardship for him. She continued to look at the array of ribbons, candles, and other decorations, picking out what she thought would look good in the inn while being mindful of price. By the time Levi returned, the clerk was ringing up the last of her purchases.

The clerk gave her the final amount, and Selah bit her lip. Was she spending too much?

But Levi didn't bat an eye as he pulled out his checkbook and paid for the purchases. After they left laden with bags, they walked down the street to the bank.

"If I chose too much, I can return some of it," she said. Several cars drove past them as they traveled on the sidewalk.

"We'll use them every year, so no worries." He paused, looking down at her. "I appreciate you taking the cost into consideration." He tilted his head. "You really are angling for employee of the month, aren't you?"

"It's a worthy goal. The competition is fierce."

Levi chuckled, and Selah laughed with him. It was nice to feel comfortable around him like this. Then again, he made it easy. But she still had to remind herself that she didn't want to feel too comfortable with him. He was her boss, not her friend.

She waited in the bank lobby while Levi took care of his business, and then they walked outside to find that the lemon-faced driver had showed up right on time. When they got back to the inn, Selah started decorating and Levi disappeared into the office.

Nina helped for a little while, tying red and green ribbon around plain white candles. "*Daed*'s taking a nap, and I need a break," she'd said. Her thick brows pinched over her eyes. "He's getting crabby." She helped for almost an hour and then went back to the house to make Loren's lunch.

Soon Delilah came into the lobby carrying a basket of food. "The decorations are perfect," she said with a wide grin. She put the basket on one of the tables in the lobby and drew in a deep breath. "They smell wonderful too. I'm sure our guests will be pleased."

Selah smiled, a bit pleased herself. She helped Delilah set out the food, a delicious-looking lunch of swiss cheese, bread and butter pickles, trail bologna sandwiches, apple slices, and home-made seasoned crackers.

"Selah," Delilah said as she closed the basket and set it on the floor, "will you please tell Levi lunch is ready?"

She paused, remembering what Levi had said about Delilah's matchmaking. But she didn't detect anything underlying in Delilah's request. His grandmother must have gotten the message. "Sure," she said. "Be right back." She stepped to the office door and knocked.

"Come in," Levi said.

"Lunchtime," she said, opening the door a crack.

He looked up from the ledger book on his desk, his brow furrowed a bit. Then he brightened. "Be right there."

She nodded and closed the door, pausing before heading back to the table. Although he tried to conceal it with his usual smile, she hadn't missed the concern in his eyes. It hit her what an important responsibility he had while his father was healing, and he was probably dealing with challenges she had no idea about. She determined that she was going to make things as easy for him and the rest of the Stolls as she could by doing the best job she could. She didn't want Levi worrying about the maid service on top of everything else.

As she sat down at the table with Delilah, Levi came out of the office. Instead of looking concerned, he appeared cheery. "I'm starving," he said, lowering himself into the chair opposite his grandmother. "Everything looks *gut*."

After they prayed, Delilah's eyes widened. "I forgot the tea," she said. "I made some earlier in the prep kitchen."

"I'll get it." Levi started to get up, but Delilah stopped him.

"Selah, you *geh* get it. You can also serve it. This will be *gut* practice for you, for when our first guest arrives tomorrow."

She had forgotten all about the temporary serving job. "Of course." She went to the kitchen, where she placed the pitcher of tea and three glasses on a tray. Then she served the tea to Delilah and Levi with ease.

"Excellent service," Levi said, picking up his glass. He gave her a sly look.

"Pouring tea isn't that difficult." She had to smile at his expression. When she looked at Delilah, the woman seemed confused, her perplexed gaze dashing back and forth between Levi and her. Then she shook her head and picked up the small jar of pickles.

"Trail bologna. *Mei* favorite sandwich." Levi took a large bite.

"Selah, after we see to stocking all the rooms this afternoon, we'll need to *geh* over the particulars of the hostess job," Delilah said. "You'll need to learn how to greet the guests, make sure they feel comfortable, show them to their rooms, ask them about food allergies—"

"Food allergies?" Her stomach started to churn. She thought all she'd have to do was serve them breakfast.

"Here's the list." Delilah reached into the pocket of her apron and pulled out a folded piece of paper. "All the duties are there. You'll need to memorize them before tomorrow."

Selah scanned the paper. The list was lengthy. The tasks weren't too difficult, but there was room for error. If she messed up on the allergies, she would be in big trouble.

"Don't worry," Levi said, his voice low and encouraging. "It'll be a piece of cake for you."

She put the list in her apron pocket. Cleaning she could do. Pouring tea was a no-brainer. But the hostess job sounded like a lot of responsibility. She hadn't been the best at being responsible of late.

I've changed, remember? I'm not that same person. I am responsible. She looked at Levi and said, "Piece of cake."

Cevilla spent most of the day fretting, and she was unhappy about that. Cevilla Schlabach didn't fret. But she hadn't seen Richard all day. She'd half expected him to come back and apologize for leaving so suddenly without telling her where he was going. What if something happened to him? He wasn't a spring chicken. She'd even peeked outside her bedroom window, which had a view to his driveway. His car had been there all day. What was he doing cooped up in that house? Of course, she could go over there and find out, but she didn't. She wasn't the one who left. *Even if it was* mei *fault he did.*

She'd also been arguing with herself about going to see Freemont. This morning the idea of talking to the bishop about Richard had seemed like a good one. Now she wasn't so sure. She didn't want to involve someone else in her problems, especially Freemont. He had enough responsibility with his bishop duties—not to mention rebuilding his farm, which had burned down last year. It was winter, but there was still much to be done, and she didn't want to infringe on that.

But he was also a married man, and he might have some insight into Richard's reluctance to talk about his daughter as well as his future. She needed a male perspective, and Noah was too young. Freemont wasn't exactly elderly, but he was in his early fifties, and that made him experienced enough for her.

Suppertime came and went, without Richard. It was too dark outside to spy on his driveway again. "That's it," she said, getting up from her chair. She would go talk to Freemont tomorrow. She'd always been a woman of action—and waiting around for Richard to realize how foolish he was being irritated her.

She heard a knock on the door, and her heart leapt. He'd come over after all. She shuffled to the door, her cane thumping on the wood floor. "You've finally come to your senses," she said as she opened the door, a blast of frigid air nearly knocking her off her feet. "Delilah?"

"Goodness, it's freezing." Without waiting to be invited in, Delilah bustled past Cevilla. "Not fit for man or beast out there."

Cevilla shut the door. "What are you doing here?"

Delilah spun around, already taking off her bonnet. "I've made another mistake," she said, her eyes lighting up behind her glasses, which were a little foggy around the edges of the lenses.

"You don't look too upset about it." Cevilla hobbled to her rocking chair and sat down.

"I'm positive now that Levi and Selah do like each other." She dashed to sit down on the couch. "One hundred percent positive."

"That's great." She could barely muster any enthusiasm, but not because she didn't care about Selah and Levi. She rubbed her throbbing temples. "Now really isn't a *gut* time—"

"You have to help me get them together. Levi's already put down his foot, so whatever we come up with has to be clever."

"Delilah, what about letting God handle this, like you agreed to?"

"God needs a nudge every once in a while." She peered over her glasses.

Cevilla glanced at the front door again, wishing Richard would walk in. Surely one argument couldn't end an entire relationship—could it?

"You're not listening to me, Cevilla." Delilah huffed. "You're being a little rude."

"Rude?" Cevilla snapped. "You come over here—uninvited, by the way—and start making demands for me to help you with Levi and Selah, who just yesterday you were saying didn't like each other, and I'm rude?" She gripped the handle of her cane. "You aren't the only one with problems, Delilah."

"Oh." Delilah's shoulders slumped slightly. "I see."

Cevilla sighed. "I'm sorry. I shouldn't have said all that." When Delilah rose from her seat, she said, "You don't have to leave. We can figure out something for Levi and Selah."

"Peppermint," Delilah said.

"What?"

"Peppermint tea. That's what you like, *ya*?"

She nodded. "*Ya*."

"I'll be right back."

Cevilla sighed as Delilah dashed off to the kitchen. She'd been here enough times to know where everything was to make tea. She had to admit her little outburst had helped her feel better. She wasn't angry with Delilah, but she had pent up her emotions all day, and it was exhausting. She was too old for all these topsy-turvy emotions.

Delilah came back with one cup of tea and handed it to Cevilla. "Now," she said, settling herself on the couch, "tell me what's wrong."

Cevilla took a sip of the tea and then set the cup on the side table beside her chair. "I don't know what to do about Richard."

"Can you be more specific?"

She heaved another sigh. "He hasn't asked me to marry him yet."

"Ah."

"I'm at *mei* wits' end." She turned and looked

toward the window, growing silent, which she almost never was except during church.

"Are you expecting him to propose?" Delilah asked.

"*Ya.* I suppose. Oh, I don't know what I'm expecting. I just know I'm tired of waiting for him to make a decision. Time's short, you know."

"I certainly do." She glanced down at her lap. "It seems to pass faster with each day, doesn't it?" She looked at Cevilla. "Maybe that's why you and I are both in a hurry. You to get married, me to marry off *mei grosskinner*. We know how fleeting life is."

"Sometimes I just want to lasso Richard, take him to Freemont, and tell him to baptize him."

"I wouldn't put that past you. I wouldn't put it past me if I were in *yer* situation." She laughed. "I know how hard it is for you to be patient, Cevilla. But the reality is you can't control Richard's decision about joining the church. That's between God and him."

"I'm not used to feeling helpless," she said, her voice uncharacteristically weak and soft. "I've been giving *mei* need to control over to God, but the more this drags on, the harder it is to do that." She shook her head. "How many times have I given others that same advice? God is in control. I know that here." She put her hand over her heart. "It's *mei* head that's not getting the memo."

"Maybe *yer* heart too."

127

She fidgeted with the cuff of her sleeve. "I found love after seventy years. And I can't do anything about it."

"But isn't that the definition of faith?" Delilah said. "Giving everything over to the Lord, even during the hardest times? The uncertain times? When there's *nix* you can do, all you have is faith."

"You're right." Delilah wasn't telling her anything new. Yet it was so hard to put into practice right now. "Let's forget about Richard and talk about Levi and Selah."

Delilah shook her head. "I've changed *mei* mind."

"Again?"

"For sure this time. I need to practice what I just preached. I can't, and shouldn't, do anything about those two. If they're meant to be together, God will put them together."

"Without our interference?"

She smiled. "*Ya.* As much as it pains me to say it, without our interference." She rose from the couch. "I'm sorry I barged in on you again."

"No apologies needed." It took a moment, but Cevilla got to her feet. "You can come over anytime, Delilah. You just saw me in a sour mood, that's all." After she walked Delilah to the door, she said, "*Danki.* You really helped me."

Delilah took her hand and squeezed it. "That's what friends are for."

128

Chapter 8

On Friday afternoon, Jackson pulled his car into the gravel driveway in front of the Stoll Inn. His father might drive a brand-new BMW, but Jackson was content with his used sedan. He didn't have any car payments, the insurance was cheaper, and it wasn't like his father had ever offered to buy him a new one. If he did, Jackson would refuse. When it came to Dad, strings were always attached. He looked at the inn in front of him. *Case in point.*

To the left was a small, empty gravel lot for parking. He had his pick of spots, so he chose one before turning off the engine. But he didn't get out. He still couldn't believe he was doing this. He'd thought about backing out, but better him doing the dirty work than his father. His dad was out to destroy. Jackson would give him only enough information to shut him up.

Resigned, he grabbed his duffel bag off the passenger seat and then got out of the car and faced the inn. The air was freezing, much colder than it had been yesterday. A light dusting of snow covered the ground, the surrounding trees, and the roof, creating an idyllic scene. He clicked a button on his key fob and the car beeped, locking the doors. That probably wasn't necessary out in the middle of nowhere, but it was a habit.

When he entered the inn, he noticed a welcoming scent of cinnamon spice and something baking. Banana bread, maybe. Or some kind of cake. Hard to tell, but it smelled good. He surveyed the lobby, which was half the size of the lobby in his father's hotel yet didn't feel confining. Cozy was a better term, which also applied to the fire in the dark-blue woodstove. Split logs were stacked in a leather and iron holder on the hearth, and a picture of nine painted quilt blocks in red, white, and blue had been hung above the stone firebox. Christmas decorations abounded, but they weren't overdone or overly complicated. They were plain, especially compared to the excessive sparkly and tacky decorations Ashley had insisted his father use in the hotel lobby. The lobby also held several small tables with chairs, he assumed for the breakfast they served.

He turned and rang the small silver bell on the counter. A carousel with postcards sat next to it, and an organizer with information brochures was attached to the wall near the door. He recognized the brochures advertising attractions, restaurants, and craft shops in the greater Holmes County and Akron area. They had many of the same ones at the hotel.

A guy about his age appeared from a small

room behind the counter. He had silver metal-rimmed glasses and a blond bowl-cut hairstyle, and he wore a blue pullover sweater. An Amish woman who looked similar in age followed and then stood slightly behind him. She wore a light-purple dress and the white bonnet-looking hat Jackson had noticed all Amish women wore. They both looked like something out of the 1800s.

The man held out his hand to Jackson, his expression friendly and bright. "Levi Stoll. You must be Mr. Talbot."

He shook Levi's hand, a little surprised he was recognized right away. "I am. But call me Jackson. I have a reservation for the weekend."

"Got you right here." Levi tapped an open guest book with his index finger. Not a computer in sight, although Jackson did see a solar-operated calculator.

Levi turned to the woman behind him and motioned her forward. "This is Selah. She's our hostess."

"In training." She gave Levi a brief glance and then smiled at Jackson and handed him two pieces of paper. "Could you fill out these forms, please?"

He took the papers and nodded. He didn't really have to look at them, knowing they were prob-ably similar to the check-in forms they had at the hotel.

"We're glad you're here," Levi continued,

"although we thought you might cancel since they're calling for a lot of snow this weekend."

"I had no idea." Maybe he should have checked the weather forecast before he left Barton.

"Five inches, at least. Good sledding weather, if you like that sort of thing. We have a few sleds available."

Jackson hadn't been sledding since he was a kid. He looked at Levi, trying to judge if the guy was serious. Both he and Selah seemed to be. "Um, we'll see." Jackson filled out the forms and then signed them before handing them back to Selah.

"Will you be paying with a credit card?" Levi asked.

He glanced at their ancient, manual, sliding credit card machine. "Cash." He dug his wallet out of his back pocket. At least his father had paid for this charade. He couldn't wait to stop living off Dad's dime.

After Jackson took care of the bill, Levi turned to Selah and handed her a ring of keys. "Show Mr. Talbot his room, please—room three, the one with the nicest view."

She paused, seeming a bit uncertain. Then she nodded. "Of course. Follow me, please."

He followed her up the staircase to the first room on the right. She opened the door and stepped aside for him to enter. "Um, here's the room."

Jackson walked inside and looked around. He

could tell the gas heater on the wall was brand-new, but it was designed to look old-fashioned. A queen-sized bed covered with a blue-and-white quilt that matched the wall paint was in the center of the room, pushed up against the wall. From the lamp light already turned on, he assumed they had electricity. He turned to Selah. "Do you have Wi-Fi?"

Her brow lifted, and then she shook her head. "No. No TV, either. Just electricity. There's plenty of reading material, though." She pointed to a small bookcase lined with books. "We also have some games, puzzles, and magazines in the lobby near the breakfast tables." Her eyes widened. "Oh, speaking of breakfast, we serve hot food from 6:30 to 10:00 Monday through Friday. On Sundays we have coffee, tea, and pastries."

He nodded. "Sounds good."

"It is. Delilah's an excellent cook. I should show you the bathroom." She rushed to the door and opened it. "You should have everything you need in here," she said, her smile a little off-kilter. "If you need anything else, let us know."

"I will." When she started to leave, he said, "Can I have a key?"

"Oh. Right. The key." She took one off the key ring and handed it to him. "Sorry. Like I said, I'm in training."

"It's all right," he said, taking the key. He almost told her about Lois, who even after so many years in the hotel business had forgotten to give guests their keys, but he caught himself before blowing his cover. He'd make a terrible spy.

She opened the door, then started to close it, then opened it again and poked her head inside the room. "Enjoy your stay."

"Thanks." After she left, this time for good, he set his duffel on the luggage rack on the other side of the room. He checked out the bathroom, and as Selah had said, everything he needed was there, from fluffy white towels to travel-sized toiletries. He went back to the bedroom area and looked around. Amazingly he was already feeling less stressed, probably because there wasn't construction buzzing around him or his father making him miserable.

Jackson pulled out his laptop and sat down on the comfortable light-green tufted chair in the corner of the room next to the bookcase. He could think of a million things he'd rather do this weekend than spend it here. Not that he had anything against the Amish. And from what little he knew about their lifestyle, he thought they couldn't be that much different from him. Sure, he was all about computers and tinkering with cars, and he felt naked without his cell phone. They didn't use computers or drive cars and . . . Well, he didn't know what they used for phones, if they used phones at all. At least he'd brought his computer and an extra battery with him, and he'd use his cell as a hotspot since they didn't have Wi-Fi.

Despite all that, he had a favorable first impression of the place, which would infuriate his father. He grinned. The weekend might not be so bad after all.

Selah cringed as she paused at the top of the stairs. Could she have been any more awkward? Soon after Christian had dropped her off this morning, refusing to let her walk in the frigid cold and telling her he would pick her up after work, Levi explained that she would assist him when their guest arrived. She had spent last evening memorizing the list Delilah gave her, but she hadn't been prepared to show Mr. Talbot—Jackson—his room by herself. Everything she'd memorized had flown out of her head.

Then there was the fact that he was English. His sandy-blond hair was longer than most English young men she'd met wore theirs, but at least it wasn't stringy or messy. He wore a red-and-black-checked shirt with the sleeves rolled up, a white, long-sleeved T-shirt underneath, and faded jeans and hiking boots. She didn't have the best track record with English men. *Specifically* one *English man.* Fortunately Jackson seemed like a nice guy. Not all English men were like—

She sucked in a breath and pushed Oliver out of her mind. She'd finally come to the point when she thought about him less and less, but Jackson had tripped her memories. That had sometimes led to problems with her emotions, something she couldn't afford to deal with right now. Gathering herself, she went downstairs. Levi was still standing behind the counter, looking at a hospitality magazine. He'd seemed even more relaxed than usual since the inspection the previous afternoon had been a complete success.

He glanced up at her. "How did it *geh*?"

Should she tell him she messed up? Then again, she didn't want him to worry that she had made a bad impression. "Fine," she said, her voice sounding tight. "Just fine."

"Did you remember everything?"

She stopped in front of the counter. "Most of it," she squeaked out.

"*Gut* enough for me." He closed the magazine. "Don't be so tense, Selah. We're all going to make mistakes because we're all learning. If we forget something or say the wrong thing . . ." He cleared his throat. "Anyway, the important thing is to do the best we can. *Nee* one is perfect."

His words calmed her a little. "You're right."

"I've got another job for you." He went into the office and then came out with a box of brochures. "*Daed* ordered these last week, and they need to be folded. He thought it would be a *gut* idea to distribute them around the businesses in Barton—as long as we get permission from them."

"That's a job I can do." She smiled at him, and

of course he smiled back. Something about Levi Stoll's smile was irresistible. He could charm anyone—well, except for Marge the taxi driver, and Selah doubted that woman had smiled more than once in the past year. She'd seen how easily he talked to Jackson and welcomed him. Levi might think he had a lot to learn, but when it came to working with guests, he was a natural.

Before she took the box to one of the tables, she asked, "How is *yer vatter* doing?"

"Better. He's still in quite a bit of pain, especially when he puts any weight on his leg. He has a follow-up appointment next week with his surgeon." His forehead creased with concern. "I'm sure he's fine, but I'd like for him to be out of pain."

"Me too." She paused. "Do you think he would like to help me fold these?"

"Sure. *Nix* wrong with his hands."

She tucked the box under her arm. "I'll be back."

"Selah," he said as she started to walk away.

"*Ya?*"

"*Danki* for thinking of *mei daed.*"

Nodding, she smiled at him, and then she headed for the house. He didn't have to thank her. She was glad to help his father. Although she hadn't worked here long, the Stolls had made her feel more welcome than she'd felt in her parents' home back in New York. If kindness

137

and a welcoming spirit were the secret to an inn's success, Levi and his family didn't have anything to worry about.

Levi watched Selah as she left the lobby. Her shoulders had been drooping when she came down the stairs, and he was glad he'd been able to reassure her that she didn't have to be perfect. He was far from perfect, that was for sure.

But he had noticed that even though Selah was more relaxed around him after they'd cleared the air between them, there was an underlying tension when it came to her job. She could out-clean his grandmother, which was a feat in itself, yet she'd looked like a frightened deer when he'd asked her to show Jackson Talbot his room. And he remembered how desperate she'd been when she thought he might fire her. Clearly this job was extremely important to her.

Nina walked into the lobby. "Selah is doing the nicest thing," she said, leaning her elbows on the counter. "She and *Daed* are folding those brochures he ordered together. He hasn't been this happy since the accident."

He smiled. "Glad to hear that."

"I've been a little worried about him." She fidgeted with one of the strings on her *kapp*. "I told him not to feel bad that he couldn't help us, but he still does."

"You know *Daed*. He doesn't like to be laid up.

Remember when he burned his hand a few years ago? He couldn't work for two days, and he just about went *ab im kopp*. He was also limited when he sprained his wrist the other week. He'll be in a better mood once he's off the crutches."

"You're right." She started rearranging the brochures in the rack. "How is our new guest? Selah said he was here, but she didn't say much else."

"Seems like a nice fellow. A lot younger than I thought he would be." From the way he'd sounded on the phone when he made the reservation, Levi had thought Jackson Talbot was a middle-aged man. "He's been in his room since he arrived."

She placed the brochures about the *Behalt*, the Amish and Mennonite heritage center in Berlin, in the first slot of the display. "If he's new in the area, we should recommend this place to him. I've been meaning to visit myself, out of curiosity." She turned to Levi. "I'm glad you hired Selah," she said, grinning.

Back to her, I see. He had to make sure to measure his words, or she would start teasing him again. "*Grossmutter* did, not me."

"Still, she seems to fit right in with us, doesn't she?"

He flattened his gaze. "Don't start."

"I'm not starting anything." She held up her hands, her expression guileless. "I'm stating a fact. Don't you agree?"

"This is a trap, isn't it?"

139

Nina laughed. "Interesting," she said, and then she walked away.

"What's interesting?"

"*Nix*," she called out before disappearing.

He yanked on the hem of his sweater. Nina could be such a pain. She was right about one thing—Selah did fit in. At first he hadn't been so sure, but now he was. He couldn't help but smile. He was glad his grandmother had hired her too.

Cevilla stared out the kitchen window, watching the snow fall from the sky. What had been a gentle snowfall earlier in the day was turning into a near whiteout, the thick flakes coming down in fast clumps. She hoped Richard was safe and warm in his house.

She gave her head a quick shake, reminding herself that she wasn't wondering about Richard anymore. He hadn't come by for his usual breakfast, and she wasn't chasing him down. She washed her plate and glass from lunch and then dried and put them away. When she turned to an empty kitchen, she made her way into the living room and sat down in her rocking chair. She had lived alone for more than sixty years and had never been bothered by the silence. Now it seemed almost thunderous, but that was mostly because of the throbbing headache she'd had for two days.

Cevilla picked up her crochet, made a few stitches, and then set it down again. She also didn't feel like reading, not even her Bible. She had a long afternoon and evening in front of her if she didn't find something to occupy her. Other than thoughts of Richard.

She heard a knock on the front door, and frowning, she got up from her chair. She wasn't fool enough to think it was Richard. But surely it wasn't Noah coming to check on her in this blizzardy mess. Calling the cell phone he'd insisted she have for emergencies after she refused to move in with him and Ivy, he'd been in touch as soon as the snow started to fall. She was fine, she had insisted, and yes, she had enough wood to last several days.

The knock grew louder, and she shuffled faster. "I'm coming," she yelled, quickening her steps. She loved her nephew, but his overprotection was annoying at times. Her arthritis was also acting up with the frigid weather, which made her move slower than normal.

Finally she opened the door. But Noah wasn't standing there. Richard was. Stunned, she didn't say anything for a moment. Then when she started to shake from the cold, she exclaimed, "What in the world?"

"Are you going to let me in?" he said, his voice muffled beneath a thick candy-apple-red scarf. The rest of him was covered head to toe with a padded winter coat, snow pants, and brand-new snow boots. In fact, everything had to be brand-new since he wouldn't have needed snow gear in Los Angeles.

She motioned for him to come in, and once he was inside, she shut the door. "What are you doing here?" she said, still shivering.

"Checking on you." He leaned on his cane and pulled down his hood. His cheeks were red, and his eyeglass lenses were fogging up. He was also gasping for breath.

Alarm ran through her as she fully realized the toll walking to her house in heavy snow and freezing temperatures had taken on him. "Foolish old man," she said, going to him and grabbing his hand, which was covered with a thick mitten. "Sit by the stove and warm yourself."

He followed as she led him to the chair on the other side of the stove from hers. Then he sat down and unwound his scarf.

"Only a nincompoop would be out in this kind of weather," she said, scolding him as her own heart rate escalated. "What if you had gotten lost? Or been frozen to death?" Fear gripped her at the thought.

"I'm well insulated." He breathed in, and then added, "Plus, I'm only next door. How would have I gotten lost?"

"Have you lived so long in California that you forgot about the storms we'd get in Arnold City? Remember when that farmer lost his way going to his barn during the blizzard of '49?"

"Oh." His complexion turned a little gray. "I guess I did forget about that. But no matter, I'm here now." He looked her up and down, scowling a bit. "I see you're fine—and also in a typical mood."

"My moods aren't typical," she huffed. The nerve of him, risking his life to check on her only to turn around and insult her. "And I'm not sure my welfare is any of your business anymore."

"Cevilla." He let out a sigh, his expression haggard. "We've gotten off track, haven't we? I'm not even sure how it happened."

She knew how, but since she held most of the blame, she didn't point it out. "I'll make us some tea while you warm up." As she shuffled to the kitchen, a sliver of warmth pierced her cold heart. He did care about her. It was hard to be annoyed with him for that.

Once the kettle whistled, she steeped their tea. Richard had bought her a cute but simple antique tea cart from Noah and Ivy's store, which had come in handy when they took tea or a snack in the living room instead of in the kitchen. When she returned to the living room, Richard had taken off his coat and gloves and hung them on the coat tree near the front door. He was back sitting next to the woodstove reading *The Budget* as if he'd been here all day instead of risking life and limb to come over. *As if everything between us is hunky-dory.* "Tea is ready," she said through gritted teeth.

"Okay." He continued to read, not making a move to reach for the tea.

Cevilla pressed her lips together. "Are you trying to rile me?"

He peeked over the newspaper. "Perish the thought."

"Ooh." She shuffled over to him and snatched the paper out of his hands. "I don't know what you're up to, Richard Johnson, but it stops now."

A flicker of annoyance crossed his eyes. "I can say the same thing for you."

"What?"

He leaned forward. "You've been cranky and cantankerous, more so than usual—"

"Than *usual?*"

"*And* lately we haven't had a decent conversation that hasn't ended with you in a huff."

She thumped her cane against the floor. "You're the one who took off yesterday morning, remember? I hadn't seen you since—not until you just walked through that door."

"You know where I live." He lifted his chin. The window in the living room shook from the roaring wind.

As the winter storm gathered steam outside, Cevilla's temper flared. "Then why are you here?" Her voice cracked, and she turned around. Bother, she was on the verge of tears. Was this how their relationship was going to end? With petty arguing? Verbally dancing around the real

144

issues that were keeping them emotionally apart?

"Because not only was I worried about you, but I can't stand this tension between us."

She heard him get up from the chair and then the thump of his cane against the wood floor. Still, she didn't turn around. Not while tears were welling in her eyes.

"Cevilla."

Silence.

"You picked a fine time to clam up." He sighed. "I don't want to be apart anymore." He touched her shoulder. "Please. Look at me."

She wiped at her eyes and then faced him. Behind his glasses she could see the sincerity and depth in his eyes, the deep wrinkles at the corners creasing farther.

"I also don't want to fight anymore," he said. "We've been apart for so many years. Good years . . . and with different lifestyles. It may sound morbid, but time between us is short. We've talked about that before."

A lump formed in her throat. All she could do was nod.

"I know you've been waiting on me to make a decision. I also know you want to talk about Sharon. It's been hard on you. I can see that now." He tenderly cupped her cheek. When he had first done that months ago, she'd been self-conscious about her wrinkles and saggy skin. Not anymore. "Can you wait a little longer for everything to fall into place? Or is that asking too much?"

Guilt washed over her in waves. Her impatience had struck again, turning to hard resentment in her heart. She could barely stand herself, and no wonder he hadn't wanted to be around her. "I'm sorry," she said, looking up at him. "I've been behaving terribly."

"Not terribly." He moved his hand and made a small space with his thumb and forefinger. "Maybe a little badly, though."

"I've always said I want your decision about the church to be between you and God. But I keep inserting myself in it." She took his hand. "Can you forgive me?"

"Of course. But you haven't answered my question. Can you wait? And can we enjoy being with each other until the time is right? Because I don't think I can handle these arguments and the tension between us."

"I don't like it, either. I can wait. As long as it takes."

He hugged her. "Thank you," he said, and then he took a step back. He glanced at the cart. "The tea is probably cold by now. I'll give it a warm-up."

She nodded, and he pushed the tea cart back to the kitchen. He looked a little silly, his tall, lean frame hunched over while he used his cane with his other hand, making steering the cart a little awkward. *Adorably awkward.*

There she went again, acting like a besotted schoolgirl. But that's how she felt sometimes when she was around him. Then she had turned into a spoiled brat, which she was determined not to be anymore. He would make a decision about the church in his and God's time. And when he was ready to talk about Sharon, she would be ready to listen.

She lifted her head and closed her eyes. *Help me have patience, Lord. I don't want to lose him. But if I keep trying to rush things, I will . . . and I don't know how I could live without him.*

Chapter 9

When Jackson arrived at Stoll Inn two hours earlier, he'd been glad he had plenty of work to do. He hadn't signed any contracts yet, but he'd been in touch with a few people about his web and IT services. Two people had asked for proposals, which was a good sign. With a dose of luck and lots of hard work on his part, he would get his business off the ground. The competition was strong in his field, but all he needed were a couple of clients and some great references to stand on his own two feet.

Despite all that, he hadn't made much progress on the proposal and website mock-up he was working on, because his gaze kept drifting to the window. He was fascinated by the big, fluffy flakes falling at a steady pace. He'd seen plenty of snow before, even the heavy snowfalls common during northeastern Ohio winters. But there was something about sitting in a quiet room watching the snow, surrounded by silence except for the hum of his computer. Work was the last thing he wanted to do, so he gave up.

He shut down the laptop and set it on top of the bookcase, remembering his father's scheme. As much as he didn't want to give his father any ammunition against Stoll Inn, he knew if he didn't tell him something, Dad would come out here himself. Jackson might as well get a feel for the place, and he had to admit his curiosity was piqued.

He grabbed his coat and went downstairs. The lobby was still empty. Wasn't this their opening weekend? They must have done more to get out the word than put that one ad in the paper. Maybe the weather had something to do with the lack of guests.

He turned and looked at the woodstove. He couldn't remember the last time he'd been in front of a real fire, but the burning wood and crackling flames reminded him of camping with his parents when he was a young kid. Those were happier times. Will I ever be that happy again?

"Would you like some banana bread? I made it fresh today."

He turned and saw a squat, grandmotherly woman looking up at him, holding a plate laden with thick slices of banana bread. That was what he smelled when he arrived. It looked delicious. "Yes, please," he said, taking a slice.

"I'm Delilah Stoll." Her smile stretched from ear to ear. "Welcome to our inn."

"Jackson Talbot."

She gestured to a table against the wall. "There's fresh coffee over there if you'd like. Decaf and regular."

He glanced in the direction she pointed and saw

two black carafes and small baskets with creamer and sugar. Spoons poked out of a small, light-blue piece of crockery. Instead of the Styrofoam cups his father's hotel provided, white ceramic mugs stood available on a tray.

"We also have tea bags, hot water, and fresh local honey. Feel free to help yourself." She paused. "Unless you'd like me to get a beverage for you."

"I can get it myself." He usually drank coffee, but tea sounded good.

"I'll just set this over here, then." She put the plate of banana bread on the table and then turned around. "Enjoy your stay. If you need anything, let us know."

"I will, thanks."

Placing the banana bread on a napkin, he made himself a cup of black tea and poured a liberal amount of honey from the squeeze bottle next to the small basket of tea bags. Then he took a bite of the banana bread. Wow. Soft, moist—even still warm.

When he finished his snack, he put on his coat, hat, and gloves and opened the front door. The burst of cold air that slammed into him almost took his breath away. He wouldn't be able to stand out here for long, much less walk around and inspect the grounds. Even if it were warmer, the thick cloud cover and increasing snow would make the late afternoon seem almost like nightfall. And that was despite the sensor light that turned on when he stepped onto the porch and the single pole light sure to come on in the parking lot.

Jackson stayed outside as long he could stand the whirling wind and frigid cold, and then he hurried back inside to warm up. The lobby was still empty, but he was glad for that. He sat down on the comfortable sofa in front of the woodstove and took off his winter gear, laying it beside him. He stretched out his legs in front of him, more relaxed than he'd been in a long time. No construction, no dust, no dirt, no loud noises. In fact, this was the cleanest place he'd ever seen.

Stoll Inn was looking better and better to him. Perhaps his father did have something to worry about.

After she finished folding the brochures with Loren, who had fallen asleep with one of them half folded in his lap, Selah spent the rest of the day making sure the inn's mudroom was clean and pristine. Jackson wouldn't see the mudroom, of course, but that didn't stop her from making it spotless. She made one last survey of the space and then picked up her small bucket of cleaning supplies. She glanced at the clock on the wall. It was fifteen minutes past four, and her day didn't end until five when Christian was expected to pick her up.

She opened one of the doors to the wall cabinet that housed the cleaning supplies, sheets, towels, office supplies, and toiletries. The room was also large enough for the washing machine and dryer, along with a large bin for soiled laundry. Yesterday afternoon, when Delilah had shown her how to operate the machines, the older woman had approached them with a mix of fear and reverence. "Never thought I'd see the day I'd use one of these things," she'd said, wrinkling her nose. "But it can't be helped. Once we have a lot of guests, we'll have a lot of laundry to do."

Selah had never operated anything other than a wringer washer, but the machines were simple enough. Still, when she pulled the rags and towels from the dryer and started folding them, she missed the fresh-off-the-line scent she was used to. Using the fancy machines also made her feel a little bit lazy, although that would probably change when she had to do several loads a day.

She decided to do a quick mop of the mudroom again, which didn't take long, and then she washed out the mop and bucket. After drying the bucket, she put it away in another cabinet. She had just put the dirty cleaning rag into the laundry bin when Levi walked into the mudroom. "Christian's on the phone for you," he said.

"Oh?" Her brother typically didn't like to use phones. Maybe he was letting her know he would be late picking her up. Or maybe something was wrong. Her chest contracted. Maybe something happened to Ruby—

Stop. She was catastrophizing, something she learned about in therapy. The only thing she knew for certain was that Christian was on the phone, nothing else. No need to panic, not without reason.

He glanced around the mudroom. "Did you clean in here again?"

She nodded, calming herself. "A little."

"It was already clean."

"Apparently not that clean, since you noticed."

"I noticed because the floor is still wet."

Selah eyed the floor. Unlike the rest of the inn, which had high-quality hardwood floors, the mudroom was painted concrete, and the wet spots that hadn't dried yet were visible.

"*Nee* one can say you don't do *yer* job well." He smiled, but she noticed the weariness in his eyes. "You can talk to Christian in *mei* office."

She followed him into the lobby, still reminding herself that a phone call didn't necessarily mean a problem. Levi turned around and put one finger over his lips. Then he pointed to the couch in front of the woodstove. Their lone guest lounged there, asleep, his arms crossed over his chest and his chin touching the top of it.

Selah nodded and walked as quietly as she could to the office. Levi picked up the cell phone and handed it to her before leaving and shutting the door behind him.

"Hi, Christian," she said, forcing herself not to ask him if anything was wrong.

"Hello, Selah. Have you noticed the weather lately?"

"It's hard not to notice." On her way to the office, she'd seen the pileup of snow outside. It had risen about a quarter of the way up the glass front door.

"You need to make arrangements to stay there tonight."

"What?"

"It's perilous for me to drive in this weather, and from the way the storm is progressing, it's only going to get worse throughout the evening."

"You want me to stay here?"

"You do work at an inn. Quite fortuitous, actually."

Selah frowned. She didn't see anything fortuitous about this situation, and her brother's characteristic stilted speech was becoming annoying. "I don't want to impose on *mei* bosses."

"Selah, you don't have a choice. I can't pick you up. The drifts here are already over a foot high."

"If I'd walked here this morning like I wanted to, I would be on *mei* way home now."

"Now you're being irrational." His tone grew tense. "Are you okay? If you're struggling, I can figure out a way to get to you."

She hung her head. They both knew what he

was referring to. And that he would risk the weather to get her if she was in trouble moved her heart. He was coming out of his unemotional shell. "I'm not having issues," she said, evening her own tone. "I'm fine. It's just that I haven't been at this job for very long, and I don't want to get fired."

"I doubt taking shelter in a blizzard is a fireable offense. I'm sure the Stolls won't mind if you stay. It's the only safe and logical choice."

He was right. She didn't want her brother or his horse to get stuck in the storm because she was being nonsensical. "I'll stay."

"*Gut.* I'll pick you up tomorrow if the weather is permissible."

"I work tomorrow."

"Then I'll pick you up at the end of *yer* workday. If there is a problem, I will call you again." He paused. "And if you need to, you can call me anytime. You know that, right?"

"I do." She smiled even though he couldn't see her. "Everything will be fine. I will be fine."

"All right. Have a *gut* evening, Selah. Try to relax, okay?"

"Speak for *yerself*," she said, weakly teasing him. "I'm not the only one wound tighter than a top."

"I think I've made excellent progress." He sounded offended.

"You have, thanks to Ruby."

"*Ya.*" His voice softened by the slightest degree. "All thanks to her."

She clicked off the cell phone, which was a small flip phone without a fancy screen like most of the cell phones she'd seen in the hands of the English. She stared at it. Her hesitation to stay at the inn had nothing to do with the Stolls—at least not much. She hadn't stayed with anyone other than her parents and Christian and Ruby since her diagnosis, and she didn't want her employers to discover it.

But her brother was right. She was being irrational. What could possibly happen to reveal her anxiety and depression? That was a secret she would always keep to herself.

When she walked out of the office, Levi was standing at the front door looking at the whirlwind of snow. She moved to stand beside him, wondering how she ever thought she would be able to walk home in the cold chaos outside.

"Everything all right?" he asked, keeping his voice low.

She handed the phone to him with a smirk. "When it comes to *mei bruder*, that's a loaded question."

"Huh?"

"Just a joke." She looked out at the snow again. "I have a small favor to ask," she said, unable to look at him.

"Sure. But I want to tell you something first."

He gestured to his office. "We should *geh* back in there. Don't want to wake up Jackson."

Alarm rose in her, but she tamped it down. Like when Christian called her, just because Levi wanted to talk to her didn't mean there was a problem. She had to learn to get a grip on jumping to the worst conclusion. Considering her reactions during the past half hour, she should start looking for a new therapist. She had put off finding one, but as soon as she was settled in her job, she'd begin her search.

He left the door slightly ajar. "Call Christian back and tell him not to pick you up. We have plenty of room for you to stay here. This weather isn't fit for anyone to be out in it."

She should have known Levi would have thought about this already. "That's what I wanted to ask you. Christian can't pick me up, and he wanted to know if I could wait out the storm here tonight."

"I'm glad he's being practical." Levi gave her a knowing look. "Although something tells me you would be on *yer* way home by now if you had walked here this morning."

"Um, possibly. I'm not as sensible as *mei bruder*."

"I wouldn't have let you leave anyway."

She looked up at him, still seeing the fatigue on his face. And behind his glasses, genuine concern shone in his eyes. She shouldn't be surprised, because this was Levi, but she was. Surprised and touched.

He took a step back from her, shuffling some papers. "You have *yer* pick of the three empty rooms, by the way." He opened the door and peeked out. "Jackson must have gone upstairs."

"I wonder what he'll do about supper?"

"Now you're thinking like a hostess. I like that." Levi grinned. "We'll invite him to eat with us. Easy solution."

"You always make things seem easy."

He shrugged. "I don't see the need to make them complicated." He looked at the ledger books on his desk, frowning slightly. "Although sometimes I can't avoid it." He looked back at her. "Why don't you *geh* to the *haus* and let *mei grossmutter* know what's happening? And tell her I'll be there soon. Just finishing up some paperwork before I find Jackson."

"But it's not five o'clock yet. I should come back."

"No, I'm letting you off early. Oh, and one more thing."

"*Ya?*"

"If you offer to pay for *yer* room tonight, I will revoke *yer* employee of the month privileges."

She laughed. "What privileges?"

"The ones I haven't figured out yet." He grinned but then grew serious. "I mean it, Selah."

She could tell he did. "I understand."

"I'll be there soon, Jackson in tow."

Selah nodded and then left the office, still smiling about the nonexistent privileges. But he'd been right—she had planned to pay for the room. The fact that he had anticipated that should have bothered her, but for some reason it didn't. She knew Levi didn't file away details to use against people. That wasn't in him. Unlike Oliver.

Levi sat down at the desk. He should be cleaning up the piles of papers and receipts scattered over it, filing them back in the drawer where his father kept them. He had gone through every scrap of paper today, trying to understand the inn's financials. From what he could tell, his father hadn't been irresponsible with money. The debt was a result of unexpected costs. Now that he had a clear picture of what was going on, he figured that even with the pending medical bills, if they had consistent business at the inn, they could pay off their debt in a decent amount of time and without having to ask for anything from the district's community fund. The fund was always an option, but they hadn't been able to contribute much to it since they moved here. It didn't seem completely right to benefit from it except in an emergency. Right now, this wasn't an emergency, and if he could help it, they wouldn't have one.

Yet his optimism about the future was tempered

by the weather. They might have had more than one guest if a blizzard hadn't been coming, which would have been a great start. Then again, if his father had miscalculated in one area, it was in advertising. A small ad in the local paper wasn't going to bring in enough guests. Levi had gleaned some ideas from the hospitality magazines his father subscribed to, but he would have to figure out how to adapt them for an Amish inn.

There was no reason to dwell on that now, though. It was almost suppertime, and he still had to invite Jackson to join them. He left the papers on the desk and shut the door. Tomorrow was another day.

Levi went upstairs and knocked on Jackson's door. When Jackson opened it, Levi said, "No one's going anywhere tonight in this storm, so you're welcome to have supper with us."

Jackson tilted his head. "I've got a candy bar in my duffel. I should be fine with that."

Levi scoffed. "A candy bar isn't going to get you through the night." He paused. "We don't usually do room service, but if you'd like that instead, we can bring supper to you."

Rubbing his chin, he said, "That's too much trouble. I'll join you, thanks. Are you eating downstairs?"

"We have a house behind the inn. That's where we live, so we'll have the meal there."

"I wondered if you guys lived on the property."

He quickly added, "Are you sure you want a stranger in your home?"

"You're not a stranger," Levi said with a grin. "You're our guest. I'll wait for you downstairs."

"You don't have to wait. I'll grab my coat." Jackson swiped his coat off the bed and closed his door. "Guess I don't need to lock this."

"Unless you want to. I promise no one here will snoop through your things, though, if you're worried about that. It's only me and my family and Selah."

"She's not your sister?"

Levi almost laughed. He and Selah didn't look anything alike. Her dark-brown hair and blue eyes contrasted with his lighter hair and green eyes. "No, she just works here."

They went downstairs, and Levi took his coat from a peg in the mudroom, slipped it on, and led Jackson to the house. The wind blew the snow sideways, and Levi had to squint against the flakes flying into his eyes. Talk about brutal. This matched any winter storm he'd experienced in Wisconsin, and he'd seen many.

When they got inside the house, they shook the snow off their bodies in the mudroom and removed their boots before going into the kitchen. Selah was setting the table, and *Daed* was already seated, his leg propped up, his color better. But he still looked tired. Levi made the introductions.

"Glad you can join us," *Daed* said, shaking Jackson's hand. "We're always happy to have guests, whether here or at the inn."

Levi introduced Jackson to Nina, who was at the counter slicing fresh bread, and then turned to his grandmother. "And this is my grandmother, Delilah."

"We've already met," she said, picking up two pot holders and then taking a large pot to the table.

"Over banana bread," Jackson said. He grinned. "Which was delicious. Thank you."

Delilah beamed. "You're most welcome."

Levi liked this guy. He was friendly, but not in a fake way, and he had made his grandmother smile, which always earned bonus points. Levi still didn't know why Jackson was staying at the inn by himself on the worst weekend of winter so far, but then again, it was none of his business.

"You've already met Selah too." Levi gestured to her, glad to see that she looked a little more relaxed than she had when he'd insisted she stay. Good thing Christian had also told her to stay, or she really might have bolted into this crazy weather.

"Why don't you sit here, Mr. Talbot?" Delilah pointed to the seat next to Selah.

That was a surprise. Levi was sure his grandmother was going to seat him next to Selah since he still didn't trust her not to meddle. Then again, maybe she really intended to keep her word.

"Call me Jackson," he said. "Mr. Talbot is my father."

Levi didn't miss Jackson's slight scowl, which vanished as fast as it appeared.

Then he watched Selah as Jackson sat down next to her. Her shoulders stiffened the slightest bit, almost imperceptibly. But Levi had noticed. Why did she have that reaction to Jackson, the same reaction she had to him when they first met? Aloof. Tense.

His gut suddenly twisted. One piece of the puzzle finally fit into place. Who hurt you, Selah Ropp?

Chapter 10

Selah tried to relax as Jackson sat down next to her. Her reaction to him made no sense. She couldn't spend the rest of her life being tense around every English man she encountered. Or around any man, for that matter. Still, she gripped the hem of her sweater as he gave her a slight smile. *Get it together, Selah.*

When she faced forward, she was looking directly at Levi. She'd been so preoccupied with her reaction to Jackson that she hadn't realized he'd sat down across from her. His head was tilted, and he was gazing straight at her. Her uneasiness increased as if he had somehow caught a glimpse of what she was trying so hard to hide. She clutched at her sweater again.

"What's in the pot?" Loren asked.

"Cabbage stew." Delilah sat down at the opposite end of the table.

"Do you like cabbage stew?" Nina asked Jackson. "People either like it or can't stand it."

"I don't think I've ever had it before," he said. "I do like stews, though."

"We enjoy it very much." Delilah adjusted the napkin on the basket that held the bread slices Nina had cut earlier.

"Especially with lots of vegetables and beef chunks," Loren added.

Selah glanced at Loren. She was glad to see that, although he still had dark circles under his eyes, he had an appetite now. When he had fallen asleep while they were folding the brochures, Nina hadn't wanted to wake him for lunch. "He hasn't been eating much lately," she'd said. That seemed to have changed tonight, thankfully. Turning her focus on Loren and away from Jackson and Levi helped her settle down a tiny bit.

"Shall we pray?" Loren said.

"Pray?" Jackson glanced around at everyone.

"We pray before each meal," Delilah said.

"You can join us if you want to," Levi told him. "But our prayers are individual and silent."

He seemed bewildered by the idea. "What do I pray about?"

"Just thank the Lord for our food." Nina smiled.

He paused and then nodded. "I'll give it a shot."

Selah closed her eyes, pleased that Jackson had joined them in prayer. She quickly thanked God for the meal and added a request for help to keep her wits about her the rest of the night.

When everyone had looked up, Delilah ladled the piping hot stew into heavy, white soup bowls and served them. Then she said, "I think this is a good time for us to get to know each other."

Both Levi and Nina groaned. "No, it's not," Nina said. "We already know each other."

"But our guests don't know us very well, and we don't know them very well." Delilah handed Nina the breadbasket. "Tell us something about yourself, Nina."

Nina's eyes rolled so far into her head that Selah worried she might hurt herself. "I'm Nina," she said in a bored, put-upon tone. "I like bread." She started to hand the basket to Levi, but he pushed it back to her.

"That doesn't count," he said, smirking. "Who doesn't like bread?"

"Ashley," Jackson muttered.

Delilah turned to him. "Beg your pardon?"

"My father's girlfriend. She eats nothing but carrot sticks and grass."

"She sounds more like a horse than a girlfriend," Nina said.

Jackson burst out laughing. "I doubt she's ever seen a horse in person."

"Hard to imagine that." Loren blew on the stew in his spoon. "But I know that's not uncommon for people who aren't Amish, particularly those who were raised in big cities."

"I think she's from Columbus," Jackson said. He shrugged. "Anyway, a little something about me. I work with computers, and my goal is to have my own website and computer consulting business. Everything is run by computers nowadays."

"Not everything," Loren said. "A few of us resist."

"More than a few," Delilah added.

"Nothing wrong with that," Jackson said. "Sometimes I think I'm too plugged in."

"Plugged in?" Nina took another slice of bread.

"I spend too much time on the computer."

"Maybe this weekend you can unplug," Levi said.

Jackson nodded. "I was thinking the same thing."

"Thank you for sharing," Delilah said.

Selah smiled a little. Delilah sounded like Ruby did when she was teaching her elementary students.

"Your turn, Levi." Delilah shoved the bread-basket at him.

Levi took a slice and put it on the saucer next to his soup bowl. "There's not much to tell," he said, looking at Selah. "What you see is what you get."

"That's not an acceptable answer," Nina said.

He turned to her. "And 'I like bread' is?"

"You should tell everyone about the time you won the relay race in first grade." Nina lifted her chin, her grin impish.

"Oh, that was wonderful." Delilah took a sip of iced tea and looked adoringly at Levi. "You were so happy to have that little blue ribbon. You had the biggest smile on your face for a week."

Levi pressed his fingers against his forehead. "I don't believe this."

Loren laughed. "She's right. You even showed your ribbon to Moonbeam, remember?"

"Moonbeam?" Jackson asked.

"His cow." Nina started to chuckle. "His bestest friend in the whole world."

"All right, all right." Levi's cheeks were red, but he started to laugh. "If you guys are finished embarrassing me, we can move on."

"Here's one thing you should know about me," Loren said, looking at Selah and Jackson. "I'm grateful to be here. Not just because of my accident, but because I think moving to Birch Creek was the best decision I ever made." He turned his gaze to his family. "That we made."

Selah couldn't help but smile again. There was so much warmth among the Stolls, even when they were teasing Levi. Her family meals were never like this—light, friendly, and loving. *More like stone silent.* The last trace of tension slipped away.

"It's your turn, Selah." Delilah smiled. "Tell us a little about yourself."

"Other than the fact you work here," Nina said with a smile. "We all know that."

Selah suddenly froze, her calm disintegrating. She'd known she would have to say something, but now that everyone was looking at her, she clammed up. What was she supposed to say? That she was in therapy for depression? That she had made a huge mistake nearly two years ago that almost ruined her life? That she looked at every man under thirty with suspicion? Sure, they would really want to keep her around after she told them all that.

But she had to say something, anything, or they would think she was *seltsam*. "I . . . I'm really happy to be here too." Her cheeks flamed hot as she grabbed her spoon and focused on her stew. She almost melted with relief when everyone else started eating. The getting-to-know-everyone game was over, thank the Lord.

When she lifted her gaze, Levi was looking at her with a slight frown. He didn't miss anything, did he? She dipped her head, her appetite gone. She didn't have to worry he might think she was *seltsam*. She was sure he already did.

While the rest of his family and Jackson continued to eat and talked about the storm, which by the sound of the howling wind shaking the kitchen window seemed to be getting worse, Levi kept his eye on Selah. She was barely eating. Her cheeks glowed red, and when she'd had to talk about herself, she'd looked like a fawn pinned down with fear. Her walls were up again, only this time he sensed a crack in the foundation.

He glanced at everyone else at the table. Jackson was already on his second bowl of cabbage stew, and *Grossmutter* was explaining the preparation process to him. *Daed* was quiet but still eating, which was a good sign. Nina grabbed a third slice of bread, which normally would have earned her a pointed look from their grandmother, but *Grossmutter* was too busy enjoying her conversation with Jackson.

Picking up his spoon, he looked at Selah again. She was staring at her bowl now, confirming his suspicions that something was wrong. Usually his grandmother's typical icebreaker was well received, as Jackson had proven. But not by Selah. Over the past few days, he'd seen her friendly side, and she could even be playful at times, something he found appealing. So why had she gone silent after *Grossmutter* asked her to talk about herself?

"Hey, Selah," Nina said, breaking Levi out of his thoughts, "instead of staying at the inn tonight, why don't you bunk with me?"

"That's a great idea," *Grossmutter* said before turning to Jackson. "As long as you don't mind being at the inn by yourself in this storm, Jackson. You're welcome to stay with Levi if you'd like."

Jackson shook his head. "Storms don't bother me, so I'm good."

Nina grinned. "This will be so much fun. Just like a slumber party."

Selah's eyes suddenly grew bigger than the saucers on the table. "Uh, yes. It will be . . . fun."

Levi saw her throat moving back and forth

and her mouth opening slightly as if she were breathing through it and not her nose.

"Excuse me," she said, pushing from the table. "I'll . . . be right . . . back." She fled out of the room.

"Is she all right?" Levi saw *Daed* frown.

"She doesn't have to stay with me," Nina said, looking a little hurt. "It was just a suggestion."

"I'm sure she's fine," *Grossmutter* said, but then she pressed her lips together. "Maybe she had to *geh* to the restroom," she whispered to Nina, loud enough for everyone to hear.

"How's the weather in Wisconsin?" Jackson said quickly. "I bet you guys have seen your fair share of storms."

"Oh, we certainly have," *Daed* said.

Levi slipped out of his seat as his father began to regale Jackson with tales of Wisconsin winters. He headed for the bathroom, figuring his grandmother was right. He'd just wait for Selah to come out so he could make sure she was okay. But as he passed the stairs, he saw her sitting on the bottom step, her hand over her chest.

"Selah?" He crouched in front of her. "What's wrong?"

She shook her head, but her hand stayed where it was.

"Are you in pain?"

"*Nee.*" Her breath came in gasps. "I'm . . . fine."

"You're not fine."

171

She finally looked at him, her eyes still wide, her breath uneven. "I'll . . . be fine. This will . . . pass."

On impulse, he took her free hand. "Selah, please. Let me help you."

Selah's worst nightmare was coming true. When Nina suggested she stay with her in her room, she'd suddenly remembered that she didn't have her medication with her. She usually took it before she went to bed because it made her sleepy. She never missed a dose, and her doctor had stressed that she had to take it every day and at the same time. But there was no way she could get it now. And that was when she started to panic.

Without thinking, she gripped Levi's hand, waiting for the anxiety to pass, telling herself that skipping one dose of medicine wouldn't send her spiraling. But what if it did? What if she couldn't calm down? What if she lost her job? What if everyone found out about her past, her mistakes, her diagnosis? Why wouldn't her heart stop slamming against her chest?

"Selah. I'm here."

She met Levi's gaze and locked on. His hand tightened around hers, and the roaring in her ears subsided.

"I'm here," he repeated. "I'm here."

Her heartbeat started to slow. His touch, his

words, calmed her. When she could breathe again, she said, "I . . . I don't know what happened." Which was partially true. She'd never felt like that before, as if she were having a heart attack.

He moved to sit beside her, still holding her hand. Then he took a handkerchief out of his pocket and dabbed her forehead.

She took it from him and wiped her face. She hadn't realized she'd been sweating, and now she shivered.

"You're cold. I'll get a blanket." He started to get up.

But she held on fast to his hand. "I'm okay. I just need a minute."

He nodded and sat back down. After a little while he said, "Was it the cabbage stew?"

She turned her head. "The stew?"

"It looks like it didn't agree with you. You barely ate any at supper."

If she hadn't felt so ashamed that she'd melted down in front of him, she would have laughed. He was giving her an out, and he didn't even realize it. "*Ya*. It must have been the stew. I should probably lie down."

"Go up to Nina's bedroom," he said. "Unless you want to *geh* back to the inn and stay there."

She shook her head. Jackson would be there, but she didn't want to be in her room alone. She was thankful that Nina had made the offer to share her bedroom. "I'll stay with Nina. And I'm

173

sure this will pass." She straightened and looked at the handkerchief. "I can't give this back to you like this."

"Keep it. And I mean it this time." He kept his gaze on her. "*Geh* on upstairs to Nina's room. It's the first one on the right. I'll tell the *familye* you're not feeling well."

"*Danki*," she said softly.

He gave her hand a squeeze and then stood. "I'll wait here until you get to her room. There's a bathroom right next to it."

"You don't have to."

"I know. But I want to."

Something in her heart thawed. He was so kind and thoughtful, and she soaked up both like a dried-up sponge. She stood and went upstairs, her legs a little shaky. When she looked back at Levi, who was still at the bottom of the stairs, she nodded. He nodded back and left.

Selah went into Nina's room and sat on the edge of the bed. She was exhausted, and her body started trembling again, this time from being in the cold room. She pulled down the covers and snuggled under them. She'd get up when Nina came upstairs. There was only a twin bed, but she could make a pallet on the floor with a few blankets and a pillow. The inn had plenty to spare.

As she lay there, she could still feel Levi's hand in hers. But before her heart softened any more, she vowed not to fall for him. It would be too easy. And too complicated. She had so many problems, and with the new experience she'd just had, everything was worse. Levi didn't need her issues, and she didn't need to put her problems on him.

Chapter 11

Jackson stood in the lobby of the inn, unsure what to do. He'd been given a prime opportunity to snoop around without any of the Stolls knowing what he was doing. They were so trusting. He could be a homicidal maniac for all they knew. *Or I could be like my father.*

There was the dilemma. If he rummaged around the inn trying to find something to use against the Stolls, he would be just like his dad, which he'd vowed he would never be. But if he came back with nothing, his father might book another room and come here himself. He might also be so angry that he'd fire Jackson from the only job he had. He didn't want to work for his father, but it was better than collecting unemployment.

He took off his cap and shoved his fingers through his hair. This family was so nice, he almost thought they weren't real. He'd enjoyed getting to know everyone tonight, and he felt bad that Selah wasn't feeling well. Levi explained that when he came back from checking on her, which Jackson thought was interesting. When Selah left the kitchen, Levi had practically run after her. He wouldn't be surprised if there was something going on between those two.

But that wasn't his concern. He was concerned

about betraying this honest family who had showed him more warmth and acceptance than his father had in years, and he'd been here less than a day. He sat down on the couch. Now he was the one not feeling well.

His gaze landed on the small wicker basket in front of him. Delilah had insisted on packing some snacks, along with another helping of apple pie, which Jackson had learned was Loren's favorite. "Can't have you getting hungry," she said, handing him the basket. Then Levi had walked here with him and gone upstairs to make sure his room was warm enough with the gas heater. Despite the heavy snow and wind, the place still had power. That was a miracle right there.

But the woodstove supplied all the heat on the first level, and while the lobby was still warm, it wouldn't be by morning. "We'll be here bright and early to restart the fire," Levi told Jackson before he left for the night.

Jackson stood. He wasn't going to sit down here and figure out what to do now. He grabbed the basket and went up to his room. Levi had left on the light, and Jackson examined his phone. No service, which was to be expected. He got undressed and readied for bed. He wasn't tired, so he perused what was in the bookcase. For some reason he was drawn to the Bible. He picked it up, and then he lay down on the bed and started to read.

He still believed his father could learn a lot from the Stolls, but he was beginning to realize he could too.

Selah opened her eyes but saw nothing. Nina's bedroom was pitch black, which surprised her because she didn't remember turning off the battery-operated bedside lamp. She felt for the small flashlight she'd noticed on the side table and turned it on, cupping the light so it wasn't too bright. Nina was camped out on the floor, sleeping on a pile of blankets on a rag rug in the middle of the room, the top of her head barely visible as she snuggled under a heavy quilt. *I'm supposed to be on the floor, not her.* But she wasn't about to wake her to switch places.

She shivered, wishing she could dive back under the covers but needing to use the restroom first. She was still wearing her dress, sweater, *kapp*, and stockings, of course, but they weren't much protection against the coldness of the upstairs. She'd hurry to the bathroom and then get back under the cozy covers.

As quietly as she could, she snuck out of the bedroom and opened the door. When she gently closed it behind her and turned around, the door to another bedroom, opposite the bathroom, opened. Levi stepped into the hallway, carrying his own pocket flashlight. Of course he would have the same idea at the same time. That was the way the night had been going for her.

He padded over to her, wearing a dark-colored sweatshirt and what looked like baggy pajama pants. "You okay?" he whispered.

She nodded. "I just had to . . ." She tilted her head toward the bathroom door. "You know."

"Ladies first."

Selah couldn't see his face clearly in the dim light, but she imagined he was smiling as usual. She headed for the bathroom but then turned around. "*Danki*," she said. "For helping me earlier."

"*Nee* thanks necessary. I'm glad I could."

A wave of guilt washed over her. She'd lied to him about why she hadn't felt well, and for some reason she felt she had to be honest. He deserved that after being there for her. She crossed her arms over her chest, trying to ward off the chill. "I didn't have an upset stomach," she whispered, barely able to say the words.

"I know."

She looked up at him. "You do?"

He nodded. "But we'll just keep that between ourselves."

She leaned against the doorjamb with relief.

"Selah," he said, taking a step toward her. "If there's something about the job or the inn that bothers you, I'd like to know. I don't want you to end up not liking it here."

He was making it hard to keep her heart in check. Forgetting how cold she'd been a moment ago, she said, "It's not the job, and it's not the inn. You . . . *yer familye* . . . you've all been so kind to me."

"And you're not used to that."

She swallowed. "Not all the time, no." Then she added, "I don't want you to get the wrong idea. I'm not talking about Christian and Ruby. They're wonderful."

"I didn't think you were."

"How do you seem to know everything?"

He turned off the flashlight, leaving them almost completely in the dark. "I pay attention," he said. "Especially when it comes to people I . . . people who work for me."

For a split second she thought he was going to say something else. Something more personal. Which was ridiculous. He was her boss, and she was his employee. *Always remember that.*

"I'm going back to *mei* room," he said, taking a step away from her. "You'd better hurry and get back to bed before you freeze out here."

"All right." She turned and went into the bathroom. An automatic light came on, set to dim, but it gave her enough light to see. She finished and then went back into the hallway. It was empty. She lightly knocked on Levi's door. "*Yer* turn." She didn't wait for him to come out.

She slipped back into the room and into the bed. When she was buried under the covers, she heard Nina's voice.

"Selah?"

"I'm sorry," she said, sitting up a little. "I didn't mean to wake you."

"That's all right."

"Do you want *yer* bed back?" Selah asked, feeling guilty again.

"*Nee.* I'm fine down here. I brought a hot water bottle upstairs with me, so I'm plenty warm."

"Are you sure?"

"Selah, I'm sure." She chuckled. "Are you feeling better?"

"*Ya,*" she said, thinking about Levi again. "I am."

"*Gut.* We were all a little worried when Levi said you didn't feel well."

We'll just keep that between ourselves. She smiled. "Fortunately it didn't last very long."

Nina grew quiet, and Selah figured she'd fallen back asleep. Selah closed her eyes and started to drift.

"Do you like *mei bruder?*"

Her eyes flew open. "What?"

"Just wondering."

She hesitated. "He's a *gut* boss."

"He's learning to be. *Daed* is technically *yer* boss, though. Levi will *geh* back to being the handyman when *Daed* is well enough to work again."

Selah couldn't imagine Levi being just a handyman, not that the work was beneath him.

Maintaining the inn was an important job. But he'd slipped into the role of innkeeper with such ease that it seemed tailor-made for him.

"Selah?"

"*Ya?*"

"I think *mei bruder* likes you." The covers rustled as Nina rolled over. "*Gute nacht.*"

Selah was too shocked to respond. Levi liked her? He barely knew her.

But was Nina right? Levi had not only seen her in one of her worst moments but had offered her an excuse for what happened even though he knew it wasn't the truth. He did know her, at least more than she wanted him to.

None of that mattered, though. If he found out who she really was and what she had done, he wouldn't like her at all.

"*Yer* turn."

Although Selah's voice was soft, he could hear it through the door. He'd wait a few more minutes, which was taking some effort, before he got up. A part of him didn't want to make it more awkward for her by meeting in the hallway again, but another part wanted to see her again.

He threw his arm over his eyes. He'd almost admitted to her what he hadn't even been able to admit to himself—he cared for her. That fact had been driven home when he found her shaking and terrified on the bottom step of the stairs. It hadn't taken him long to recognize what she was going through—a panic attack. A friend back in Wisconsin used to get them after he'd been in a farming accident when he was eighteen, and Levi had witnessed attacks on two separate occasions. Micah had explained what they were and had even told him how they made him feel. "Like *mei* heart is exploding in *mei* chest," he'd said. "I hope you never have to *geh* through one." He'd hoped so too.

Levi couldn't imagine what had caused Selah's panic attack since they'd only been talking at the table. But he'd never know because he wasn't going to bring it up to her again. Still, it added to his concern. Whatever had happened to her in the past—when, he now believed, someone had hurt her deeply—seemed to have had a lasting effect.

He sat up and scrubbed his hand over his face. This was a problem. He couldn't afford to like Selah. He had too much to deal with right now, and he would never get involved with an employee. But none of that affected how he felt. Somehow, he'd have to set those feelings aside whenever he saw her. He wanted her to trust him, and the only way she would do that was if he proved she could by keeping his distance. That would help him in the long run too.

His feet were still cold from the floor, and he rushed to the bathroom, finishing as fast as he could before hurrying back to bed. He turned off the small flashlight and lay there in the dark, his eyes wide open. How was he supposed to sleep with Selah just a few feet away? He hadn't seen this as a problem when Nina suggested Selah share her room, but that was before he'd admitted to himself that he cared about Selah. Even now, all he could think about was whether she was okay. Was she able to fall asleep? Or was she still feeling anxiety? How could he help her if she was?

By staying away, remember?

Levi flopped onto his side and punched his pillow. Other than to say hello to Jackson, he'd spend the next day in the office. Hopefully the snow would let up by evening and Selah would go home. They had church on Sunday at Barbara and Daniel Raber's, but he could avoid Selah there. By Monday morning he'd have his feelings under control and they'd go back to a normal employer/ employee relationship. *Easy as pie, right?*

He groaned. Who was he kidding? Nothing would be easy when it came to him and Selah Ropp.

Chapter 12

When Levi woke up the next morning, well before dawn and after getting next to no sleep, he put on his snow gear and went outside to do the morning chores. Before he went to bed last night, Nina had already taken care of feeding Rusty for him. Taking turns wasn't unusual for them, although it always struck him that she never offered to take turns cleaning the barn, just feeding the horse. That figured.

The minute he stepped outside, he faltered. The wind wasn't blowing as hard, but the frigid air sliced through his thick clothes to his skin. He grabbed the snow shovel and furiously dug a path to the barn. By the time he reached it, he was warmer. He leaned the shovel against the barn and went inside to feed the horse and give him fresh hay, and then he rushed back inside and changed into dry clothing. Even with all the work he'd just done, it was still only five a.m.

He went to the kitchen, intending to grab an apple and head straight for the office at the inn. But he was surprised to see *Grossmutter* already bustling around the kitchen. She started pouring what looked like blueberry muffin batter into a tin. Between the banana bread, the orange twists from Yoder's Bakery, and now blueberry muffins,

Jackson would get his fill of bread and pastries. He glanced out the kitchen window. Although he couldn't see much in the dark, the snow was built up around the edges of the outside window, and he could still hear the wind. "You're up extra early this morning," he said.

"It takes time to prepare a *gut* breakfast." She put the muffin tin into the oven. "Selah's over in the prep kitchen getting everything else ready."

"Oh." Since he was avoiding her, he might as well have his morning meal here, then. "What's for breakfast besides muffins?"

She turned to him. "*Geh* to the inn and find out *yerself.*"

"What about *Daed*? And I thought I'd eat here."

"I'll make oatmeal for him when he gets up." She wiped her hands on the skirt of her apron. "Why do you want to eat breakfast here instead of in the lobby?"

He sat down at the table. "I'm used to eating it here."

"Get used to eating it at the inn. I'm not making double breakfasts. There will be plenty of food for everyone there."

"Got it." But he didn't move.

"What?" she said, putting the batter bowl in the sink and turning on the tap.

"Just waiting for the shenanigans. I know they're coming."

Grossmutter turned off the water and faced

186

him. "I promise *nee* shenanigans. Or tomfoolery or meddling."

"Wait." He held up his hand. "You mean to tell me you're not going to make a sly comment about me and Selah being alone in the inn?"

"You won't be alone. Jackson is there."

"I doubt he wakes up before the chickens."

She poured a cup of coffee and set it on the table. Before he could reach for it, she sat down and took a drink from it. "You've been telling me for a long time to stay out of *yer* business. Now that I am, you're not happy about it."

"I am," he said. "I'm confused, that's all."

"Why?"

"You've never taken me seriously before."

She nodded. "I should have. It doesn't matter that you and Selah like each other—" She slapped her hand over her mouth. "Never mind. Bad habit."

"We don't like each other." He ran the heel of his hand back and forth on the table.

"So you say," she mumbled.

"*Ya*, I say. She's *mei* employee, you know. Having a relationship isn't ethical."

"She'll be *yer* coworker soon enough. *Yer daed* won't be on crutches forever."

"Still not ethical."

"So you say."

He shot up from the table. "I'm going to work."

She pushed back her chair and stood. "Take this to Selah." She handed him a stack of folded cloth napkins Levi had seen her making months before. "I forgot to give them to her before she left."

He took the napkins and grabbed an apple. So much for avoiding Selah.

Selah had overestimated how much time it would take to prepare breakfast. She had already warmed the breakfast casserole, set out several flavors of individual yogurt cups, put the fruit slush into a bowl, and sliced the bread. Just a few more tasks to do and she would be finished. She wasn't sure what she'd do after that. But hiding out in the prep kitchen was preferable to lying in bed unable to sleep, which had been the problem after she'd talked to Levi in the hallway. No matter how hard she tried, she couldn't get him off her mind. At least here she didn't have to worry about running into him first thing in the morning.

She peeked out the door to see if Jackson was up, and she wasn't surprised when she saw the lobby empty. Breakfast didn't officially start until six. She stepped back into the kitchen and stood there, staring at the clock.

"*Grossmutter* asked me to bring these to you."

Selah jumped at the sound of Levi's voice. She put her hand over her heart. "You scared me."

"I'm sorry." His eyes widened behind his glasses. "Are you okay?"

"If you mean am I going to have another meltdown, *nee*." She turned from him, embarrassed again—and irritated that there didn't seem to be anywhere for her to go without him showing up. Not that it was his fault. *How am I supposed to avoid him, Lord, if we keep running into each other?* She took the napkins from him. "*Danki.*"

He nodded, not looking at her. "The woodstove is out. I'll *geh* relight it and get more wood."

She froze. In her hurry to get breakfast started—and avoid Levi—she hadn't paid attention to the stove. The small oven in the prep kitchen had heated quickly and warmed the entire space, but the heat wouldn't warm up the lobby. "I'll do it," she said, heading for the door.

Levi blocked her way. "I said I would do it."

"But it's *mei* job."

"Lighting the stove and getting firewood isn't in *yer* job description."

She couldn't keep herself from looking up at him. "I don't remember getting a written job description."

"It was in *yer* paperwork." A twitch of a smile appeared at the corners of his mouth.

"*Nee*, it wasn't." She fought to hide a grin.

"Hmm. I'd better get busy making one so there's no confusion going forward." The ghost of a smile disappeared. "About anything."

Her gaze remained locked on his handsome face. His glasses seemed to disappear as she looked at his green eyes and honey-colored lashes. Her heart started to thrum—and not because she was anxious. She wasn't even ill at ease. She felt something else, something that drew her to him despite every protest and excuse she could come up with.

Then he moved away from her. "I, uh, better get the woodstove going before Jackson wakes up."

She blinked, her pulse still humming. She also took a step back, still trying to collect herself. "Uh, right."

He dashed out the door.

Selah sagged against the kitchen counter, willing her heartbeat to slow, her irritation high. Her attraction to Levi not only stunned her but felt stronger than anything she'd ever experienced. *This isn't good, Lord. Not good at all.* And no job description would clear up her confusion.

But if she were whole and normal, she could easily let herself fall for Levi Stoll.

When Jackson woke up, pale-gray light peeked through the gap in the window curtains. He looked at his phone, which he'd charged last night. Seven thirty. He normally didn't get up until eight, or sometimes nine, but he was wide awake after sleeping so hard that he hadn't moved all night. He stretched, shifting around the soft, comfortable quilt that had kept him extra warm.

He got out of bed, his bare feet landing on the cold wood floor, and walked to the window. He drew back the curtain, and his mouth dropped open at the sight. Snow blanketed the entire back property of the inn. The drifts were halfway up one side of a small barn and a shed several yards away from the house, and more snow was coming down. This was one incredible snowstorm.

His stomach growled, and he quickly got ready for the day and dressed in an old Cleveland State sweatshirt and jeans. He hadn't thought to bring an extra pair of shoes, so he put his hiking boots back on. Fortunately they were waterproof and warm so his feet wouldn't freeze while he was digging out his car—whenever that would be.

As he went downstairs to the lobby, he took in a deep breath. The delicious scents of breakfast filled the air. *Real* breakfast. He doubted he'd find organic fruity loops or tofu bacon in this place.

Selah walked out of the small kitchen off the lobby. "Good morning," she said. She went to the woodstove and opened the double front doors, and then she closed them again. Turning around, she said, "Would you like some breakfast?"

"That would be nice." He paused, remembering how she had fled from supper last night. "You look like you're feeling better."

"Um, yes. Much better."

"Good. I'm gonna get some coffee." He went to the beverage station and poured himself a mug of steaming caffeinated and then sat down at one of the tables. He glanced over his shoulder when Nina walked into the lobby.

"Morning," she said. "Have you had breakfast yet?"

"Selah's getting it for me." He swiveled in his chair so he could face her. He'd enjoyed seeing her tease Levi last night. He'd taken it in stride. Growing up, he'd always wanted a brother or sister. Being an only child, especially in his family, had been a lonely existence.

"My grandmother made a delicious breakfast this morning. Do you want a copy of the paper to read? We only have yesterday's, though." She glanced at the front door, half the glass fogged over. "I thought it would stop snowing by now."

"Sure. I didn't get a chance to read up on the news yesterday." Normally he checked his phone for news, but here at the inn, it wasn't hard to set his electronics aside.

"I'll get it for you." She went to the front desk and pulled out a paper from behind the counter.

"How's your father doing this morning?" he asked as she handed it to him.

"He's up and around, which is good. Cranky, which my grandmother says is also good." Her thick brown eyebrows furrowed. "She doesn't have to deal with him, though. I hope the snow is cleared out by Monday. He has a follow-up doctor's appointment in Akron."

"I'm sure they'll get the snowplows running soon."

"Usually our roads are the last ones to get

plowed. But that's the way things go." She shrugged. "Dad asked me to get a couple of orange twists for him. I'll see you later." She turned and went into the kitchen.

Orange twists? He'd never heard of those before. Jackson opened the newspaper and sipped his coffee as he perused the articles. Not many of them interested him—he didn't like politics, which was the main thing even in the local news. He glanced at the sports page, but his attention drifted as he looked up and around the lobby.

As he'd been last night in his room, he was struck by how quiet it was here. The background noise of daily life he was used to was missing— the hum of electrical appliances, the ringing and dinging of cell phones, the clamor of televisions, which seemed to be everywhere. He didn't think he could live off the grid like this, which wasn't even off the grid considering they had electricity in the inn. But being away from the stresses of life for even a little while made his problems fade into the background. He didn't realize how much he needed this.

He chuckled and folded the paper. Without knowing it, his father had done him a huge favor.

Selah placed a small cup of fruit slush on a tray, next to a heaping portion of the breakfast casserole on a plate. Since Jackson hadn't come down as early as she'd thought he would, she'd put a few items away so they wouldn't get too cold or too hot. Because of that it took her more time to get everything ready for him now. She'd have to figure out a better system before more guests arrived, or everyone would be complaining about a late breakfast.

She picked up the tray and had turned around to take it to Jackson when Nina walked into the kitchen, startling her. She gripped the tray and steadied herself. "Oh, that was close."

Nina went to her. "I didn't mean to scare you."

Selah glanced at the dishes. Thankfully everything remained where she'd put it.

"I just came to get some orange twists for *Daed*. He loves those things. Do you need any help?"

"I'm capable of preparing and serving breakfast, Nina."

Nina balked. "Sorry. I was just offering."

Selah sighed. This was the second time she'd been startled this morning, and she was getting edgy. It wasn't Levi and Nina's fault, though. Maybe missing her medicine, having a panic attack, and the lack of sleep were all affecting her. That, and her attraction to Levi. She shook her head, unwilling to dwell on that thought. "*Nee*, I'm sorry. I shouldn't have snapped at you. *Danki* for offering."

"Are you okay?" Nina frowned. "I can serve Jackson breakfast if you're still not feeling well."

She tempered her words. "I'm fine, really. A

little tired. Probably not as much as you since you slept on the floor."

"I feel great." Grinning, Nina picked up a plate and placed two orange twists on it. "I should sleep on the floor more often."

Selah suspected she was saying that for her benefit, but Nina did look happy and refreshed. She wished she could say the same thing about herself. "I better get this out to him before it gets cold." As Nina turned toward the mudroom to take Loren his twists, Selah backed out of the swinging kitchen door.

Jackson was staring at his coffee mug, the paper ignored. "I'm sorry that took so long," she said. "Here you go."

He folded the paper and moved it aside to make room. "Looks great," he said as she put the food in front of him.

She also placed a set of small salt and pepper shakers on the table, along with one of the cloth napkins Levi had given her. "Can I get you any-thing else? We have both orange and apple juice. I can bring you a glass if you'd like."

"I think I'm good." He looked up at her and then back down at the breakfast. He let out a low whistle. "This is quite a spread."

"Delilah is a good cook."

"I really enjoyed the cabbage stew last night." He grinned. "I could get used to eating like this. What are orange twists, by the way?"

"They're a type of pastry. The orange flavored dough is twisted and then baked. Sometimes there's chocolate drizzle on them. Would you like one?"

"Sure. I'm game to try anything."

"I'll be right back."

When she returned, Levi was talking with Jackson. She stilled. She couldn't go back into the kitchen when Jackson was expecting his twist. Avoiding Levi was getting harder and harder. She took in a deep breath and then walked over to them and placed the twist on the table.

"Breakfast looks good." Levi turned to Selah. "Nice job."

His words set her teeth on edge. Was he being condescending? As if she'd done something monumental by serving breakfast?

"Best breakfast I ever had," Jackson said.

Levi nodded. "That's what we like to hear. Do you need anything else?"

Selah clenched her jaw. It was her job to ask Jackson if he needed anything else.

"I was going to get more coffee—"

"I'll get it." Selah grabbed his mug off the table and stormed to the beverage station. She filled it to the brim and then nearly slammed it on his table. Hot coffee sloshed everywhere, which brought her to her senses. "Oh *nee*," she said, grabbing his napkin and wiping up the coffee. "Did I get any on you?"

Jackson shook his head. "Uh, no."

"I'm so sorry." She began to wipe furiously. "I'm really sorry."

"It's fine, Selah," he said.

But it wasn't fine. She had lost her temper over something stupid, and now she'd made an idiot of herself in front of Jackson and Levi. She couldn't look at either of them as she ran off to the kitchen.

"If Noah calls me one more time . . ." Cevilla snapped shut the flip phone and placed it on the kitchen counter. The argument had gone on for a long time, but she'd finally agreed to not just take the phone her nephew had given her but to keep it in the house, something she *really* hadn't wanted to do. Yet on days like this, when the snow was up past her knees, it was nice not to have to trudge out to the barn to check voice mail every two or three hours because her nephew was a worrywart and would panic if he didn't get a return call. It was also true that a woman her age could easily slip and fall in conditions like this, but she hated to admit that.

"He cares about you." Richard examined the puzzle piece in his hand, squinted, and then placed it in the correct spot. He and Cevilla had been working on the puzzle since after breakfast, and they would have made more progress if they hadn't spent so much time talking and laughing—about the past, of course. They discussed very little about the present, and nothing about the future.

"I know. He says he'll be over as soon as the snow eases up so he can dig us out. I wouldn't be surprised if the Yoder boys showed up too."

Richard nodded and picked up another piece. "Hope you told Noah there was no need to rush."

Cevilla smiled. She'd admitted to Noah that Richard had spent the night—on the couch. The admission embarrassed her a little, as though she'd been caught doing something improper, which, of course, wasn't true. It didn't help when Noah laughed and said, "Just make sure you two lovebirds stay out of trouble."

She frowned. Her nephew could be irritating at times. *Wonder where he got that?*

Richard's cell phone rang. He fished it out of his pants pocket and tapped the screen. Unlike her, he had a fancy smartphone. The flip phone was more than enough for her. "Hi, Meghan," he said, grinning. "Wonderful to hear from you . . . Yes, I miss you too. It's been too long since we've seen each other."

Cevilla saw the light in his eyes as he talked to his granddaughter. They had always been close, and she'd been with him when he showed up on Cevilla's doorstep last year. She took her cane and stood, mouthing the words *I'll get more tea.* He nodded and continued to talk.

She paused in front of the kitchen stove. Once again she was struck by the fact that Richard was giving up a lot to be with her. And what was she giving up? Nothing—unless she counted no longer spending most of her days on her own. Otherwise, he was making all the changes. Was that fair? Was it even right?

She'd been so focused on her own feelings that she hadn't thought about how difficult it must have been for Richard to leave everything he knew behind. He was considering not only changing his address permanently but changing his entire life—for her.

A stab of pain went through her heart as she realized how lopsided their relationship was.

When she pushed the tea cart back to the living room, Richard was still talking. He looked at Cevilla as she put the cups on the puzzle table. "Cevilla's brought our tea, sweetheart, so I'll let you go for now. I'm glad to hear everything is going well. Tell your mother I said hello . . . and that she could give me a call every once in a while."

Cevilla winced.

"Love you, Meghan . . . I'll tell her . . . All right. Bye." Richard swiped his finger across the screen and placed the phone back in his pocket. "Meghan sends her love," he said, picking up his cup of tea.

Cevilla was silent for a moment. "When was the last time you heard from Sharon?" she asked.

Richard frowned. "Been awhile." He shrugged, and after taking a sip of tea, he put the cup back down. "I'm sure she's busy with whatever she busies herself with." He smiled at her. "Meghan said she might come out for a visit soon."

"That would be nice." She saw how excited he was at the prospect, which sent off another twinge in her heart.

"You've become quiet all of a sudden," he said.

"I have?" Cevilla waved him off, trying to force a smile.

"What's wrong?"

"Nothing's wrong. I do have my quiet moments, you know."

"Not very often." He peered at her over his glasses. "Sure everything is still okay?"

"*Ya,*" she said, managing to brighten a little. They had just overcome their first major argument, and she didn't want him to worry that they were going to fight again. "Everything is right as rain—or snow, considering today's forecast."

"Good." He looked at her with an endearing gaze for a long moment. "I'm glad we got back on track, Cevilla. I don't want that to ever happen to us again."

She nodded, watching him pick up one of the puzzle pieces and search for its place, her heart filling with love. *Neither do I.*

Chapter 13

After Selah fled to the kitchen, Levi turned to Jackson. "Sorry about that."

He waved his hand. "It's no problem. She must not be feeling well again."

Levi glanced at the kitchen door. "Yeah," he mumbled. "I'm sure that's it."

Jackson calmly sipped his coffee as if Selah hadn't just splashed it all over the table. He picked up his orange twist. "This looks amazing."

If all their guests were as easygoing as Jackson, running the inn would be a breeze. "Let me know if you need anything else." Jackson gave him a thumbs-up, and then Levi went to the kitchen, making sure to open the door slowly. Selah's back was to him, but he could tell she was covering her face with her hands. "Selah?" He walked up behind her. When she didn't say anything, he touched her shoulder.

"Don't." She shrugged him off.

He took a step back, knowing he'd crossed a line. "Sorry."

Her shoulders slumped, and then she turned around. "Don't apologize, either. This is all *mei* fault." She looked up at him, pain in her eyes. "I'll get myself together, I promise."

"Selah, I . . ." He wasn't sure how to respond.

To say she was touchy was an understatement, but she also seemed confused. "Whatever is going on, you can talk to me. I won't break *yer* confidence."

"Somehow I believe that."

"Because it's true."

She backed up from him until she was against the counter. He took another step away from her, not wanting her to think she was trapped. "I think I'm just tired," she said. "I get a little short-tempered when I don't get enough sleep."

Levi didn't buy her excuse, but he nodded anyway. "Take the rest of the day off."

Her gaze shot to his. "I don't have to do that. I need to clear breakfast. I'll be fine."

"I know you'll be fine, but you're still taking the day off. *Geh* upstairs or back to Nina's room and get some rest. I'll take care of the food and dishes."

"But—"

He crossed his arms. "Did you forget I'm *yer* boss?"

Her gaze averted, hiding her eyes. "*Nee.*"

"Then why are you arguing with me?" When she started to speak, he held up his hand. "Don't apologize again. I think we're all tired and out of sorts. Except for Jackson. He seems to be really enjoying his stay."

"Thanks to *yer familye.*"

"And thanks to you. I know I said breakfast

looks good out there, but it looks really *gut*. It takes a team effort to keep this place going, even if there's only one guest. Don't discount *yer* contribution."

She nodded. "I won't."

"Now, you have *yer* duty schedule for the day." He opened the door to the mudroom, giving her what he hoped was an encouraging smile. He didn't want to be that stern with her, but he knew if he wasn't, she'd continue arguing with him. "Hop to it."

Selah paused, the lines of strain around her mouth lessening. Then they both stepped into the mudroom, where she took her coat from a peg before leaving. Just to make sure she complied, he watched out a window until he saw her going into the house. At the same time, Nina was coming from the barn. Levi held the door open for his sister, shivering a little from the cold.

"Where's Selah going?" Nina said as he closed the mudroom door.

"To take a nap. In *yer* room, I think. Is that okay?"

"More than okay." Nina leaned over and whispered, "She's a little crabby this morning."

Levi didn't acknowledge her words, but he hoped whatever was going on with Selah was a onetime thing. If not, he had another problem to deal with. But he couldn't stand the thought of firing her. He shoved that thought away. They would work things out, somehow.

"Levi?" Nina said as they walked into the kitchen.

"What?"

"Good grief, now you sound out of sorts. I was just going to ask you if you wanted to play a game of Dutch Blitz. *Grossmutter* is in the living room working on a crossword puzzle, so she's keeping an eye on *Daed*. I don't think he needs anyone to wait on him all the time, and naturally he agrees. But you know *Grossmutter*."

"*Ya*. She gets her way sooner or later." He looked at her. "I don't want to play, but maybe you could ask Jackson."

"Think he knows how?"

"You could teach him. I think he's still eating in the lobby."

Her eyes lit up. "All right. I'll ask him, and when he's finished, I'll clean up breakfast."

"I'll help."

"You will?" She tilted her head. "Where's *mei bruder* and what have you done with him?"

"C'mon, I've washed dishes before."

"I know." She laughed. "You're just too fun to tease." Then she went into the lobby.

Levi began filling the sink with water, his mind on Selah again. In a short time, he'd grown to care for her, and it didn't make much sense. He'd known women his age all his life and had never experienced a spark of attraction. But from the moment he met Selah, he'd felt something, and it wasn't just curiosity. He recognized that now. Leave it to him to fall for a complicated woman.

Shutting off the tap, he closed his eyes. *Lord, I don't know what to do other than pray for Selah. Whatever she's dealing with, please help her. And you can help me, too, while you're at it. I'm gonna need it.*

Selah lay in Nina's bed, unable to sleep even though she'd been given marching orders to do so. After she'd left the inn, she'd entered the house through the mudroom and taken off her coat. Then she'd passed Loren and Delilah in the living room, where they were reading separate sections of the paper, a pencil behind Delilah's ear. "Everything all right, dear?" Delilah asked as Selah moved toward the staircase.

Hearing Delilah's caring voice nearly undid her. She bit her lip and nodded. "I'm just a little tired. Levi suggested I take a nap."

Her graying brow lifted. "He did?"

"*Ya.* I didn't sleep well last night."

"A nap is an excellent idea." Loren set down the paper and folded his hands over his waist. "This feels a little bit like a Sunday since we're limited in what we can do."

"Speak for *yerself*," Delilah said.

"I told you I could start doing things around here. Like get *mei* own lunch."

"And risk hurting *yer* leg when you're just starting to feel better? Humph." She looked at Selah. "Enjoy *yer* rest."

Loren nodded, closing his eyes. "We'll make sure to keep the noise down. Right, Mutter? You're usually the main culprit."

She gave him a pointed look, which he didn't see, and then she fluttered her hand in the direction of the stairs.

Now Selah was underneath the warm covers, trying to fall asleep. But all she could do was fret over the disasters that had happened ever since Christian told her to stay with the Stolls. Between her panic attack and getting angry over nothing—which ended up affecting their first guest—she worried she wouldn't have a job anymore despite Levi's amiability. She might have blown this opportunity in less than a week. That had to be a record.

Her insides churned. Anger, irritation, sadness—these were familiar enemies, and they wouldn't let her go. And something else worried her. Was it possible that missing one pill would set her so far back? There had to be another reason. The prospect that something else was wrong with her escalated her anxiety.

A soft knock sounded at the door. Before she could respond, the door opened a crack and a hand poked through to set a plate on the floor. "I'm awake," Selah said. "You can come in."

Delilah opened the door, looking sheepish. "I didn't mean to wake you. I brought you a snack for when you wake up."

One thing about Delilah, she made sure no one went hungry. "*Danki*."

"Having trouble sleeping?"

"A little."

"How about some chamomile tea?"

A lump formed in Selah's throat. "*Nee* . . . thank you." Then she burst into tears.

"Oh *mei* goodness." Delilah went to her and sat on the edge of the bed.

"I'm sorry," she said. "I don't know what's wrong with me." She tried to stem their flow, but the tears kept coming.

Delilah didn't say anything. She just held her until she was able to stop, and then she took a handkerchief out of her apron pocket. The Stolls seemed prepared for everything. "Here," she said, handing it to her.

Selah wiped her eyes. "I'm sorry," she said again.

"Selah, I can't help you if you don't tell me what's wrong."

She looked at Delilah, who was the last person she ever thought she would open up to. The taskmaster, the stubborn woman who always got her way, the one Levi said could be a tyrant. But she was also caring, and Selah had never felt so cared for than in this moment. *Except when I'm with Levi.* But she couldn't tell Delilah the truth.

Then she would really be out of a job, not to mention possibly ostracized by this family. She couldn't take that chance right now.

Delilah patted Selah's knee. "I shouldn't have pried," she said. "I'll get you that tea." She rose from the bed. "It will help you sleep."

"*Danki*," Selah whispered.

Her heart started to hammer in her chest again. Levi wouldn't be here to rescue her this time. She got on her knees and prayed harder than she ever had, not stopping until her heartbeat slowed again.

It will be okay.

Those words had to come from the Lord, because in her mind, *nothing* was okay.

Levi spent all of lunch and most of the afternoon in his office, except when he took a break to get an orange twist from the kitchen and a cup of coffee. Nina and Jackson had played Dutch Blitz for a couple of hours, and she'd made sure he got some lunch. His sister was a pretty good hostess, he had to admit. But taking care of one guest was much different than caring for multiple ones. God willing, they would have more soon.

Despite holing up in the office, he didn't get much work done. He hoped Selah had been able to rest. Around four, he emerged from the office and stood by the front door. The snow had finally stopped, and the sun appeared through the mass of gray clouds, illuminating the sparkling landscape. About three feet of the stuff was in the parking lot and on the road, but only four inches or so on the front porch. There wouldn't be much daylight left, so he needed to get busy clearing the parking lot.

He turned as Jackson came down the stairs and said, "Finally, some sunshine."

"Nina and I will dig out your car," Levi told him.

"You don't have to do that today. The plows aren't out yet, and I'm not leaving until the morning."

"We have church tomorrow, so we can't do it then."

Jackson frowned and then nodded. "No work on Sunday?"

"Nothing that isn't urgent or taking care of our animals." He set his mug on the counter.

"I see. You still don't have to excavate my car. That's not typically the innkeeper's job."

"We're not a typical inn. Besides, more hands are better than few, especially since we don't have a snowblower. But we have plenty of snow shovels."

"Then I'm definitely helping." Jackson paused. "I gotta admit, I'm confused by some of the things you guys do—and don't do. Like not driving cars. What's up with that?"

Levi, unlike some Amish, had always been open to questions from outsiders. "For us, cars aren't necessary. We can get where we need to by horse and buggy, and if we need to go farther, we can hire a taxi or take a bus. Isn't that what English people do too? Use taxis and other transportation services?"

"Yeah, but it's way more convenient to have a car."

"True, but life isn't always about convenience. At least not among us."

"I noticed." He rocked back on his heels. "Convenience isn't always a good thing. Sometimes I'm so busy I can't think straight. Then I wonder, if I'm so busy, why aren't I accomplishing anything? And if everything is supposed to be so easy, why does it seem to be getting harder?" He shrugged. "Oh well. I'll get my gear from upstairs and meet you in the parking lot."

Levi nodded and went to the house to get Nina and his snow gear. When he walked into the kitchen, his grandmother was sitting at the table, her chin resting on her hand, staring into space. He wasn't used to seeing her motionless, except in church services. "Where's Nina?" he asked. When she didn't respond he said, "*Grossmutter?*"

"Oh, *ya.*" She blinked and straightened. "Nina's in the living room with *yer daed.* He's slept almost the whole afternoon. I guess he's still catching up on the sleep he missed while he was in the hospital."

"*Gut.*" He was sorely tempted to ask his

grandmother if she'd checked on Selah, but he refrained. Instead of working in his office, most of the time he'd tried to figure out how to detach himself from her. That would be difficult to do, considering he wanted to do the opposite. He wanted to spend time with her, to get to know her, to reassure her that everything would be all right. But that would be a mistake. He headed for the living room to get Nina.

"Selah's still upstairs."

He whirled around but then steadied himself. Now that his grandmother had opened the door, he was going to walk through it. "Did you check on her? Did she have anything to eat? Is she still upset?"

She held up her hand. "One question at a time. *Ya*, I checked on her, and *ya* she had something to eat. As far as being upset . . ." She got up and went to Levi. "You did the right thing by giving her the rest of the day off."

That didn't answer his question, and he had to fight the urge to go upstairs and check on her himself. "I'm going to shovel the parking lot," he said. He needed to focus on work, not on Selah.

Grossmutter nodded. "I'll get started on supper."

Levi went to the living room, where Nina lay on the couch reading a book. He glanced at his father, who was snoring away in his chair, before nudging her on the shoulder. "We're shoveling the lot," he said in a loud whisper. "Now."

"Now?"

"Now." He glanced up the stairs and then forced his mind off Selah again.

Nina groaned. "Fine. I'll meet you out there."

"Hurry up."

"Everyone's acting so *seltsam* today." She got up from the couch, scowling. "Jackson and I are the only normal people here."

"Don't forget about me," *Daed* said.

Levi whirled around. "Sorry. We didn't mean to wake you."

"That's okay." He grabbed his crutches and stood. "I need to move around anyway. If I sleep any more, I'll be awake all night." He looked at Levi and Nina. "Need any help with the shoveling?"

"Nee," they said at the same time.

"Just joking." He hobbled away toward his bedroom.

Levi and Nina headed for the mudroom to prepare for the task at hand. "Why are you so fussy?" Nina said as she put on her thick winter coat.

"Just be quiet and get dressed." He stormed outside, his coat half on. Then he stopped and took in a deep breath. When this weekend was over and Selah was feeling better, the two of them were going to have another talk. And this time they would straighten everything out once and for all.

Chapter 14

Selah stood at the window in Nina's room and put her hand against the freezing cold pane of glass as she watched Nina and Jackson dig out his car. They were on opposite sides of the snow-covered vehicle, and Nina picked up a huge shovel of snow and flung it behind her, not knowing that Jackson was there. A cascade of snow fell over him. Even though she couldn't hear what the two of them were saying, she saw Nina put her gloved hand in front of her mouth in surprise before Jackson flung a bit of snow back at her. They both started to laugh.

She couldn't even crack a smile. She would be out there right now, helping them clean Jackson's car and the rest of the parking lot, if she hadn't ruined everything.

She plopped onto Nina's bed. Instead of napping after Delilah brought her the tea, she had prayed some more. It settled her down some, but all she wanted was to go home.

She moved from the bed and paced for a few minutes before going back to the window. Jackson and Nina were still shoveling. Where was Levi? She couldn't see him, but she was certain he was also shoveling somewhere, just out of her vantage point. She couldn't imagine him not helping while Jackson and Nina worked.

A knock sounded at the door, and when she told whoever it was to come in, Delilah opened it. "Ruby just called," she said. "Christian is on his way to pick you up. She said he should be here in thirty minutes."

Selah let out an inward sigh of relief. "*Danki.*"

Delilah paused. "Would you like a drink or a snack while you wait downstairs for him?"

She shook her head, unwilling to explain that she planned to stay in Nina's room until the very last minute so she wouldn't run into Levi.

"All right. I'll be in the kitchen cooking supper if you change *yer* mind." She gave her a small but warm smile and then closed the door.

Selah waited as long as she could and then took a deep breath and went downstairs. She'd go through the kitchen to the mudroom to get her coat and bonnet, and hopefully Levi wouldn't be there.

To her surprise, neither Delilah nor Loren were in the kitchen, although a couple of pots were on the stove and the scents of cinnamon, ginger, and pumpkin were in the air. Two piecrusts sat on the counter next to a large mixing bowl. She hurriedly got her belongings from the mudroom and then dashed to the living room to watch out the front window for Christian to show up. Levi, Jackson, and Nina weren't in the parking lot now, and she figured they'd gone inside the inn. The fact that the Stolls and Jackson weren't around eased her mind a little bit. At least she could avoid an awkward scene with everyone, knowing she was the reason it was awkward.

A few minutes later Christian's buggy turned into the wide path now cleared down the center of the parking lot. She opened the door before he pulled to a stop.

"You're leaving?"

She turned to see Levi standing in the living room. His face was red from the cold, and his eyeglass lenses were fogging up from the heat coming off the woodstove. He took them off as he walked toward her. "These things can be annoying sometimes," he muttered before stopping in front of her.

"Christian's here." She shut the door a little way, not closing it completely.

"I know. What I meant was that you were leaving without saying good-bye."

Her cheeks heated. She'd been so self-absorbed that she hadn't realized that by slipping out undetected she was being rude to the people who had treated her so kindly. She looked up at him, ready to apologize.

But the words didn't come. She hadn't seen Levi without his glasses before, and while she thought he was handsome with them, he was gorgeous without them. The sparkle so easy to see when he wore his glasses was in full force now. Then it started to fade as he frowned.

"It's too cold to keep Christian waiting." He

put his glasses back on and stepped away. "See you back here on Monday."

"Monday. Right." She opened the door and dashed onto the porch, which had been swept clean. That must have been what Levi was doing while his sister and Jackson were in the parking lot. Once down the steps, she practically skated to the buggy before climbing inside. She sat back, her chest heaving.

"You seem to be in distress." Christian peered at her. "Are you okay?"

"*Ya.*" No, she wasn't okay, but if she told the truth, he would ask more questions. "I guess the cold took *mei* breath away."

"Fortunately it's not as hyperboreal as it was yesterday."

She was too tired and out of sorts to ask him what that meant. "Can we *geh* home now?"

He lifted an eyebrow and then nodded. "Of course."

As Christian maneuvered the buggy out of the parking lot, Selah resisted the urge to look back at the inn. Monday. She might be able to avoid Levi at church the next day, but it was crucial that she get her wits back by Monday. If not, she would be in trouble—for more reasons than one.

Levi thrust one hand through his hair. He'd missed a prime opportunity to talk to Selah. But seeing her leave without saying a word to any of his family had irritated him to the point where he gave up. It didn't matter that when she'd looked at him after he took off his glasses, he'd felt something shift inside him even though her image was blurry. He sensed something there, something strong between them despite his confusion and annoyance with her—which made him even more frustrated.

"Look, I'm using one crutch!" His father hobbled into the living room.

"Great." Levi continued to look out the window as Christian's buggy went down the snowplowed road.

"Don't get too enthusiastic on me, *sohn*."

Levi turned around and faced him. "Sorry. I was a little distracted."

"By Selah?"

He was about to deny it, but what was the point? He'd been lying to himself all this time about his feelings for her, and by default to his grandmother, but he couldn't lie to his father. "*Ya*. You could say that."

Daed limped to his chair and sat down. "You've had a lot on *yer* plate lately."

Levi plopped down in the chair next to him. "Not that much." He didn't want his father worrying about him.

"Oh, I don't know about that. Getting the hang of being an innkeeper isn't easy. I'm finding that out from firsthand experience. Then having a new employee and our first guest. And doing all that with *yer* usual positive attitude."

He wasn't feeling all that positive right now, especially about Selah. "It's part of the job."

"I'll be back on *mei* feet soon enough, and you'll be relieved of all that responsibility."

"I don't mind it, though." He looked at his father. "I kind of like it, actually. Now that I know what I'm doing for the most part, it's enjoyable. Of course, we've had only one guest so far. And the blizzard stopped everything, so there wasn't that much to do."

Daed nodded. "There's a lot more for you to learn. If you're interested, I can teach you. I like the idea of having someone else able to run the inn in case of things like this happening." He gestured to his leg, which he then propped up on the footstool. "Although I promise to stay off roofs from now on."

"*Gut.*" Levi leaned back in the chair. "I'll take you up on *yer* offer to learn innkeeping."

"We can start Monday, after I get back from *mei* appointment." *Daed* sniffed the air. "I can smell that pumpkin pie from here. I think *yer grossmammi* is trying to impress Jackson." He got up from the chair. "I'm going to see what else she's cooking up in there." He tucked his crutch under his arm.

"Should you be on only one crutch?" Levi asked, frowning.

"Probably not." He looked at Levi. "By the way, Selah's a nice *maedel*. I'm sure whatever is going on between you two, you'll work it out."

Daed limped out of the room, and for once in his life, Levi wasn't so optimistic.

Shortly after she arrived home, Selah ran out to the phone shanty. Most people in the community had a cell phone for emergencies, and the school where Christian taught had one, but her brother was old-fashioned when it came to technology—even if it was sanctioned by the bishop. He'd insisted on putting this shanty in when they moved here. For once she was grateful, because she was desperate for privacy.

She dialed Anne on her private number, one to be used only in emergencies. This definitely constituted an emergency.

"Hello?" Anne's calm voice came through the receiver.

"Hi." She twisted the phone cord around her finger. She'd forgotten to put on her gloves, and her hands were freezing. She stuck one hand into her pocket, holding on to the receiver with the other.

"Hi, Selah." She paused. "Is something wrong?"

"Everything is wrong!" She explained what had happened over the past forty-eight hours. "I'm sorry to bother you, but I don't know what to do."

"Take a deep breath first," Anne said. "Then we'll talk."

Selah inhaled, the cold air stinging her lungs, but it did relax her a tiny bit.

"All right," Anne said. "Now, my first question is have you found a new therapist yet?"

"No."

"Why not?"

Anne was nice, but she was also direct, which Selah knew she needed but didn't like much right now. "I haven't had the time."

"Your mental health should always be a priority, Selah. We talked about this."

"I didn't call to get a lecture, Anne." She paused. "I'm sorry."

"It's okay. You're agitated and anxious, which makes you short-tempered."

"I don't know what's happening to me," she said, a familiar hopeless feeling looming in the background of her soul. "I thought I was doing so well."

"You are. And I can promise that missing one dose of your medication won't send you spiraling the way you're describing. Don't make it a habit, though."

"I won't." She would carry her medicine with her from now on.

"Why don't you tell me how the job is going."

"It was fine until all this happened." She huddled in her coat. "I made sure not to make any mistakes." *Other than falling for Levi.*

"So you're doing your job perfectly," Anne said.

"I'm trying to."

"Are you double-checking everything you do? Are you worried that you might make a mistake and get fired?"

Selah nodded but then remembered Anne couldn't see her. "Yes. I'm terrified of that."

"Which translates to a large amount of stress. Being perfect is impossible—and trying to be perfect can lead to anxiety and agitation. But that can't be the only reason you had a panic attack." After a long pause, she said, "Is there anyone at the inn you don't get along with?"

"No, they're all wonderful. Especially . . ."

"Especially who?"

She groaned. She knew Anne well enough to know that she would gently push Selah until she answered. "There is this one man . . . Levi."

"I see. And he's special to you in some way."

Swallowing, Selah said, "Yes. He is." Then she added quickly, "But I know it's wrong to get involved with my boss."

"He's your boss?"

"Sort of." She explained the situation with the family. "Technically he'll be a coworker when his father goes back to work, assuming my job has become permanent by then. But that doesn't really change anything. I shouldn't be interested in anyone to begin with."

"Why not?"

"Because I'm . . ." She leaned her forehead against the side of the shanty. "I can't. And before you ask me *why* again, it's because I've decided to stay single."

"For how long?"

These short, peppering questions were getting on her nerves. "My whole life."

She heard the sound of shuffling papers in the background. "That's a bit extreme, don't you think? Particularly because you like someone now?"

"I have terrible taste in men. You know that."

"You made some mistakes. You can either learn from them or hide and let them inform the rest of your life. It's your choice."

Selah gasped. "Then you're telling me to quit my job?"

"That's not what I said. You wanted a fresh start when you moved back to Birch Creek. That means keeping the past in the past. You're not going to make the same mistake you made with Oliver."

Just the sound of Oliver's name grated. She cringed. "It probably won't matter. After what happened, they won't want me back."

"Or they will. You won't know if you don't show up for work. A panic attack isn't the end of the world. And when you find a therapist— which you *will* do on Monday and set up an appointment—you can figure out what triggered the event. Until then, you have some decisions to make."

"About my job?"

"Yes. And about Levi."

Selah frowned. "What do I need to decide about him?"

"That's for you to figure out. Selah, you're going to be okay. You already used prayer to help you cope, which is excellent. You can work on other ways with your new therapist." She paused again. "I'm glad you called. Keep me updated."

"All right." She did feel better, having Anne's reassurance. And she was right about finding a therapist as soon as possible. She was improving, but she still had a long way to go.

After she thanked Anne, she hung up the phone, but she didn't go back in the house even though she was shivering. Instead, she focused on a Bible verse. *What time I am afraid, I will trust in thee.* She had to turn her fear over to God so she could think clearly and listen for his guidance. Only then could she make the right decisions—about everything.

Chapter 15

As soon as Jackson returned to the hotel Sunday morning, his father pounced on him.

"Well? What did you find out?"

Jackson set his duffel bag on the floor by the front counter. He'd stopped here before going to the apartment because he'd had an idea for rerouting the network while he was at the inn, and he wanted to try it out. He glanced around. Unlike the lobby at Stoll Inn, there was no woodstove, and everywhere he turned he saw an overabundance of sparkly, cheap-looking decorations. They were a stark contrast to the sparse but homey Christmas decorations at the inn.

He reached into the plastic bowl of peppermint candies on the counter, courtesy of Lois, not Ashley, and slowly unwrapped one, stalling for time. His experience at the inn had been unexpected—and not just because of the blizzard. The Stoll family had welcomed him, a stranger, into their home and made him feel like he was their friend. It was so beyond the way his father ran his hotel, where he never mingled with guests. He'd fought with himself about what to say regarding the weekend when he saw his father, and he still wasn't sure what to do.

He knew what he couldn't do—betray the Stolls. His father tapped his foot as Jackson popped the candy into his mouth. "Nothing. I didn't learn a thing."

Dad frowned, his groomed eyebrows furrowing. "I don't believe you."

"I don't care what you believe. They run a tight ship over there. They even helped me dig my car out yesterday. Hey, why are you here on a Sunday? You're usually off somewhere with your girlfriend."

"Ashley's spending the weekend with her parents."

Jackson lifted a brow. "And you weren't invited?"

His father scowled. "Get back on topic. You had to have found out something we could exploit."

"Again with the *we* thing. There is no we."

"Even if I pay off your loans? Every single dime?"

Jackson stilled.

"I thought that would get your attention." His expression turned smug. "I'm sure you were snowed in, which means you had plenty of time to get to know the inn and the owners. Even if the inn doesn't have any obvious issues, the people do. People always do."

Speak for yourself. But his father was also dangling the enticing carrot of eliminating Jackson's debt. If he had no debt, he could move out of his father's apartment and get his own place. He'd move to another city, possibly another state. All he had to do was make up some dirt about the Stolls. They wouldn't even know how it happened.

"Think about it," his father said. "Insider information for your loans. A fair trade, I think." He tapped his fingers against the counter before leaving the lobby.

"More like bribery." Jackson slammed his fist against the counter.

A few minutes later, Lois emerged from the back. "Oh, thank goodness you're back." Jingle bell earrings dangled from her earlobes, making a tinkling sound when she moved. "Your father is being insufferable."

"Isn't he always?"

"He's worse this time." Lois straightened the bowl of candy Jackson had disturbed. "He's at loose ends since Ashley left him."

"Left? I thought she was spending the weekend with her parents."

Lois's brow lifted from behind her glasses. "That's what she said. But anyone who chooses her parents over her, ahem, *boyfriend,* is either about to break up with him or already has."

Jackson rolled his eyes, having little sympathy for his father's romantic problems. He scowled and grabbed another piece of candy but didn't unwrap it.

"You look just like him when you're cranky."

He didn't appreciate the comparison. "I have a reason to be cranky."

She patted his hand. "Tell old Lois about it."

He paused. It would be nice to get this problem off his chest. But could he trust her? "I don't know . . ."

"If it has to do with your father, my lips are sealed." She sighed. "I don't know how long I'm going to last here anyway. He gets harder and harder to deal with. I don't have to subject myself to this."

"You definitely don't." He leaned forward. "Lips sealed?"

She made a zipping motion over her mouth.

Jackson told her about his weekend with the Stolls, his father's plan, and then his father's offer to pay off his school loans. Lois listened intently, and when he was through, she clucked her tongue.

"I wish I could say I was surprised he would do that." She shook her head. "You're faced with a difficult dilemma, though." She tilted her head and looked at him, her eyes soft. "But I've come to know you better since you moved here. You're not your father's son."

He stilled. She was right. He wasn't. Yet that didn't change the reality of his situation. Even if his business was an instant success, it would take years if not a decade or more to get out of debt.

"Hey, if you've got some time, can you help me take down some of these decorations?" Lois sniffed. "They're ridiculous. And my sister calls *me* the queen of tacky."

"Sure thing." Anything to get his mind off the Stolls and his father. But pulling down Christmas décor didn't clear his mind like he'd hoped. All he had to do was tell his father something he could use to negatively affect the Stoll family's business and he could start his life completely in the black. *They will never know it was me.*

Selah's fingers trembled as she pinned her white *kapp* to her hair. She smoothed her light-green dress and put a navy-blue cardigan over it. Sunlight streamed through her bedroom window, and at breakfast Christian had reported that the temperature was indeed "temperate."

She finished dressing for church and then put on her coat and bonnet, tucked her scarf around her neck, and went outside. The temperature had warmed overnight, and a lot of the snow had melted. Christian had hitched up the buggy, and Ruby was already in the front seat. Selah climbed into the back seat and put a thick blanket over her legs.

Ruby turned around and faced her. "Did you sleep last night?"

"A little."

Her sister-in-law frowned. "I'm worried. You looked pale yesterday, and this morning at breakfast you didn't eat much."

"I wasn't that hungry. Don't worry, Ruby. I'm fine."

Ruby peered at her as Christian climbed in. She nodded and then turned and faced the front.

When they arrived for church at Daniel and Barbara Raber's home, Ruby and Selah headed for the barn where the service would be held. She immediately saw Delilah and Nina and chose to sit two benches behind them. They didn't turn around, fortunately. She owed them an apology for disappearing the way she had, but she didn't want to do that before church began.

As everyone filed in, she couldn't stop herself from glancing at the other side of the room. She didn't see Levi right away, but as she started to face the front, she saw him walk in, his father at his side. Just glimpsing him made her heart flutter. Eventually that would stop—once her heart caught up with her mind that knew she and Levi, despite the attraction, weren't meant to be together. Last night she had prayed for guidance, but the only clear direction she'd received was that she had to apologize to the Stolls and have a talk with Levi about her job. All that could wait until after church.

She focused on the service, singing the hymns and taking in their words instead of just repeating them by rote. She paid attention to Timothy Glick's sermon, and she concentrated on prayer. By the time the service was over, she felt refreshed if not confident. *What time I am afraid, I will trust in thee.* She was determined to live out that verse.

When the community members began to disperse, she hurried to Delilah and Nina. "I'm so sorry," she said, twisting her fingers together. "I shouldn't have run off like I did yesterday. I want to thank you for everything."

Nina smiled while Delilah nodded. "You're fine," Delilah said. "We all knew you were ready to *geh* home."

She was thankful they understood.

When Delilah had excused herself, Nina opened her mouth to say something, but then she clamped it shut when Ira passed by, giving him a short wave.

"I've got to run," Nina said, keeping her gaze on Ira. "I need to ask Ira if he wants to *geh* ice fishing Saturday. The pond is definitely frozen over now. See you Monday?" Before Selah could respond, Nina followed Ira out of the barn.

When Selah looked around, the barn was empty except for a few men who were busy putting all the benches away. That gave her a few minutes to collect herself before she sought out Levi. She had to be completely calm when they talked. Aloof, something she knew how to be. She'd spent much of the past two years learning how to manage her emotions, but she hadn't done a good job of it lately. That had to stop now.

All the men had left when she turned and nearly

ran into Levi. Startled, she took a step back from him. Then she made the mistake of gazing at his church clothes—a black coat over a crisp white shirt, black vest and pants, and a black hat, which contrasted perfectly with his light-brown hair. She averted her gaze from his clothing and met his eyes, which didn't help, either. She steeled herself, locking her attraction to him deep in the recesses of her heart. "I didn't know you were still in here."

He nodded, unsmiling, his expression emotionally distant. She'd never seen him like this. "Are you all right?" she asked as evenly as she could. So much for aloof on the inside.

Meeting her gaze, he said, "We're due for another talk, *ya*?"

Stoic, remember? "Ya. Let's talk."

Levi was used to seeing the reserved expression on Selah's face, but it was taking everything he had inside to act the same way. He wasn't trying to mock her or to exact any kind of just desserts. He had told himself that when he saw her today, he would simply cut whatever string was keeping them attached. He had no idea if she sensed that. Probably not, considering yesterday she couldn't wait to get away from him. But he wasn't leaving until they had an understanding between them. Again. Hopefully this would be the last time they had to straighten out anything between them.

He looked at her, trying not to stare. She was so pretty he could hardly stand it. But this morning something different was in her eyes. Distance, yes, but also a confidence he hadn't seen before. Yet he had to focus on the matter at hand. "*Are you returning to work tomorrow?*"

She nodded, her shoulders straightening. "*Ya.* If you still want me there. And I can promise that what happened during the blizzard won't happen again."

The certainty in her eyes made him believe her even though he'd expected her to say no, she wouldn't be coming in. But even if she had another panic attack, that wouldn't cause her to lose her job. He knew his family would agree. "*Gut.* You're a great maid, and we don't want to lose *yer* services."

"*Danki.*"

So far so good. No lingering gazes, and his pulse behaved itself. He could do this. "We'll be closed on Christmas and Second Christmas, of course."

"Of course."

"You don't have to come to work on those days. And you can have time off if you want to visit *yer familye* in New York for the holiday."

Something flickered in her eyes. "*Danki.*" Her voice was soft. "I appreciate that."

His heartbeat tripped. *Not now.* "Then I don't think we have anything more to discuss."

"*Nee*, we don't."

"Business as usual?"

Again, the flicker of emotion in her eyes, but her expression quickly turned blank. "Business as usual."

"Then I'll see you tomorrow."

"*Ya*, tomorrow."

He pretended to busy himself with brushing dust off the back of one of the stacked benches until he was sure she was gone. That wasn't so hard. He—his family—needed her. He didn't want to go through the process of hiring and training another maid. *I don't want to lose her* . . .

"Maid services," he said out loud to the empty barn, and then he ground his teeth.

"What?" Seth Yoder came up behind him.

"*Nix*," Levi said, jamming his hands into his pockets. "Just mumbling to myself."

"Ah." Seth looked around the barn. "Martha forgot her purse, of all things . . . There it is." He pointed to a plain brown leather purse on top of a short stack of hay bales in the corner. "She's been forgetful lately." After retrieving the purse, Seth looked at Levi. "You okay?"

"Sure. Why?"

"You're standing alone in the barn talking to *yerself*."

"I wasn't alone. I was talking to Selah. About her job. She's working at the inn now."

He nodded. "Martha told me." He put the purse

over his forearm, grimaced, and then held it from the strap like a grocery bag. "Next time *mei frau* is getting her own purse. See you inside the *haus*."

"I'll walk with you."

Levi spent the rest of the time there talking with friends who had stayed for the meal. He noticed Selah wasn't around even though Christian and Ruby were. He was sure she walked home. He smiled a little and shook his head. Although Selah was unpredictable, especially lately, her walking home alone didn't surprise him at all.

Chapter 16

January 28

Dear Anne,

   I hope you don't mind getting a letter from me instead of a phone call. I'm supposed to use the phone only in case of emergencies, but updating you on what's happened since we spoke before Christmas isn't an emergency, something I'm very thankful for.

   I went back to New York for two weeks at Christmastime. Things were the same between my parents and me, although my mother seemed to be more interested in my life in Birch Creek than she'd been in the past. Christian and Ruby stopped by for two days before Christmas, but they didn't stay long, because they were spending the rest of the holiday with Ruby's family in Lancaster. Even Ruby, who's full of energy and personality, was subdued when she was there. My parents have that effect on people.

   When I returned to Birch Creek, I had my first therapy appointment here. It's strange starting over with someone new, but I think she'll be someone I can talk to. Her name is Tera, and I'll see her once a week for now. Fortunately she takes evening appointments, so I don't have to take off work.

Speaking of work, I didn't go back to the inn until the second week of January. That wasn't my choice, though. Business has been slow for the Stolls, and even though it's almost the end of the month, they've only had three guests total. Levi and his father have been working on ways to publicize the inn. It also doesn't help that this is still the slow season.

Before I went to New York, Levi and I had a talk, and since then we've had a good relationship—that is, working relationship. His father has been training him how to run the inn, and I've made sure I'm busy with my cleaning work. Delilah is also teaching me some of her family recipes so I can help with food preparation once the inn gets busy. But things aren't the same as they were before, and I wish they were.

Selah stopped writing and erased the last sentence. She didn't want to go into why everything felt different at the inn, and it wasn't just because she and Levi had limited contact.

With so little business, everyone was in a subdued mood. There was barely enough work for her, which was why Delilah started teaching her the recipes.

She missed the sense of closeness she'd felt with the Stolls before the blizzard. She wished the warmth and camaraderie would return. And even though she knew keeping her distance from Levi was for their own good, she missed him. A lot. But she couldn't have it both ways—distance and closeness—and distance was the better choice. Her feelings would wane—eventually.

She looked at the sheet of writing paper and picked up her pencil. She had to finish this letter and put it in the mailbox before she went to work.

I haven't had any anxiety attacks since the blizzard, thank God. I always carry my medicine in my purse, which gives me some assurance. I think overall I'm doing well.

I need to close now and head to work. If you'd like to write me back, that would be nice. I pray all is well with you.

Take care,
Selah

She put the letter in an envelope, addressed it and affixed a stamp, and headed downstairs. The house was empty because Ruby and Christian had already left for school, and she grabbed her coat and bonnet and put them on before slipping on her boots. She kept a pair of work shoes at the inn so she didn't have to carry them back and forth.

When she stepped outside, the sun beamed in a cloudless sky. A winter thaw had melted the last snowfall, which had been only a few inches, nothing like the pileup they'd had before. While it was still nippy, the air wasn't bone-chillingly cold. She put the letter in the mailbox and then briskly walked to work.

Her first chore of the day was to clean the stove in the lobby since it was warm enough outside that they didn't need to have it running. The lobby empty, she assumed Levi and Loren were in the office, as they usually were, and that Delilah and Nina were in the house. Like every morning, she was tempted to knock on the office door and say hi and to stop by the house and greet Delilah and Nina. But since the blizzard, they had all seemed to hold to the invisible line between employee and employer, and she wasn't going to cross it. *I got what I wanted, Lord. But why does it bother me so much to have it?*

She had just swept the ashes into a large dustpan when the new bell above the front door dinged. Selah turned and saw Richard Johnson, Cevilla's friend, coming in. He was a regal gentleman, tall and lean with neat but not fancy clothes. Today he wore a brown leather hat, shaped different from an Amish hat, along with a chocolate-colored suede overcoat. He gripped his cane as he walked across the lobby.

"Hello, Selah," he said, taking off his hat as he approached the front counter. He stared at her. "Goodness, what have you been up to?"

"Cleaning the woodstove." She gestured to it with her hand and saw the big spot of dark soot on her sleeve. She thrust her arm behind her back.

"Well, if stoves could sparkle, I'd say you're on your way to making that happen." He grinned. "Is Levi or Loren around? I'd like to ask one of them something."

As if on cue, Levi walked out of the office. He looked at Selah for a brief second, his left eyebrow lifting, but he didn't say anything as he walked around the counter. "Hello, Richard. What brings you by?"

Richard set his hat on the counter. "I have a question for you, young man. Do you ever open for supper?"

Levi adjusted his glasses. "No, we don't. We just serve breakfast."

"I see." He stroked his clean-shaven chin. "Would it be possible for you to be open for the evening meal just one time, for a special occasion? As a favor to me?"

Levi paused. "I don't know. This is the first time we've had that request."

"I'd understand if you couldn't, but I want to do something nice for Cevilla. She's been a little down in the dumps lately." He smiled. "I was thinking of a romantic supper. Nothing fancy, of course. Simple fare, but with some flowers on the table and her favorite dessert. I thought having it someplace other than home would be a welcome change." Richard paused. "I'd rent the inn, of course."

Levi's mouth dropped open. "The whole inn?"

"Yes. Plus pay for supper and staff to serve it. I want this to be an occasion Cevilla will never forget. And I want it to be a surprise."

Selah took a step back, stunned. She also caught a flash of surprise in Levi's expression, but he quickly hid it behind a professional demeanor.

"I think it can be done," he said in an even tone.

Richard lifted one gnarled index finger. "Oh, I should have asked this first. Do you have any reservations for rooms on Valentine's Day? I believe it's on a Friday this year, if I'm not mistaken, and I'd like to have the dinner then."

"It is on a Friday. And no, we don't happen to have any reservations for that night."

"Then if you think we can arrange this, I'd like to go ahead and pay in full now."

"Of course."

Selah watched as Levi moved behind the counter. How could he be so calm about this? Even she had been praying that business would pick up, and now they had a guaranteed sellout for Valentine's Day—not to mention the chance to take part in a sweet and romantic idea. If someone rented an entire inn just for a romantic dinner with her, she'd be over the moon.

She halted her thoughts. *Remember* yer *"forever single" plan?*

Levi looked at Selah again with a blank expression and then turned to Richard. "We can go into the office and work out the details."

"Sounds good."

Selah figured Loren must not be in there since the office was big enough for only two people. When she finished cleaning the woodstove, Levi and Richard were still inside. She surprised herself by being so curious about their conversation. Did Levi even know how to put on a romantic dinner for two? Delilah would no doubt manage, but she wasn't the one who'd just made a promise to Richard.

The business side of the inn wasn't her concern, though. She picked up her large pail of ashes, her broom, and the dustpan and went to the mudroom. After emptying the ashes outside and putting everything away, she went to the public restroom on the main floor of the inn to wash up.

She looked in the mirror, horrified. Her sleeve wasn't the only thing dirty. Her face and neck were covered in soot, and so was her *kapp*. No wonder Richard had been surprised when he walked into the inn and Levi had looked at her so strangely. She scrubbed off the dirt the best she could and then went outside and brushed the soot from her dress. She also attempted to neaten up her *kapp* without taking it off. She had a clean one at home, and she would scrub this dirty one later.

When she went back to the lobby, Richard's car was gone and the door to the office was closed. She was tempted to knock on it and find out what ideas Levi had for Richard and Cevilla. But instead, she started washing the stone tile hearth and the walls around the stove.

As she worked throughout the day, she couldn't stop thinking about the dinner. Several perfect ideas went through her mind, from appetizers to décor to the main menu. All very simple of course, but memorable. And what if they made the inn available for other special occasions, especially when the weather was nicer? The more she thought about it, the more she thought the idea held promise. It would take some discussion and planning, but in her opinion, it seemed doable.

Levi, as usual, had made himself scarce, and she hadn't seen him again by the time she left for the day—not even at lunch. She paused at the counter before going home and looked at the closed office door, her ideas ready to spill out. Was it her place to suggest something for the inn that didn't have anything to do with housekeeping? More importantly, would Levi listen to her? He was so distant, she wasn't sure. Yet she was proposing ideas for the business.

As she walked home, she continued to argue with herself. But by the time she turned into her driveway, she had decided. Tomorrow she would speak to Levi about her ideas. She'd drive herself *ab im kopp* if she didn't.

"Cevilla, I just don't know what to do."

"Make a right up here." Cevilla pointed to the intersection a few yards away. She'd been surprised when Delilah showed up on her doorstep and invited her to go to Schrock's Grocery. Cevilla wasn't in the mood for company or for a trip to the store, but Delilah wouldn't take no for an answer. Now Cevilla knew why. The woman had been chattering nonstop about Levi and Selah. *Again.*

"I know *mei* way to the store, Cevilla. I'm talking about *mei grosssohn* and Selah."

Her tone was snippy, but Cevilla didn't hold it against her. "Didn't we discuss this before? That you were going to hold *yer* tongue and mind *yer* own business?"

"You have *nee* idea how hard that is."

Oh yes, I do. Her relationship with Richard had been back on track—until last week when she'd found a letter that had fallen out of his coat pocket. Despite knowing it was wrong, she'd read it before putting it back. Those written words had changed everything, but because she'd promised Richard she would let him manage his own business, she hadn't said anything to him. That didn't help the guilt and despair she felt inside, though.

"Cevilla, are you listening to me?" Delilah sighed. "Honestly, every time I've tried talking to you lately, you haven't paid attention." She paused, turned right on the black asphalt road, and then continued. "I know something is wrong. Why don't you just admit it?"

"I wish you'd mind *yer* own beeswax, Delilah."

Delilah sucked in a breath. "Well, that was rude."

"Well, I'm tired of being polite. Obviously you want me to tell you to *geh* ahead and interfere with Selah and Levi. Fine. Here's me giving you permission." She turned and looked out the window. Delilah's buggy still had its winter screen on it, but that didn't stop the sun from warming the inside of the vehicle. If Cevilla wasn't so irritated, she would have enjoyed the nice winter day.

"What kind of advice is that?" Delilah snapped.

Cevilla sighed. "The only kind I can give. Look, if you really believe the two of them belong together—"

"I do. Although I did have a bit of a concern at one point."

She had to admit her curiosity was piqued. "But you don't anymore?"

Delilah shook her head. "*Nee*. And I'm frustrated that they're getting in their own way."

"That's usually what happens in these situations."

"I know." She looked at Cevilla. "But this is different from when I've tried to set up Levi with any other woman. I can see how much he cares for her, and it's obvious Selah feels the same way about him."

Cevilla could see the distress in Delilah's eyes. "You really are upset, aren't you?"

"I am." She sniffed. "I know I'm nosy and a busybody and I like to be in control. It's been pointed out to me more than once by *mei familye*, and I'm working on doing better, with God's help. But Loren, Nina, and I have also grown to care about Selah. I'm afraid . . ." She frowned. "I'm afraid they'll both end up brokenhearted when they don't have to be."

Nodding, Cevilla touched Delilah's hand. "Do you have a plan in mind?"

"Not yet." She pulled into Schrock's parking lot. "I'm open to suggestions."

Cevilla sat back in her seat. It was hard to come up with romantic high jinks when her own emotions were in a tailspin. "I'll pray about it," she said. "You pray too. God may reveal to you that you need to stay out of it."

"If he hasn't said anything about it by now . . ." Delilah shook her head. "You're right. And I'm going to listen to whatever he has to say. But he's been quite silent lately."

After she pulled into one of the parking spaces with hitching posts, she stopped the horse and then looked at Cevilla. "You don't need to worry about Richard, by the way."

"Who says I'm worried?"

"It's written all over *yer* face. You look like you've been sucking on sour grapes for a month."

She touched her cheeks. "I look that bad?"

"You look fine. But I can tell." She smiled, her eyes filled with satisfaction. "And I also have a sixth sense about these things."

"Oh dear, that sounds familiar," Cevilla muttered. How many times had she said that to unsuspecting future couples?

"And *mei* sixth sense says you and Richard will be fine."

Cevilla nodded, but she wasn't sure. Her own sixth sense had taken a leave of absence, and she didn't know if it was ever coming back.

"Let's do some shopping." Delilah smiled, the strain at the corners of her eyes gone. "I might even treat you to some ice cream."

"In January?"

"Anytime is the right time for ice cream, *mei* friend."

The morning after Richard stopped by, Levi was tired of hiding out in the office. And that's exactly what he was doing—hiding. Even his father, who had finished teaching him about running the inn, had pointed out that Levi was spending too much time tucked away. "Is everything all right?" he'd asked when he returned from a trip to Barton with Nina the day before.

Richard's visit had given him a chance to change the subject, and by the time he'd finished telling his father about the dinner and full rental of the inn, *Daed* was thrilled. "An answer to prayer," he said, and he thumped his cane on the floor, which reminded Levi a little bit of Cevilla. *Daed* would have to use the cane for several months, and he still had to take it easy, but his leg was healing faster than the surgeon had anticipated. They were all thankful for that.

And now here he was, back in the office, the only place he could be where no one other than *Daed* would question him. Speaking of questions, his grandmother had been unusually quiet lately. In fact, everything seemed off and tense with his family and Selah, but he had chalked it up to the lack of business. He still felt optimistic, though. When the weather warmed up, they'd be turning people away.

He wished he had the same positive attitude when it came to his own feelings for Selah. Keeping his distance from her was the most difficult thing he'd ever done—which was why he was always holed up while she did her work. He couldn't risk seeing her for more than a brief glimpse, because he was afraid of losing his resolve. He missed the way things had been between them the short time before the blizzard. He'd missed her when she was in New York, and he had missed her when she wasn't working. He plain missed her, and he had the sinking feeling it would be a long time before he stopped.

He slipped off his glasses and rubbed his eyes. It wasn't as if he didn't have anything else to think about. He and his father had hoped that their four prior guests, who had all seemed to enjoy their stay, would spread the word about the inn. But if they had, the result wasn't more customers. He and *Daed* had been coming up with marketing ideas. Trouble was, they weren't very good.

Levi put on his glasses and pulled out a pad of paper and a pencil. He was tapping the pencil on the desk, trying to think of another idea, when he heard a light knock on the door. "Come in," he said, still focusing on the blank paper and willing his mind to get creative. Only when he looked up did he remember that the only person who knocked on the office door was Selah.

She stood there in the doorway, clasping her hands like she normally did when she was nervous. He remembered the way she looked when Richard stopped by yesterday. She'd been covered almost head to toe in soot. He hadn't been expecting that. Even looking like she'd jumped into a pile of ashes, she was still the prettiest girl he'd ever seen. And now, standing a few feet from him, fresh and clean in a light-purple dress and stark-white *kapp*, she was beautiful.

"Uh, hi." Great. He sounded like a frog had taken up residence in his throat. He cleared it and then placed one hand on the pad of paper before shooting up from the chair. The pad slipped from under his hand, hit the wall, and fell behind the desk.

Her lips twitched a little.

He regained his balance, crossed his arms, and leaned against the corner of the desk, trying to act casual. *And probably failing.* "What can I do for you?"

"I wonder if I could talk to you for a minute. It's about Richard's visit yesterday."

Levi couldn't turn her away when she was the one who approached him, especially about inn business. "Sure. What about it?"

"Do you mind if I sit down?"

He gestured to the empty chair near the desk and then carefully sat down before he did something else stupid. She was here to talk business, and he would be professional. "I have to admit I was surprised by his request."

"Me too, but I think it's so sweet." A dreamy look appeared in her eyes. "Very romantic."

Levi's breath caught. Her expression was relaxed, her eyes sparkling. *Keep it professional.* He grabbed another pencil off the desk and started tapping it against his knee.

"I was thinking," she continued, looking at him again, "and I realize that I don't have a right to give an opinion about how the inn should be run—"

"Selah," he said, stilling the pencil. "You work here, just like the rest of us. *Yer* opinion does matter. What do you have in mind?"

He listened as she explained her idea of booking the inn for special occasions, and not just for Valentine's Day. "Engagements, graduations, *familye* reunions, maybe even weddings," she said. "Small parties, of course. I think we could fill a need for English people who are looking for a place to have a simple celebration at an affordable price. We'd have to set guidelines, of course. But most people who'd consider an Amish inn a venue would be looking for an unpretentious, wholesome experience."

She sounded like a seasoned marketer, and he liked her idea. But they couldn't afford to do anything too risky right now. "First let's see how it goes with Richard and Cevilla."

"Oh. All right."

He could tell he'd burst her bubble, and that was the last thing he wanted to do. "I don't mean that we can't do what you're suggesting," he said. "But I have to discuss it with *Daed*, and of course *Grossmutter*. I'm sure Nina would be on board."

"Are you on board?" Her eyes locked on his.

His heartbeat sped up a notch. This was the side of Selah he was really attracted to—forthright and confident. A little challenging too. "*Ya*," he said, unable to pull away his gaze. "One hundred percent."

Selah grinned. "That's *gut* to know."

Oh, he was in trouble when she smiled at him like that. He tapped the pencil on his knee again with lightning speed as he averted his eyes. "Uh, do you want to discuss anything else?"

"Actually, *ya*. Did Richard want anything specific for his special evening?"

"He left it up to me. Said I know Amish customs better than him and that he would *geh* overboard if he had to plan it."

"Do you know what you're doing?"

He laughed and finally looked at her. "What do you think?"

"I'm more than happy to help . . . if you want me to."

"*Ya*," he said, faster than he intended. He gripped the pencil. "*Grossmutter* and Nina seemed a bit taken aback when I told them I'd agreed to Richard's request. I'm sure they'd appreciate hearing *yer* ideas. You can get together with them to discuss the details."

"I'll do that." Then she looked at her lap again, her hands clasping. For some reason the confident Selah seemed to disappear. "*Danki* for letting me help."

"You don't have to thank me."

"But you're *mei* boss. I think I do." She stood and headed for the door. Then she turned around, the spark of determination back in her eyes. "Let's give Richard and Cevilla a special supper they'll never forget." She opened the door and walked out.

Levi tossed the pencil onto the desk. He couldn't even have a business conference with Selah without his emotions getting the best of him.

Chapter 17

The buzz of the alarm woke Jackson, and he groaned as he grabbed his cell phone from the bedside table and switched it off. Through bleary eyes, he glanced at the time and date. Six thirty a.m, February 13. He put the phone back on the table and let his head drop against the pillow. Why did he even bother setting an alarm on weekdays? His father didn't care what time he showed up for work. But he'd made a New Year's resolution to stick to regular work hours, and except for a few instances, he had. But he'd never been an early bird, even scheduling all his college classes for after ten. *Coffee. I need coffee.*

He stumbled into the kitchen, awake enough to notice his father had already left the apartment. Dad had started going to the gym after his breakup with Ashley. Jackson didn't know what had happened there, since he and his father weren't talking after Jackson refused to tell him anything useful about the inn.

Making that decision had been easy. Granted, he could have done more snooping, could have questioned the Stolls more about their business. They were so trusting that they probably would have told him anything. But he couldn't do it— and not just because it was wrong. The Stolls were good people. They didn't deserve to be spied on much less have their business negatively affected. His father had been so incensed that Jackson thought he would kick him out of the apartment. He hadn't, thank God, but Jackson suspected that had more to do with his need for technological help than with family loyalty. Jackson didn't care. He was just glad he wasn't out of a job and out on the street.

After downing an extra strong cup of brew, he took a shower, got dressed, grabbed his computer bag, and drove to the hotel. The website and network overhaul were almost finished, and Lois was so excited with Jackson's work that she threatened to quit if he left. "The network hasn't cut out since he started working here," she told Dad. "Do you know how lovely it is not to hear twenty complaints a day about the internet?" His relationship with his father might be in the toilet, but at least his job was safe. Most importantly, he could live with himself.

He walked into the lobby and smiled at the mini Valentine tree Lois had put on one corner of the counter. Valentine's Day was tomorrow, but for Jackson, it had always been an ordinary day. He'd dated a few girls in high school and college, but nothing serious, and he always managed to be single on V-Day. He wanted to establish his business and have his own place before he considered dating someone. Right now he was focusing all his energy on his job and getting clients. He had one so far, but he would need several more.

Jackson went to the continental breakfast buffet and picked up a granola bar and an apple, and then he walked over to Lois.

"When are you going to get a haircut?" Lois pursed her lips and scowled.

"Good morning to you too." Self-conscious, he touched the back of his hair, which was still damp from the shower. "When I turn into Rapunzel," he said, grinning.

"Very funny. It's almost past your shoulders now. I have half a mind to take the scissors after you myself. I do have my cosmetology license, you know."

Today she was wearing a red sweater with a huge lace heart on the front, heart-shaped light-up earrings, and bright-pink lipstick. Her maroon-colored hair was streaked with the same shade of pink.

"I'll make an appointment with the barber," he said.

"Promise?"

"Promise." *Maybe.* His hair was at the point he could throw it up in a ponytail, which kept it neat. Besides, he didn't want to spend the money. But if he ever saw Lois with the clippers, he'd give in to the cost. "How's things?"

"Excellent. We've booked almost two floors for the weekend."

"Really?" He bit into the apple, wondering how Stoll Inn was doing.

"Really. I guess word got around that the construction is almost completed." She smiled, but then her smile faded. "I tried telling your father, but he just blew right past me and went into your office."

"*My* office?"

"Okay, his office, but you spend more time in there than he does." She set a bowl of wrapped chocolate hearts on the counter. "Want one?"

"Maybe later." He took another bite of the apple and headed for the office. It was just around the corner from the front desk, and when he walked inside, he saw his father typing away at *his* computer with two fingers.

Jackson balked. "What are you doing?"

His father clicked off the screen and glared at him. "None of your business."

"If you're fooling around with my computer, it is my business."

"*My* computer," his father said. "My computer, my hotel, my apartment. Don't you forget that." He shot up from the chair and stormed past him into the hallway.

"How could I forget it?" Jackson muttered. He placed his backpack on the desk and sat down in front of the computer, checking the history to find out where his father had been. The man had looked too guilty to be innocent. It was a review website, which made sense. He must have been checking the reviews for the hotel. Jackson scanned them. They were mostly complaining about the endless construction, but there were some good reviews, and the average was decent. The only construction in progress now was an overhaul of the indoor pool, which really did need to be done. Once that was completed, Jackson figured the good reviews would outnumber the bad by a wide margin. Stay Inn was a good hotel—with a courteous staff despite their boss.

He was about to click off the site when he saw the recent search results. Stay Inn . . . and Stoll Inn. Of course, his father would read their reviews. His curiosity getting the best of him, he clicked on the Stoll Inn link. *Oh no.*

The inn had dozens of one-star reviews, but as he read each one, he realized they were all fake. They were also similar in writing style and tone even though the reviewer names were different. "He didn't," Jackson mumbled, continuing to read.

The inn reeks of smoke.

Dirty. I thought I was going to throw up.

Toilet clogged on the first day. No response from the maintenance staff. We immediately checked out.

Mold, mold, everywhere mold.

I will never, ever stay at this dump again.

Jackson sat back in the chair and shoveled both hands through his hair. His father stressed how important reviews were, enough that he trusted only himself to reply to reviews, telling Jackson and Lois not to go near them. His father had to be the one who'd written the bad reviews for Stoll Inn. If he wasn't so angered by the deception, Jackson would have admired his persistence. Every review had to come from a different email address. But confronting him would be pointless. He'd deny it—or worse, rationalize what he'd done.

Jackson took out his laptop, pulled up the website, and then sent an email about the reviews to the webmaster. Hopefully the site would take them down. He closed his laptop and sighed. Reporting the fakery was all he could do.

Wait. That wasn't all he could do. He shot out of the office. "I'll be back in a little while," he told Lois, who waved in return, not looking up from her computer screen. He jammed on his coat as he went through the automatic double doors.

He got into his car and headed for Stoll Inn, seething. His father could be a jerk to him. Jackson was used to it. But he drew the line when it came to undermining innocent people. That he wouldn't stand for.

• • •

"And after they finish with the salad," Levi said to Nina, "you'll bring out the steak."

"Isn't it too cold to grill?" Nina's face drooped as she leaned her cheek on the palm of her hand.

"*Nee.* It's only two steaks, so it won't take long."

"Filet mignons, and they're small," Selah added. The three of them sat at the kitchen table going over the plans for Richard and Cevilla's supper tomorrow night. Selah had done most of the planning, and Levi had approved her ideas. They included a white tablecloth on one of the tables, a bud vase with a single red rose, and red velvet cake for dessert. *Grossmammi* agreed to make the side dishes—mashed potatoes, green beans sautéed with diced tomato, and pickled beets.

"He's putting on quite the display, isn't he?" she'd said last night over rhubarb cobbler.

"He wants to do something special for her," Nina said, pointing out the obvious. "But I don't think Selah's ideas are too fancy."

"It's unbecoming for a couple their age."

"I thought you two were friends," *Daed* had said, looking at her with concern.

"We are. But I didn't realize this was going to be such a fancy supper."

"It's not . . ." *Daed* sighed. "Just make the side dishes, please."

259

"I will." She sniffed and cut a large bite of the cobbler with the side of her spoon. "And they will be delicious."

Levi was sure they would be. He wondered if his grandmother was envious of Cevilla. *Grossmutter* had never hinted that she was interested in remarrying, but maybe seeing Cevilla receiving special treatment from Richard made her rethink her stance. If so, Levi could add that to the list of uncharacteristic behavior she'd been displaying recently.

"What if I ruin this for them?" Nina said, bringing Levi out of his thoughts.

"You won't," Selah said.

Levi looked at her. As they'd been planning the dinner for the past two weeks, Selah had blossomed. That made her even more attractive to him, which he hadn't thought possible. But instead of focusing on hiding his feelings, he decided he was better off just being himself. That seemed to be working for him and Selah. They were much more relaxed around each other now.

"But I'm clumsy," Nina said. "I dropped the french toast tray the other day, and I forgot to give the guest we had last week the extra towel she requested." Now that their father didn't need full-time care, Nina had taken back the hostess job from Selah, with mixed results.

"She didn't seem upset about that," Levi said. Although Nina couldn't keep making those kinds of mistakes. She wasn't that much of a klutz, but for some reason she turned into one whenever she had to deal with guests.

"Would you like me to serve them instead?" Selah asked.

Nina sat up, her expression brightening. "Would you?"

Levi grimaced. He hadn't anticipated her working that night, knowing the family could manage serving the dinner. "You would have to work late," he said.

"I don't mind. I'd like to see how things turn out." She smiled.

His heart jolted, but he ignored it. This wasn't the first time her smile had gotten to him, and it wouldn't be the last. He smiled back, like he would have with anybody else. *But she's not just anybody.* "All right, then. Make sure to note the overtime." When she started to protest, he gave her a stern look, and she stopped.

"This is great, Selah," Nina said. "You're much more graceful than I am, and you remember little details. You planned this whole thing, and it's wonderful. I don't want to mess up all *yer* hard work or Richard's surprise. And don't worry, I'll clean up everything." She sat back in her chair. "I feel better now."

Levi did too. The supper would go off without a hitch with Selah in charge.

Daed hobbled into the kitchen, leaning on his

261

cane. Although he didn't have much pain anymore, he still dealt with stiffness. "Levi, Jackson Talbot is over in the lobby."

"He is?" Levi glanced at Selah and Nina, and both sets of eyes were wide with surprise. They hadn't seen or talked to Jackson since he'd stayed at the inn.

"*Ya*. He says he needs to talk to you right away."

He got up and looked at Selah and Nina again. "You two work out the rest of the details. I want everything in place before tomorrow night."

"Whatever you say, *boss*." Nina smirked.

Levi walked to the inn, where Jackson was pacing back and forth in the lobby. "Hi," he said, approaching him. "Glad to see you again."

"I'm glad to see you, too, although I wish it was under better circumstances." He scowled.

Levi listened, his dismay growing as Jackson explained about his father writing bad reviews of the inn. "I know he's the one who did it," he said. "I emailed the site, and hopefully they'll take down the reviews. They should, since fake reviews are against their policy, but I don't know how long it will take them to do it."

"But we're not on the internet," Levi pointed out. "We don't have a website, and we don't book anything online. The internet reviews shouldn't matter, then."

"That's not how it works. Ninety-six percent of people read reviews before booking a place to stay.

They're averaged by stars, five being the highest, and right now you have all one stars, thanks to my dad. With that low rating, you won't get anyone to click on your listing much less book a room."

Levi frowned. "How did we get a listing?"

"Someone must have put it on there. I don't know—maybe my dad did that too. I'm not sure what the rules are. Not that my father plays by any rules but his own."

A knot formed in the pit of Levi's stomach. Was the review site the reason business had been almost nonexistent? "I didn't know your father owned Stay Inn."

Jackson's face reddened. "I have to fess up. My father booked my weekend here so I could spy on you."

The knot tightened. "Why?"

"He wanted dirt so he could ruin your business. Or even shut you down. Who knows?" He held up his hand. "I promise I only told him the truth, that this is a great place to stay and you're going to be exploding with business in the future. I guess that set him off." Jackson looked at him. "I hope you believe me."

"I do." Levi saw the sincerity in Jackson's eyes. Besides that, he knew he was a straight shooter. He wouldn't lie about something like this, not when he was here trying to help.

"We need to do something to get back at my dad. He has to know he can't get away with this."

Stunned, Levi said, "Are you talking about revenge?"

"First, I'll start with flooding his hotel with horrible reviews. Then I'll cancel the bookings we do have. It's about time he had a taste of his own medicine."

"That isn't right, though," Levi said, alarmed.

Jackson looked at him, exasperated. "Doesn't the Bible say an eye for an eye? This is the perfect time for that."

"Why is that the one Bible verse everyone seems to remember?" Levi shook his head. "We don't exact revenge on others. I'm sorry this happened, but please don't write bad reviews or cancel bookings on our behalf."

"You're just going to let this go?" He held up his hands. "How can you do that? He's trying to ruin your business."

He thought about how to explain his conviction to Jackson. He wasn't happy to hear about what Mr. Talbot was doing. He was downright mad about it, and he had to fight not to lose his temper over it. He took a deep breath. But getting mad or taking revenge wouldn't fix the problem, and it sounded like they had a big problem. "I trust that God will make our inn the success he wants it to be," he said as calmly as he could. "I have faith that he will."

"Even when someone is trying to destroy you?"

"Even then. We must always forgive."

Jackson blew out a long breath and took a step back from the counter. He shook his head. "All right. I won't do anything other than talk to the review site people if they get back to me. I'll keep pestering them until they take down the reviews. That's not revenge. That's honest business practice." He looked at Levi. "You and your family deserve a chance to make your inn a success. I'll even write an excellent review for you—which will be the truth." He half smiled.

Levi leaned against the counter, relieved. "Thank you, Jackson."

Selah and Nina walked into the lobby, and Nina's face brightened when she saw Jackson. She said hello, and the two of them started talking as if they were old friends.

Levi moved away and Selah joined him. "They get along well, *ya*?"

"*Ya*." That didn't surprise him. When it came to friendship, Nina had always gotten along with men better than with women, mostly because she was a tomboy. But he wasn't paying that much attention. His mind was swimming with what Jackson had told him. Despite reading all those hospitality magazines, he'd had no idea about internet reviews, and he was sure his father hadn't, either. Eventually he'd bring it up to *Daed*, because if that's how potential guests found the inn, they'd have to have a listing, and they would have to work it out with Freemont to make sure it was okay. His head started to pound. He just wouldn't tell his father about this now. *Daed* was worried enough as it was.

"Levi?"

He turned to Selah. "*Ya?*"

"Are you all right?" She moved closer. "You look like you're in pain."

She was close enough that he could smell the soap she used to clean with, along with a sweet scent that calmed his frayed nerves. "Just a little headache," he said, turning partway to face her.

"Can I get you an aspirin? Some tea?" She leaned closer. "Sometimes drinking a full glass of water helps me."

"*Nee*," he said, unable to pull his gaze from hers. "I'm already feeling better."

She glanced down and then looked up at him with a small but lovely smile that not only took away his headache but threatened to steal his breath.

"I've got to head back to the hotel," he heard Jackson say. "I usually work in the office all day, and I don't want Dad to suspect I know what he did."

Reluctantly Levi pulled his attention away from Selah. "Thanks again."

"What did he do?" Nina said, looking from Jackson to Levi.

Jackson's expression turned panicky. "You

know, people could learn a lot about running a hotel from you guys."

"Aw, thanks," Nina said.

Jackson opened the front door. "I'll be in touch," he said, and then he dashed out.

Before either Nina or Selah could ask more questions, Levi said, "I've got work to do in the office."

"I'll see if *Grossmutter* needs any help," Nina said.

"And I guess I'll . . . clean," Selah quipped.

"Everything's already clean." Nina hooked her arm in Selah's. "Come help us in the kitchen."

Levi watched as the two of them left. Nina might usually get along with men better than women, but she had taken to Selah right away. Which wasn't hard to do once Selah let down her guard. The hard part was getting away from her—although it was becoming clearer and clearer that he didn't want to do that.

As he sat down at the desk, though, for once his thoughts weren't totally on Selah. He still couldn't believe what Jackson's father had done. How could anyone be so dishonest? The best response was to pay attention to their own business and remember that God was in control. But with the lack of guests and income at the inn, that was becoming difficult to do. *Mr. Talbot might have succeeded in putting us out of business before we've hardly started.*

Chapter 18

"Where are we going?" Cevilla asked as Richard pulled out of the driveway.

She and Richard still had a steady relationship. They still ate their meals together. He still read in the evenings while she crocheted before he went home for the night. But he had also attended the Mennonite church again, and they hadn't talked about the future since the blizzard. Yet for once Cevilla's unease didn't have to do with her impatience. She couldn't get the letter that had fallen out of Richard's coat pocket off her mind. He was considering giving up so much for her, and she'd chastised herself more than once for not fully realizing that sooner. She was becoming selfish and self-absorbed in her old age, the exact opposite of Amish values. All because of romance. No, not romance. Love.

She still loved Richard, more than ever. And because she loved him, she had to let him go. She'd planned to do that tonight, but he'd put a kink in that plan by insisting they were going out.

"It's a surprise," he said now, his grin noticeable even in the dim light of the car.

She managed only a halfhearted smile in return.

They drove in silence until he pulled into the parking lot of the Stoll Inn.

"What are we doing here?" she asked, completely befuddled as he parked near the entrance.

"Like I said, it's a surprise." He reached for his cane in the back seat and then opened his car door before coming around the other side of the vehicle to open her door. When she started to get out, he held out his hand. She took it, feeling warm and secure. Her heart started to crumble.

"I don't like surprises," she muttered as she followed him to the inn.

"Trust me, you'll like this one." He held her hand as they made their way slowly up the steps, ignoring the accessible ramp on the other side of the porch. She hadn't been here since she'd visited Delilah to satisfy her nosiness about the completed renovations. She'd been impressed. But she couldn't see the exterior very well in the dark, despite the automatic lights that lit their path. That wasn't anything new—she'd had trouble seeing in the dark for a few years now. When they reached the top of the steps, Richard let go of her hand and opened the door.

"Happy Valentine's Day!"

Cevilla's jaw dropped at the sight of Selah Ropp standing in the lobby, grinning with delight. She was such a pretty girl, especially when she smiled. Wait, did she say Valentine's Day? "Richard," she said, turning to him, "what is going on?"

"Come in, both of you." Selah gestured for them to enter.

When Cevilla walked into the lobby, she halted, stunned. She had almost forgotten all about Valentine's Day over the years. It wasn't a holiday the Amish necessarily celebrated, although she had when she was a child and still English. But right now she couldn't be in a less romantic mood. Her nerves twisted and tangled. The lobby was decorated for a romantic supper, with a fire in the woodstove, candlelight everywhere, and a lovely set table in the middle. Delicious smells wafted through the air. Was somebody grilling? "I . . . I . . ."

"She's speechless," Richard said, beaming as if he'd just discovered how to achieve world peace.

After taking their wraps, Selah moved to stand by Levi, who was looking handsome tonight. They made a lovely couple, and even though they weren't interacting with each other, something about them being together was natural. Her sixth sense tingled. No wonder Delilah was so frustrated with the two of them.

"So far so good," Richard said.

Cevilla's sixth sense deflated like a child's balloon after a bully popped it. What had this man gone and done?

"Please sit down." Selah guided them to the table, which was covered with a white tablecloth and had a vase holding a lovely red rose in the center.

Cevilla looked at Richard. "What did you do?" she said, finally finding her words.

Levi pulled out a chair for her. "Just a little something special."

"For my special lady," Richard added as she sat down, and then he took the chair across from her.

She would have groaned at his corny line if she wasn't so overwhelmed. She stared at him. Never in a million years would she have thought he'd do something like this.

The next few minutes were a blur as Selah brought their drinks, followed by a basket of rolls. Richard took one, spread it with butter, and then handed it to Cevilla, the grin still on his face, his eyes gleaming in the candlelight.

"Uh, thank you." She took the roll and put it on her plate. "Richard, you didn't have to do this."

"I know, but it's Valentine's Day. I didn't want to make too much of a fuss, but I couldn't let it go by without making it special."

I wish you had. He'd ruined her plan. They couldn't talk now. Not only were Levi and Selah here, but a guest could come down the stairs at any moment. Which made her wonder. Where were the rest of the diners? "I didn't realize the Stolls served an evening meal here. I thought they only served breakfast."

"Usually they do."

When he explained how he had rented the inn and persuaded Levi to prepare a one-off dinner, Cevilla gripped her napkin. Who knew what else he had up his sleeve? *I have to tell him before*

271

this goes too far. Her mouth felt like cotton, but she had to go through with it. She put her napkin on the table and said, "Richard . . . we need to talk."

Selah peeked through the cracked door of the kitchen to check on Cevilla and Richard. She couldn't believe how giddy she felt over this elderly couple's romantic dinner. It was nice to be happy and excited about something for once. When Nina said she felt nervous about serving the supper, Selah had jumped at the chance to do it instead. For the first time in a long time, she felt normal—and pleased that she had contributed to this special occasion.

The only hiccup had been Levi, and that wasn't his fault. Trying to keep her feelings for him under wraps was exhausting, and it seemed that the harder she ignored them, the stronger they were. Planning the supper had been a good diversion, even though they had worked on it together. Nina was a good buffer, plus Selah was focused on making sure everything was perfect, which made it easier to set her emotions aside. But when she saw Levi right before Cevilla and Richard arrived, her equilibrium flew out of whack. He had showered and changed clothes, and when he stood by her, she caught the scent of soap and freshly laundered clothes, plus something that was uniquely him. Her emotions went into overdrive, and she was thankful when their guests arrived.

Soon she would bring out the first course—a simple salad with oil and vinegar dressing. She had read about fancy suppers, and some of them were so overboard. She couldn't believe people ate things like fish eggs and twenty-four-karat-gold-covered chocolate. That was far too excessive. Just splitting a normal Amish meal into different courses made things different but not too extreme.

She saw Richard lean forward and smile as he talked to Cevilla, who still looked as shocked as she had when they arrived. That surprised Selah. She thought Cevilla would have relaxed by now. Then again, maybe it took longer for such a big surprise to wear off for someone elderly. Richard seemed pleased, which was good.

"Aren't you being sneaky."

She turned to see Levi walk up behind her. He had come through the mudroom, where just outside the back door he'd set up the grill to cook the steaks. "I'm checking on our guests without being obvious," she said, carefully letting the door close.

"Oh. That's what it's called." His green eyes twinkled behind his glasses. "He really managed to surprise Cevilla."

"That he did. I just hope she's happy about it. She still looks stunned." She went to the other side of the kitchen and placed several cherry tomatoes, cut in half, on top of the salads. Then she drizzled oil and vinegar over the lettuce leaves before adding three homemade croutons on top of each one.

"Need any help with those?"

"*Nee.*" She placed the salads on a serving tray. When she turned, she brushed his side with her arm. "Sorry," she said, moving past him to get a set of the salt and pepper shakers on the opposite counter.

"*Mei* fault. I was in the way."

She tried to keep her eyes down and focused on the seasonings, because if she looked up at him while they were this close, she didn't know what she would do. The kitchen was barely big enough for her and Nina or Delilah, but Levi was larger and taller than them both, and his presence seemed to fill the room.

"I better check on the steaks." He slipped out through the mudroom.

She blew out a breath, glad he was gone but wishing he was there just the same. She'd have to talk to Tera about how to handle her intense feelings at her next therapy session. Last time she'd seen her new counselor, she thought she could handle them herself. But lately they had become so all-consuming that she didn't know what to do. She put the salt and pepper shakers on the tray and returned her focus to their guests. She wasn't going to spoil their evening.

When she brought out the salads, her heart squeezed a little at the sight of Cevilla and Richard. She could see how they were meant to be, not only because of his grand gesture but because of how he looked at her and listened to her. They really were a sweet, loving couple . . . who were suddenly arguing.

"You what!" Richard sat up straight in his chair, his eyes wide. "You can't be serious."

"I'm very serious." Cevilla's chin lifted, her look imperious. In contrast to Richard's angry expression, she was the picture of calm. "You can drive me home now."

"I will not drive you home!"

Selah froze halfway between the kitchen and their table. Now was not the time for the salad course.

"You will explain yourself, woman." Richard threw his napkin on the table.

"How dare you call me *woman*!"

"How dare you tell me it's over!"

"What in the world?" Levi said, appearing beside her.

"I don't know," Selah said, backing away. "They were fine a second ago."

"It's over because it needs to be." Cevilla's chin fell slightly. "I'm asking too much of you, Richard. I know your daughter doesn't approve of me."

"Sharon has nothing to do with this."

"I read her letter."

Richard froze, his bushy gray eyebrows narrowing. "You what?"

"We should *geh* back into the kitchen," Levi said.

Selah felt his hand tug on her elbow, and she followed him. Once in the kitchen, she set the tray on the counter. "What went wrong?" she said, staring at the salads she'd so carefully prepared. "Did I overdo the decorations? Would another kind of bread have been better?" Her hands started to shake, and she clasped them together.

"Selah, we both heard Cevilla say something about reading a letter and Richard's *dochder*." Levi put his hands on her shoulders and gently turned her to face him. "Everything you planned is perfect." He glanced over his shoulder at the closed door. "But Cevilla and Richard clearly aren't."

"I wanted this to be wonderful for them," she said, feeling the warmth from his hands calming her.

"I'm sure it's a misunderstanding," he said, but he looked uncharacteristically somber. "They need to work it out, and then they can get back to the festivities of the evening."

"I hope so." Despite her better judgment, she again cracked open the door and peeked out. Her heart sank as they continued to argue. *I guess Richard wasn't the only one with a surprise.*

● ● ●

I'm not going to cry. I'm not going to cry.
Richard's outburst had startled Cevilla, but it
hadn't completely surprised her. He had a right
to be angry. She should have kept her mouth shut
and tried to get through the evening. But she
never would have been able to without speaking
her heart.

"How did you find the letter?"

She stared at the uneaten roll on her plate. "It
fell out of your coat pocket."

"And you believed you had the right to read it?"

"I know I shouldn't have read it. But I'm glad I
did." She regained her composure. "I know how
Sharon really feels about me."

Richard sighed. "She has . . . issues."

"With me."

"With everyone. No matter who I date, she has
something negative to say."

This was the first time she'd heard him mention
past girlfriends. "How many women did you date
before me?"

His head shot up. "Are we really going to do
this now?" He reached for her hand. "Let's just
enjoy tonight, okay?"

"No, it's not okay." She pushed back from the
table, and she would have popped up from the
chair if her popping days hadn't been over. Her
joints creaked as she moved to stand. "You always
do this."

"Do what?" he ground out.

"Change the subject. Avoid the topic. Pretend everything is all right."

"It was," he said, his voice growling with anger, "until you read my personal correspondence."

He was deflecting again, even though he was right. "Take me home, Richard."

His mouth dropped open. "Cevilla, I—"

"Now."

He didn't say anything else as he stood. "I need to thank Levi and Selah."

"I'll go to the car."

As he walked toward the kitchen, she grabbed her coat. Then she stepped outside, stopping on the porch, her chest aching. *Oh Lord, what have I done?*

"Don't worry, Richard," Levi said after the man explained that they would have to cut supper short for the evening.

Selah gripped the counter behind her. This was awful. Not only had the two of them not made up, but they were leaving.

"I appreciate everything you young people have done for us tonight, but Cevilla . . . Well, she's not feeling well."

Levi nodded. "We can do a rain check. Or a refund."

"You keep the money. And you two," he said, pointing at Selah and Levi, "enjoy those steaks."

He turned and, on unsteady legs, walked back into the lobby.

"I'm going to see them out," Levi said to Selah. "I want to be sure they get to their car safely."

She nodded, and her heart went out to the two of them. She said a quick prayer, asking God to help them work out their problems.

There was a knock on the back door, and Selah slipped through the mudroom to open it. Delilah came in, huffing, carrying the side dishes. Nina was behind her with the dessert. "I can't believe Levi made me come through the back way," Delilah said, as though the family didn't always come in the back way. "In *mei* own establishment."

"He didn't want you to interrupt Cevilla and Richard's meal." Nina set the cake on the counter.

"Humph." Delilah shoved the containers at Selah.

"You're just irritated because you can't spy on them."

She whirled around. "Me?" She placed a hand on her chest. "Spy?"

"*Ya.* You." Nina laughed.

"It doesn't matter," Selah said softly. "They left."

"Who left?" Delilah asked.

"Cevilla and Richard."

Delilah's brown eyes flamed, and she bit her bottom lip. "How dare they? What? Our food isn't *gut* enough?"

She shook her head. "They had a fight."

Delilah paused, her bluster disintegrating. "They did?"

"Oh *nee*," Nina said. "What happened?"

"I don't know. One minute they were fine, the next they were fighting." She looked at the salads. Maybe it was her imagination, but the lettuce looked like it was already wilting. "Then they left."

"I see." Delilah grew quiet.

"What are we going to do with all this food?" Nina asked.

Selah averted her gaze. "Richard said for me and Levi to enjoy it," she whispered.

"What? You're not talking loud enough, Selah."

She looked at Nina. "He told me and Levi to eat it."

"Oh." Nina's expression turned sly. *"Oh."*

"Nina," Delilah said, taking her granddaughter by the arm, "let's *geh* back to the *haus*."

"Can't I have a slice of cake first?"

"*Nee.*"

"Selah and Levi aren't going to eat all that."

"I said *nee*. Now let's *geh*."

Nina turned and gave Selah a thumbs-up before Delilah dragged her out of the kitchen.

This couldn't be happening. Selah stood there for a minute, trying to comprehend what had occurred. She looked at the salads, the containers of beans, beets, and mashed potatoes . . . the cake.

She couldn't eat Cevilla and Richard's romantic supper. That wouldn't be right.

When Levi returned to the kitchen, Selah looked at him. "How are they?"

"Giving each other the silent treatment." He looked at the food on the counter. Then his brow shot up. "The steaks!"

"What?"

Levi flew out the back door. A few minutes later he brought back a plate with what looked like two pieces of charred leather. "I turned the gas off a little while ago, just to keep them warm." He stared at the ruined meat. "*Gut* thing, or they would have caught fire." He set them on the counter, thin tendrils of smoke rising from each one. Then he looked at Selah. "What do we do now?"

"Take the food back to the *haus* and throw away the steaks. I'll call Christian to come pick me up."

"You're not going to eat?"

She gaped at him. "*Nee.* I'm not going to eat someone else's romantic dinner." Unwittingly she lightly slapped his arm. "What's wrong with you?"

"I don't waste *gut* food."

Selah looked at the steaks, her lips twitching. "So you're going to eat those?"

Levi picked up the plate. "Dare me to?"

"Of course not." She took the plate from him

and set it down. Then she looked up at him, her partial smile fading. "I . . . I don't want you to get sick."

"I don't think you can get sick from burnt food." He gazed at her. "But *danki* for caring."

That brought her to her senses, and she started to pull back from him, but he caught her hand before she could. "Don't call Christian. Let me take you home."

"I don't want to inconvenience you."

"Trust me," he said, still holding her hand. "You're not." Finally he let go. "I'll *geh* hitch *mei* horse to the buggy."

"What about the food?"

"That's Nina's job, remember?" He walked into the mudroom and out the back door.

Selah shivered and looked at her hand. Had he realized he was holding it? Certainly not, or he would have let go sooner.

Yet despite his holding her hand being an accident, and despite how the romantic supper had turned out, and despite being worried about Cevilla and Richard, she was looking forward to Levi taking her home. And for once, she didn't ignore that feeling.

Chapter 19

Levi steadied his hands as he hitched up the buggy. He shouldn't have held her hand. But she was always pulling away, and he couldn't let her this time. Once he had her, he couldn't let her go . . . until he realized what he was doing. And now he was taking her home, which would be fine if he could get himself together.

He drew in a deep breath, finished hitching Rusty to the buggy, turned on the battery-operated lights, and pulled out of the barn. Selah stood in the parking lot, huddled in her coat and black bonnet, waiting for him under the automatic lights. He pulled up beside her, and she climbed in. He noticed she was sitting as far away from him as she could. Great. He had offended her. Best thing to do was pretend it hadn't happened. He pushed up his glasses and guided the buggy onto the road.

Other than the jangle of the reins, the *clip-clop* of the horse's shoes on the pavement, and the creaking of the rocking buggy, it was silent—and that was getting to him. "You know," he said, his mouth ignoring his mind telling it to shut up, "tonight wasn't a complete disaster."

"How do you figure that?"

"Well, now we know we can put on a special

event, even if this one didn't work out." He glanced at her. "I told you I'd let you know about *yer* suggestion after we did this supper."

She shrugged. "I guess."

Just so he could keep the awkwardness from completely engulfing them, he was about to ask her if she wanted to discuss any other ideas. But then a car came out of nowhere, speeding toward them. It blared its horn, scaring the horse. On instinct, Levi grabbed Selah, pulling her close. The reins dug into his hand as he tried to control Rusty, but he kept his arm around Selah until the horse came to a halt.

He looked down at her, tucked into the crook of his arm. They were stopped under a streetlamp, and he could make out her wide, fearful eyes. "Are you okay?" he asked, tightening his arm around her.

"*Ya.*" She sounded breathless. "I'm okay."

"That was a pretty big scare," he whispered.

"It was."

His heart thumped in his chest, and not just from the car that almost hit them. He knew he should let her go, but he couldn't. She wasn't looking away. She wasn't moving away. Her eyes were locked with his, and even though he knew he shouldn't, he leaned down and kissed her. To his surprise, she kissed him back. He'd never felt so happy—*so right.*

He finally slowed the kiss, and they parted.

Then they must have come to their senses at the same time, because they scrambled to opposite ends of the seat.

"I . . . I have to check on Rusty." He clambered out of the buggy and took a big breath. *What have I done?*

Selah touched her lips, still feeling the effects of Levi's kiss. His perfect kiss. Which she shouldn't have succumbed to. But once he kissed her, she couldn't stop herself. And now all she knew was that she wanted to kiss him again. "I can't," she whispered, trying to catch her breath. *My job, remember? Being single, remember? Living alone with no problems . . .*

None of that mattered, at least not now. From behind the buggy screen, she saw him petting Rusty, talking in his ear. He patted the horse's flanks and climbed back into the buggy.

"Unbelievable," he muttered. "If that guy had hit us . . ." He picked up the reins, made sure no one else was on the road, and continued toward Christian's house.

Selah stared straight ahead, but then unable to stand it anymore, she shifted her eyes to Levi. He was also looking out front, his expression unreadable, at least in the dimness of the buggy. A tiny battery light illuminated the floorboard, but that was it. It wasn't enough for her to gauge what he was thinking—or feeling.

Her eyes darted to the buggy screen, and she kept her focus on that until he pulled into her brother's driveway. When the horse stopped, she paused. Should she apologize? Jump out of the buggy and pretend nothing happened? Talk it out with him, like her therapist always told her to do when she had a problem? Ugh, why was she thinking about her therapist now?

"Selah."

She turned and found him facing her. A county road crew had installed three streetlamps on the road right before Selah moved back in, and one of them was at the end of the driveway. She searched his face for some hint of what was going on in his mind, but his expression was inscrutable. "What?" she finally asked.

"I hope that what happened back there won't come between us in our working relationship. The car . . . I was just worried something had happened to you."

So you kissed me to find out? But she bit her tongue.

"You're a valuable employee," he continued. "I don't want something . . . insignificant to keep you from returning to work."

Their kiss was insignificant to him? When it had touched her very soul?

He wasn't much different from Oliver. She realized that now. "I'll be there in the morning," she said, her throat tight as she got out of the buggy. Before she could hear him say anything else hurtful, she hurried into the house.

"You're home early," Ruby said when Selah dashed inside.

"Headache." She ran upstairs to her room and shut the door. Levi was doing her a favor. She had veered from her goal, and she was *not* going to let the fact that he was a complete jerk keep her from her job.

Her fists clenched, and she shut down her heart. And she would never, *ever* open it again.

Jackson flipped through the TV stations in the apartment living room, but as usual, nothing good was on. He glanced at the clock. Nine p.m. His father wasn't home, and Jackson didn't care where he was. He was still angry about the fake reviews. He'd been stewing about them since yesterday, but he didn't bring it up with his father. The only reason he didn't was Levi. He didn't get how the man could be so calm, other than he didn't fully understand the magnitude of what bad reviews could do for a business. The dude wasn't stupid, but he was naive. Jackson also hadn't heard from the webmaster of the review site, and the reviews were still up.

He sat up on the couch, some home improvement show droning in the background. There was another thing he didn't get about Levi. How could he instantly forgive Jackson's father like that? Maybe he wouldn't if he knew Dad, but Jackson had a feeling that wouldn't matter. Earlier that evening he'd done a little perusing on the internet about the Amish and was surprised at how much information he was able to glean. They were fairly popular folks, considering they kept to themselves. What he read about the importance of forgiveness in their faith made Levi's reaction more sensical, although Jackson couldn't imagine himself forgiving that easily.

Grabbing the remote, he restlessly scanned the TV channels again, catching several Valentine's Day commercials. He figured his father must be out romancing some twentysomething woman. The thought made his stomach turn.

He was about to turn off the TV when the apartment door burst open and his father staggered in. Jackson smelled the whiskey on him right away. Dad left the door open and fell into the nearest chair.

Jackson got up and shut the door. "Did you drive home like this?"

His father nodded, hanging his head.

Anger welled up within him. "You could have killed somebody—or yourself. Why didn't you call me? I would have picked you up."

"I'm fine." He looked up at Jackson, bleary-eyed. "Get me a beer, will ya?"

Jackson rolled his eyes and went into the kitchen, where he filled a glass with water from the tap. "Here," he said, handing it to his father when he returned to the living room.

"That's not beer."

"Drink it anyway."

His father shoved away Jackson's arm. Jackson set the glass on the side table next to him. "Where's your date?"

His father let out a sound that resembled a growl. "Still at the bar." Then he started to sob.

"Oh brother." Jackson sat down on the couch as his father cried, unable to look at him. Talk about uncomfortable. When his father stopped drunk-crying, he looked at Jackson. "Get me a beer."

"I said no."

"Good for nothing . . ." His eyes rolled, and then he passed out.

Jackson stared at him. It would serve Dad right if he left him there. Then he'd have a hangover and a sore neck. He muttered an oath as he lifted his father, putting his arm over his shoulder, and dragged him to his bedroom. Jackson plopped him onto the bed, and his father let out a big snore.

He shut the door partway and went back into the living room, where he parked himself in front of the TV again. He couldn't go to bed, not with his father passed out. He remembered a fellow student in college being so drunk that he passed out and vomited. He could have choked to death if one of his fraternity brothers hadn't been there. He turned the volume down low and started flipping through the channels, settled in for a sleepless night. Another Valentine's Day commercial splashed across the screen, all hearts and flowers and sappy romance. "Happy Valentine's Day to me," he muttered as his father sawed logs in the other room.

Chapter 20

Cevilla woke up late the next morning, her heart broken. The handkerchief she used to dry her tears was still in her hand. Richard had dropped her off last night after a stone-silent ride in the car. He made sure she got in the house all right, and then he drove away. She didn't even look to see if he'd gone home. She went inside and straight to bed, where she had a long, overdue cry.

Now with sunlight streaming through her window, she was filled with regret. Other than the Lord, Richard was the best thing that had ever happened to her, and she had shoved him away after he'd gone to all the trouble to surprise her with a romantic dinner. But had she truly made a mistake? If they couldn't discuss the important issues in their lives without fighting or deflecting, then how were they to have a long-lasting relationship? What if in a year or two he regretted a decision to marry her and was stuck with her for the rest of his life, separated from his daughter?

When she heard a rapid knocking on the front door, she was tempted to ignore it. But then she realized whoever was banging on the other side of the door didn't plan to stop. As she hurriedly dressed, she tried to readjust her *kapp* after sleeping in it. But then she gave up and just headed to the door. "I'm coming, all right?" she snapped. "Hold *yer* horses."

She unlocked the door and opened it, and then she groaned. "Not you again."

Delilah gave her a once-over. "You look dreadful."

Leave it to Delilah to give her a boost of confidence. "What do you want?"

"To knock some sense into you." Once again, without waiting for an invitation, Delilah breezed inside.

Cevilla shut the door, leaning on her cane. "If you're expecting tea this time, forget it."

"I'm not expecting anything, other than for you and Richard to make up."

"That's not happening."

Delilah sat down on the couch. "Why not?" Then she shivered. "It's freezing in here."

"I just woke up. Or rather *someone* woke me up."

"At this time of day? You've practically slept it away." Delilah stood and started putting logs into the woodstove.

Cevilla glanced at the clock on the wall. Eight thirty wasn't exactly sleeping the day away, but she kept that to herself. "Look, I appreciate you taking care of the stove and caring about me and Richard, but I'd like to be alone right now."

"You've been alone for a hundred years." Delilah shut the woodstove and smirked.

"I have not." She hobbled to her chair and sat down. Every joint in her body was stiff, but the heat from the stove would help. "I have always had the Lord."

Delilah nodded. "That goes without saying." She sat down again. "We went to a lot of trouble for you two last night. I thought it was a bit overboard," she said, looking at her fingernails before pinning Cevilla with her gaze, "but the *kinner* wanted to make sure it was special."

"I didn't know Richard was doing that for me. I didn't mean to waste their efforts."

"And mine. I made the side dishes, and *mei* famous beets."

"Beets?" Cevilla's stomach turned. She couldn't stand beets.

"I'll bring you three jars next time I come by."

Good grief, she planned to stop by again? "That's not necessary—"

"Let's not get off track." She held up one plump finger. "I will not allow you to throw away a man like Richard. You love him, and he loves you. Case closed."

Cevilla looked down at the basket of crochet by her chair. She hadn't picked up her yarn and hook for over a week. "Sometimes love isn't enough."

"Do you really believe that? Would you have said that to Martha and Seth? Noah and Ivy?"

"No, I wouldn't have, but that was different.

They didn't have the obstacles I do." When Delilah laughed, Cevilla scowled. "What's so funny?"

"Every relationship has obstacles, from beginning to middle to end. *Nee* couple is immune from them. The successful ones work it out. The ones who don't try . . ." She clucked her tongue. "I never thought you would back down from a challenge, Cevilla Schlabach."

Cevilla sighed. "Maybe I'm too tired to fight this one."

Delilah's expression softened. "It's that bad?"

"Richard hasn't decided if he's going to join the church. At least he hasn't said anything to me about it. He refuses to discuss it or the future." Her shoulders slumped. "On top of that, his *dochder*, Sharon, is convinced I'm only out to take his fortune."

"Now, that's ridiculous." Delilah scoffed. "How much money does he have, anyway?"

"Close to a billion."

Delilah gasped and then started to cough. "You're joking," she said when she'd sufficiently recovered.

"Not at all. But I wouldn't care if he didn't have a quarter to his name."

"But a billion dollars, Cevilla—"

"Money isn't important. You know that."

"It is when you don't have it," she mumbled.

When Delilah didn't clarify, Cevilla continued.

"It's one thing to ask him to give up his church. It's another to ask him to give up his *familye*."

"Is that what you did?"

"Huh?"

"Did you ask him to give up his *familye*?"

Cevilla paused. Had she? Of course, his becoming a member of the Amish faith was a given. They couldn't marry unless he did. But had she asked him to give up his family? "*Nee*. I would never do that."

"So it's possible, then, that he knows exactly what he's doing? That he thinks being with you is worth whatever conflict he has with his *dochder*? Because *nee* man would rent out an entire inn and set up a romantic dinner on Valentine's Day unless he had made up his mind."

Her hand went to mouth. "You think he was going to propose?"

Delilah shook her head, pressing her fingers to her temples. "If I didn't believe before that you were single all *yer* life, I would believe it now." She looked up at Cevilla. "*Ya*, I'm sure he was going to propose. And then you went and soured the milk."

"I—"

"Now, you *geh* right over there and tell him you're sorry and that you'll do whatever he wants you to do to make it up to him. At our age, that's a limited list, so you shouldn't have any problem reconciling."

"Delilah—"

"I'm serious, Cevilla. I'm not leaving until you set things right with him." She crossed her arms.

Cevilla imagined Delilah sitting on her couch like a plump hen for the rest of the day. *No thank you.* "Fine, I'll *geh*." She got to her feet. "You have to be the most stubborn, pushy person on the face of this earth, Delilah Stoll."

Delilah grinned and rose. "Takes one to know one. I'll get *yer* coat."

A short time later, Cevilla stared at Richard's front door. His car was in the driveway, but that didn't guarantee he was home. The overcast sky, combined with a chilly wind and the fact that for once she had no idea what to say to him, made her want to flee to the warmth of her own home. She'd figure out a way to kick out Delilah when she got there.

Wait. Cevilla Schlabach didn't flee. She didn't cower, she didn't run, and she certainly didn't let other people push her around. Her gaze narrowed with determination, and she knocked soundly on the door, which immediately opened. Startled at the quick response, she gripped her cane, nearly losing her balance. He must have been standing right behind the door. She cleared her throat. "Richard."

"Cevilla."

"May I come in?"

He let her inside, and then she followed him into

the small living room. Richard's house wasn't much bigger than hers, and he had built it that way, despite having a sprawling mansion in Los Angeles. Meghan had designed the home with simple furnishings—a light-gray rug on the hardwood floors, his old, beat-up recliner that was over thirty years old positioned near a woodstove similar to Cevilla's. He had air-conditioning, which he rarely used, and electricity, but for the most part, the home was close to a typical Amish one. Even then, he spent most of his time at Cevilla's.

"May I take your coat?"

She looked up at him, startled for another time by his appearance. Richard was fastidious about his appearance, but this morning he was still in his bathrobe with the belt barely tied, his hair was sticking up in places, and his eyes were bleary. "Did I wake you?"

He shook his head. "I didn't sleep much."

"Me either."

They looked at each other for a long moment, and an awkwardness that had never been between them before filled the room. Finally he said, "I don't know about you, but I need to sit down."

"Oh. Of course." She slipped off her coat, and when she struggled with one sleeve, he helped her out of it before hanging it on a peg by the door. Then they sat down, him in his recliner, her on the couch. Again, they were both silent, not looking at each other.

Then Cevilla felt a nudge, deep inside, prompting her to speak. "I'm sorry, Richard. I shouldn't have read Sharon's letter."

"You're right. You shouldn't have." He turned to her. "But you did, so we might as well talk about it."

She peered at him. "You want to *talk* about it?"

He nodded and then stared at the floor. "I thought about what you said last night. That I don't want to discuss important things. And you're right, I don't. Because in my experience, that only leads to conflict." He met her gaze again. "I don't want conflict between us, Cevilla. If that takes talking over the things I've been putting off, then I want to do that."

Nodding, she felt a bit of her anger and tension lift. "Thank you."

"I wish I would have thrown that letter away. I knew Sharon was going to be a problem." He combed his fingers through his hair. "I've tried talking to her on the phone, but she hangs up on me. I wasn't there for her when she was growing up. I was too involved in my business, in making money and being successful. I accomplished both of those goals, but I'm ashamed to say that it was at the cost of my daughter." His eyes filled with tears. "She's spoiled, entitled, and manipulative, and it's my fault. Nancy did the best she could, but she and Sharon's personalities clashed. She didn't know what to do with a strong-willed daughter, and I was no help."

Cevilla nodded as Richard wiped his eyes with the back of his hand. "You did the best you could," she said.

"Don't cut me any slack. I messed up and put material things before my only child. I was a terrible father. She would be the first one to tell you that. Sharon never lacked for money or toys or cars or clothes. But none of that took my place, and I've been trying to make it up to her ever since. After her divorce, I also vowed that I would be the father to Meghan I wasn't to Sharon."

"You still are." Cevilla knew firsthand how much Meghan adored her grandfather. "We all make mistakes, Richard. You learned from yours, and that's what matters."

"I guess." He tugged at the belt of his bathrobe. "But she's never forgiven me. And those things she said about you in her letter? Ignore them. We both know you're not a gold digger and a bad influence." He let out a bitter laugh. "You couldn't be further from either."

"I don't care what she called me," Cevilla said. "I just don't want to come between you and your family."

"You won't. Meghan loves you, and just because Sharon lives in a house I paid for and spends my money, doesn't mean we have a relationship."

"Maybe you should try calling her. You could invite her out for a visit, and she and I could get to know each other."

He looked horrified. "I wouldn't put you through that."

She lifted her chin. "I'm no wilting flower, Richard. You should know that by now."

He stared at her for a moment and then nodded. "It's too early to call," he said. "Why don't you go home, and I'll be over in a little while after I shower and get dressed."

Cevilla got up from the couch and shuffled to the window. She peeked outside and then shook her head. "Bother. She's still there."

"Who?"

"Delilah. She said she wasn't leaving until you and I worked things out." She let the curtain fall over the window and turned around. "I guess I haven't been here long enough for her satisfaction."

"Seems you've met your match," he said, smiling. "But I know you won't admit it. How about some breakfast while we wait her out? Then we'll call Sharon together. She can at least meet you over the phone."

"I'd like that."

He stood, went to her, and wrapped his arms around her. "I love you, Cevilla. I promise that from now on I'll talk things out with you." He pressed a kiss to the top of her head and looked at her. "Speaking of which, there's something important we need to discuss. But not right now."

"Soon?" she said.

"Very soon."

She laid her head against his chest. "I love you too." Then she pulled away. "Now, let's eat. I'm starving."

Levi stared at the black coffee on the table in front of him and then pushed it away. He glanced at the clock. Selah was supposed to be here half an hour ago, and she was never late. His stomach churned. He wasn't surprised that she hadn't shown up, and he didn't blame her. Last night he'd made the biggest mistake of his life, and Selah had suffered for it.

He hadn't slept a wink, replaying the ride with Selah over and over in his mind. What had he been thinking? Not about the kiss. He'd been thinking about kissing her for a long time before the near-miss car accident had made him draw her into his arms. The kiss had been more than he imagined, and it had been almost agony for him to pull away.

But then he had to ruin everything. Their tentative friendship, her job at the inn, the possibility that sometime in the future they might become something more than friends . . . In a moment of panic and confusion, he'd cut her deeply with his words. He smacked his forehead. *Why did I do that?*

His father walked into the lobby, his cane thumping against the floor, a mug of coffee in his other hand. "Where is everyone?" he asked, crossing the room. "I can't find *yer grossmutter* anywhere, and Nina seems to have disappeared too. I thought Selah would be here already." He chuckled. "It's more of a ghost town than usual around here."

Levi didn't laugh. He could barely shrug. "Nina went to Ira's for a little while to help Mary put together some care packages for a mission group in Millersburg. *Grossmutter* took the buggy and left. She didn't say where she was going. And Selah . . ." He took off his glasses and rubbed the bridge of his nose. How was he supposed to tell his father—and the rest of the family—that he had run Selah off? That he'd kissed her, insulted her, and then expected her to come back? *No, I don't expect her to come back.*

"Selah what?"

"*Nix.*" He put his glasses back on and started to stand. "I've got some firewood to split." Yesterday morning a delivery truck had brought a load of wood cords. His father had overordered, thinking they would go through firewood faster. To save money, they hadn't fired up the wood-stove unless necessary, like they'd thought it was last night.

The evening had been a disaster in more ways than one.

"The wood can wait." His father sat down across from him and put his mug on the table. "Something's wrong. Really wrong. I haven't seen you this down since . . . since *yer mamm* died."

The pain in Levi's heart wasn't similar, but it was as intense.

"I know you're worried about our finances, but don't be. They might look bleak now, but business will pick up. Or the Lord will have a different plan for us and let that be known in his time." He paused. "But our lack of guests isn't what's bothering you, is it?"

He thought about lying. It would be easier, and he could keep his pain to himself. They would find another maid—not that they especially needed one right now—and he and Selah wouldn't see each other except at church, where she could easily avoid him. After what he did, she wouldn't want to have anything to do with him. Eventually his pain would subside even though right now it seemed unlikely. *More like impossible.*

"Did something happen between you and Selah?" *Daed* asked.

Levi nodded. "*Ya.* I really messed up." He clenched his hands. "She's not coming back—"

"Sorry I'm late!" Selah had come through the front door, still wearing her coat and grasping her purse. "I overslept." She looked sheepish. "I guess it was from all the excitement last night."

Daed nodded. "It was an interesting night, to say the least."

"That's for sure. I thought I'd work in the flower beds today. They're full of weeds and leaves and need some tidying up." She kept her gaze on *Daed*. "Unless you need me for something else."

"That's a great idea." He turned to Levi. "What do you think?"

All Levi could do was nod and stare at Selah. If she'd had trouble sleeping last night, she didn't look like it. Her cheeks were rosy from the cold, her blue eyes as bright as her smile. He remembered the devastated look on her face last night, and it was as if she were a different person this morning. Did that mean she'd forgiven him? That she realized he was an idiot and didn't mean what he said? Dear Lord, he hoped so.

"I should probably figure out what seeds and annuals to order," *Daed* said. "We planted plenty of bulbs last year, but we need to refill the hanging baskets and plant some flowers around the two oak trees out front. A few pots on the porch would be nice too." He rose. "I'll *geh* take care of that right now."

As *Daed* left, Selah walked to the front door. Levi jumped up from his chair. "Selah?"

But she walked outside, the glass door shutting

behind her. Thinking she hadn't heard him, he followed her. "Selah!" he called as she flew down the porch steps, setting down her purse along the way.

No answer. She went to the far side of the inn, crouched in front of the flower bed, and started pulling weeds.

Was she ignoring him? Forgetting that she had every right to do so, he marched over to her. "Selah."

She continued to yank out weeds.

Fine. She wanted to give him the silent treatment? Great. It wasn't like he wasn't expecting it. That would make everything easier. He turned around and went back to the inn. When he got inside, he calmed down. He didn't have the right to be mad at her, and she had every right to ignore him. But he was grateful she'd returned to work. He knew how important this job was to her, and he was glad she hadn't let his stupidity keep her from it.

Selah leaned back on her heels and let out a heavy sigh. She knew she was acting like a child, but ignoring Levi was the only way she could both deal with him and keep her job. If she even looked at him, she would lose her temper, melt into tears, or do both at the same time.

Although it was chilly out, the brisk air helped her remain calm. She dug her hands into the cold dirt and focused on pulling out the weeds. It wasn't long before her hands were stiff, and she wished she had put on gardening or work gloves. But she kept working until her fingers were numb—just like her heart.

The sound of crunching gravel made her turn around, and she saw Nina jogging toward her from the parking lot. "Hey, Selah," she said when she knelt next to her.

"Hi." She glanced at Nina and gave her a small smile before going back to work.

"So . . ." Nina put her palms flat on top of her legs and grinned. "What happened last night?"

"You know. You were there."

"Not the supper, although I do hope Cevilla and Richard worked things out. They missed a great dessert, if I do say so myself. That was *mei* first time baking a red velvet cake." She nudged Selah. "I'm talking about *after*."

"After?" Selah tossed a handful of weeds in a pile behind her and then scooted down to the next section of the bed.

Nina followed. "You know. The buggy ride? With *mei bruder*? But don't be too detailed, because, ew."

Selah looked at her. "He took me home. End of story."

"Really?" She looked disappointed.

"Really." She grabbed a stubborn weed and yanked.

"Huh. I thought—"

"Do you want to help me with these?"

"I would, but at breakfast *Daed* asked me to stack the firewood after Levi splits it." She dug her thumb into the dirt. "*Nix* happened?"

"*Nix.*"

Nina stood. "Huh," she repeated. "See you at lunch, then." She went into the inn.

Selah scowled. What had Nina thought would happen? That Levi would kiss her? That they would be a couple by now? She grabbed at the first plant she saw and gave it a hard pull. Only when it was out did she realize she had just destroyed a perennial.

Her head fell to her chest. She wasn't sure she could do this. Ignoring Levi was hard enough, but if his family had the idea that the two of them were getting together . . . And where would they have gotten that idea anyway? From Levi? She'd seen no evidence that Delilah had meddled. Her anger burned. What exactly had Levi said about her behind her back?

She jumped up from the ground and quickly brushed off her dirty hands. In the distance she heard the faint sound of an ax sinking into wood. She stormed to the back of the inn, where Levi was standing in front of a flat stump, a short log positioned on it vertically. She waited until he was finished chopping, knowing there would be a chance for serious injury if she startled him. She was furious with him, but she didn't want him to get hurt. When he tossed the split pieces aside, she marched to him.

"Let's get one thing straight," she said, looking directly at him. "There will never be anything between us, so you can stop talking to *yer familye* as if there could be."

His brow flew up. "What are you talking about?"

"I don't know what kind of game you're playing with me, but it stops. Now."

"Selah," he said, dropping the ax on the ground. "I don't play games."

She crossed her arms. "*All* men play games. But I am not a toy." She fought to keep her tone even. She had wanted to say the same thing to Oliver but never had the chance. "I'm here to do *mei* job. That's it."

"There you guys are."

She turned around to see Jackson walking toward them. He waved as he approached. "How's it going?"

"Great," Levi ground out. "Couldn't be better."

"Glad to hear it. Hey, man, I've got a favor to ask you."

Selah slipped away. When she made it to the front yard of the inn, she felt dread instead of relief. Levi had seemed genuinely confused by what she was saying. Oliver had been a master liar, but she doubted Levi had a deceptive bone in his body. Still, she wasn't sure she was entirely wrong. He was playing games with her, but maybe he didn't realize it. Looking at her in a way that made her feel special and then treating her like an employee. Being there for her when she needed him during her panic attack and then keeping his distance. Kissing her and then telling her it was nothing.

But it didn't matter whether he knew he was being fickle. The fact remained that she couldn't take it anymore. She turned around and stomped back to Levi. Ignoring Jackson, she tapped Levi's shoulder.

"What do you want?" he said, sounding more irritated than she'd ever heard him. But she didn't care.

"I quit!" She turned around, stalked to the front porch to grab her purse, and headed for home.

Chapter 21

Right before lunch, Richard pulled out his phone. "I think Sharon is up by now. She and Meghan are probably having breakfast together. Meghan usually works from home on Saturdays."

Cevilla sat at the kitchen table and folded her hands as Richard dialed the number. "What are you going to tell her?"

He peered at the phone screen through the bottom of his glasses. "That we're getting married."

Her mouth dropped open. "What?"

"Marriage. You know, holy matrimony. Man and woman. Husband and wife. All that stuff. Ah, here's Sharon's number. Looks like it's been awhile since I last called her."

"This is your idea of a proposal?"

Richard set the phone down on the table and looked at her, his expression calm. "Well, I did have a special evening planned for this occasion, but we know how that turned out. And I'd get down on one knee, but I wouldn't be able to get back up."

"But what about the church?"

"I'll be joining soon. I talked to Freemont about it a month ago, and we started classes last week. That was also part of last night's surprise. Thanks for sticking a pin in the balloon."

She let his words sink in. He was joining the Amish, on his own accord, without her pestering him—at least too much. And he wanted to marry her. Butterflies took wing in her stomach and then settled down when she spied the phone. "What will Sharon and Meghan say?"

"Meghan will be happy, of course. As for Sharon . . . I don't know. But like I said, this is my life and my decision. She'll have to get on board with it." He picked up the phone again. "Ready to meet my daughter?"

Cevilla nodded, excited despite what Sharon had said in that letter. "I can't wait."

A few moments later, Richard had tapped in the number and put the phone on speaker. "Hello?" A sophisticated female voice answered.

"Hello, Sharon, dear. How are you?"

"Father."

Cevilla cringed at the tightness in Sharon's voice. With one word the conversation was already on the wrong foot.

Yet Richard seemed to take it in stride. "Is Meghan there with you?"

There was a pause. "I am now." Meghan's light tone was a total contrast to her mother's. "Hi, Grandfather. How are you? How's Cevilla?"

"We're both good." He met Cevilla's gaze and smiled. "I called because I have an announcement to make."

"You're getting married!" Meghan practically shouted into the phone.

"Meghan," Sharon said. "Don't be foolish."

"She's not foolish," Richard said. "I am getting married."

"It's about time," Meghan said.

Cevilla's heart warmed. At least one person was happy for them.

"Is this a joke?" Sharon's voice blasted through the phone.

"No," Richard said evenly. "I—we—are both serious."

"Father, how could you?"

"Easy, Sharon. Cevilla is right here, listening. Would you like to say hello?"

"Certainly not."

Richard rolled his eyes and then mouthed to Cevilla, *I told you.*

"When is the wedding?" Meghan asked as if her mother hadn't just been insulting.

"Meghan, don't encourage him."

Cevilla could imagine Sharon clutching her pearls or rubbing her temple at the very least. She was also feeling left out of the conversation. "We haven't discussed details, but we'll have the exact date soon," she added.

"You're serious, Father?" Sharon said.

Frowning, Cevilla looked at Richard. Sharon was deliberately ignoring her, something Cevilla usually didn't put up with. But for Richard's sake she would keep her mouth shut.

"Yes, I'm serious. I want you to meet Cevilla before the wedding."

"I can't possibly take the time off." Sharon sniffed.

"Time off from what?" Richard asked. "You don't have a job."

"I have commitments."

"The Garden Club and your hairdresser can wait a week." He sighed.

After a heavy silence, she said, "I'll come on one condition."

That sparked a bit of hope in Cevilla, and from Richard's sudden cheerful expression, he felt the same way. "What condition?"

"That I take you back home."

"I am home," he said, gripping the phone.

"LA is your home. You belong here, with us."

"I belong with Cevilla."

Apparently Sharon and Meghan weren't the only stubborn ones in the family. *Those apples hadn't fallen far from the tree.*

Richard continued talking. "Let's get some things straight, Sharon. Number one, I'm not going back to LA. Two, I'm in love with Cevilla, and I'm going to marry her. And three, week after next, I'll be baptized in the Amish church."

"You're going to be Amish?" Meghan asked.

"Yes. I've done my research and I've prayed, and I believe that's what the Lord wants me to do. I'm as sure of that as I am about how much I love Cevilla. We have a second chance, and I'm not going to let that slip by."

"That is so sweet." Meghan sniffed. "I have tears in my eyes, Grandfather. I'm so happy for you."

"Meghan, stop it!" Sharon shrieked. "Father, clearly you have dementia and can't make your own decisions. I'm going to have you tested as soon as you come back to LA."

"Help," Richard murmured, looking at Cevilla.

That was all Cevilla needed to hear. She grabbed the phone and put it to her ear.

"You don't have to do that," he said. "It's on speaker."

"Oh." She held the phone away from her and spoke into it. "Listen here, young lady. Who gave you a doctor's license?"

"I beg your pardon?"

"If your father has dementia, or any other health issue, I will accompany him to the doctor. I will be his wife, and I will take care of him, just as he takes care of me. We have fine doctors in our area, so you can trust that he will be in good hands."

"I don't trust any such thing."

"That, my dear, is your problem."

Sharon huffed into the phone. "Let me speak to my father."

"Mother," Meghan said, "why don't we cool off a little and talk about this with Grandfather and Cevilla later?"

"I have my psychiatrist on speed dial," Sharon

yelled, ignoring Meghan and Cevilla. "I'll have you committed if I have to!"

"I think you need a new psychiatrist," Richard groused. "This one is clearly not helping you."

"You're impossible." Her voice sounded scratchy. "Can't you see what all this is about, Father? She wants your money. I bet one of her children is behind all this."

"I don't have any children," Cevilla said quietly.

"Sharon," Richard said, "is it out of the realm of possibility that my fiancée loves me for me and not my bank account?"

Silence on the phone, then, "I plan to talk with my lawyer."

"Do you have him on speed dial too?" Cevilla clamped her hand over her mouth. She didn't mean for that to slip out.

Sharon ignored the comment. "That woman won't get a dime of our money."

"*Our* money?" Richard's face twisted with anger. "You mean the money you worked all your life to earn? The years you spent sacrificing precious time and relationships for?"

"How can you throw a lifetime away over some woman you barely know?"

Cevilla now knew Richard was right. His daughter was unbearable. She held his hand as he closed his eyes.

"This is my life, Sharon. I will live it how I choose, and I choose to be here with the woman I

315

love, joining the faith God has led me to be a part of. I had hoped you would support my decision. I don't have that many years left."

"Grandfather," Meghan said, her voice thick, "I don't like it when you say things like that."

"I'm not trying to hurt you, dear. But there's no reason to beat around the bush. This wedding is happening."

"And I promise I'll be there," Meghan said. "Just tell me when."

"Thank you, Meghan. Sharon, I want you here, too, but only if you're supportive." He squeezed Cevilla's hand. "Can you do that for me?"

Cevilla held her breath, her eyes blurry with tears, as she and Richard waited for his daughter's answer.

"I can't," Sharon said, and then she ended the call.

Richard slid his finger across the screen. He continued to hold Cevilla's hand but didn't say anything.

Cevilla cleared the lump from her throat. "Maybe we should postpone—"

"No."

"She probably needs some time to absorb the news."

He turned to her. "She's had plenty of time. I didn't move here on a whim."

"But it's a big adjustment."

"She's a sixty-year-old woman. She'll adjust."

He sighed. "I've apologized to Sharon many times over the years. I've tried to reason with her. I've asked for her forgiveness. In the end she makes the same decision. I can't put my life on hold waiting for her to come around. That's not fair to me or to you. We're getting married, and that's final."

"Yes, sir," she said, getting up and putting her arms around the back of his shoulders.

He touched her hands. "It hurts," he whispered. "I can't deny that."

"I know." She kissed the top of his ear. "God is a God of miracles. We can pray he'll change Sharon."

Richard nodded. "He's the only one who can."

"Selah quit?"

Levi shrank back in his chair as all three of his family members, gathered around the kitchen table, stared him down. He'd decided to wait until after lunch to tell them. "*Ya*, Nina. She quit." His hands clenched under the table. He'd known Selah was angry when she marched toward him and Jackson. Jackson had moved out of his apartment and wanted to rent a room at the inn, which Levi had just agreed to. Then he had his feet knocked out from under him when Selah made her announcement, acting like Jackson wasn't even there.

"She didn't give notice?" *Daed* said, scratching his chin.

"She didn't say good-bye?" *Grossmutter*'s expression was a mix of confusion and disappointment.

"What did you do, Levi?" Nina glared at him.

He held up his hands. "I didn't do anything." Talk about a big fat lie. But he wasn't about to tell his family that he'd kissed Selah, then hurt her feelings, then tried to act like *nothing* had happened. Some things had to remain private even among a nosy family like his.

"You had to have done something—"

"That's enough, Nina." *Daed* gave her a stern look. "Employees leave jobs all the time. We'll just have to hire someone else."

"But there's *nee* one like Selah."

Levi had to agree with that. "I'll call the paper and place another ad."

"*Nee*, I'll do it," *Daed* said. "I'm going to call them anyway about running another ad. We're giving a 20 percent winter discount to anyone who books a room from now until April."

"A discount?" *Grossmutter* shook her head. "We can't afford discounts."

"We have to get guests in here somehow. Winter is the slow season. I just hadn't anticipated how slow."

Guilt slashed at Levi. He still hadn't told his father about the fake bad reviews. He'd meant to ask Jackson if they were still online, but then Selah showed up. His head started to pound. *If only I hadn't kissed her.* But that wasn't true. He didn't regret the kiss, only his words and actions afterward.

Daed picked up a few crumbs from the table and put them on his empty plate. "At least we have Jackson staying with us again."

"For how long?" Nina asked.

"He didn't say." Levi stared at the half-eaten tuna fish sandwich on his plate. "For sure a week. After that, he didn't know."

"I hope you gave him a discount," *Grossmutter* said.

Levi frowned. "I thought we couldn't afford discounts."

"This is Jackson we're talking about." She got up from the table and started to clear it. "Of course he gets a discount."

Nina got up and helped *Grossmutter*, her expression somber. In a short time she and Selah had grown close. His thoughtless actions had unexpected consequences, and he could see he wasn't the only one affected by her quitting.

"Nina, you'll have to work both the hostess and maid jobs the best you can until we hire someone else," *Daed* said, "but we'll all help. Selah helped confirm that even with only a few guests, doing both jobs is just too much work for one person. I hope it doesn't take too long to find someone."

"All right." Nina put the dirty dishes in the

319

sink and turned on the tap. For once she wasn't complaining about the hostess job.

Levi cleared his own plate, ignoring Nina's harsh look. *Grossmutter* wiped down the table but didn't look at him. Great. She blamed him too. But why did they automatically think this was his fault? Had Selah complained about him? No, he knew she wouldn't do that. His sister and grandmother were upset, and right now they needed him to be the scapegoat—even though they had no idea how close they were to the truth.

That evening after supper Selah walked out to the patio, sat down in one of the wooden Adirondack chairs Christian had purchased last summer in Holmes County, and looked at the sky. It was chilly and she was wearing only her sweater, but she barely felt the cold. She'd spent the afternoon kicking herself for what she'd done. Why had she let her temper get the best of her? She should have at least given notice and worked until they found someone else. Now she had not only lost a job she enjoyed but put people she cared about in a tough position.

She closed her eyes. *Lord, I thought I was done being impulsive and angry. I have such a long way to go.* That admission made her think that even though she'd gone about it the wrong way, she'd been right to quit. With the way things were between her and Levi, she would have lost her cool at some point, and they would have had to fire her anyway. At least she wouldn't have that on her résumé when she applied for another job.

Selah slid down in the chair, which was already low to the ground. Appropriate, since she hadn't felt this low in a long time. Her heart hurt, which irritated her more, because despite being angry with Levi, she still cared about him. For both their sakes, she still wished things were different between them. That line of thinking was useless, but she couldn't help it.

"Selah?"

She turned her head and saw Ruby coming outside carrying a blanket. "Hey," she said.

Ruby covered her up. "Christian told me you quit *yer* job at the inn."

She nodded. She had told Christian in private right before supper, and to his credit he only nodded and didn't press her further.

"I thought you liked working there." Ruby settled in the chair next to Selah and put her hands in her coat pockets.

"I do—did." Selah huddled under the blanket. "But it was time for me to move on."

"You were only there a couple of months."

"I know. But I don't think being a maid is for me." That said, if she found another cleaning job, she would snatch it in a heartbeat. Her goal hadn't changed—she still wanted to move out and have her own small house. That plan would just be deferred longer than she expected.

"Selah," Ruby said, shifting in the chair, "I know I shouldn't pry . . ."

Then don't. But she held her tongue. She'd been plenty rude to Ruby in the past for no good reason other than Selah had been miserable. Like now. Her sister-in-law didn't deserve her disrespect.

"But I don't understand why you would leave a job you enjoyed and so desperately wanted. Did something happen with the Stolls?"

Selah turned away. "You could say that." She hesitated. "One Stoll in particular."

"Levi?"

She turned to her. "How did you know?"

"Because you've been out of sorts since he dropped you off last night."

"Why do you have to be so observant?"

Ruby chuckled. "It's a job requirement when you spend all day with young *kinner*. You wouldn't believe what they try to get away with sometimes." She grew serious. "If you don't want to talk about it—"

"I really don't." She paused. "But I should. It helps when I talk things out." She blew out a breath. "This is embarrassing."

"You're talking to me here, Selah. Embarrassing is *mei* middle name."

Selah chuckled. Ruby had managed to get herself into a few pinches since Selah had known her. She'd even inadvertently destroyed Christian's classroom one day when she substituted for him after he sprained his ankle. Not only had he forgiven her for that, but the incident had been the start of their relationship. "I made a mistake," Selah said. "One I promised myself I wouldn't make."

"What's that?"

"I fell for another guy."

"Levi."

Selah nodded, rubbing her fingers on the hem of the soft blanket. "After Oliver, I promised myself I would avoid relationships with men altogether, friends or otherwise. Especially otherwise. But it didn't take long for me to fall back into *mei* old habits."

"Is Levi like Oliver?"

She shook her head. "I didn't think he was. Now I'm not so sure."

Ruby didn't say anything for a moment. "I thought you said Oliver was a jerk. I can't imagine Levi harming a fly."

"I didn't think so either. But then he kissed me—"

"Wait. What?" Ruby sat straight up. "He kissed you?"

She shouldn't have let that slip out. "*Ya.*"

"Did he force himself on you?" Ruby's tone held an angry edge.

"*Nee*. Of course not. He'd never do that."

"*Gut.*" Ruby sat back. "Because if he had, he and I would be having words. Lots of words."

Selah smiled, warmth flooding her. Knowing her sister-in-law would protect her, and by extension Christian, helped ease her pain. But not completely. "It was what he said afterward that hurt." She explained his behavior after the kiss.

"Ah." Ruby chuckled. "I see what's going on here."

"You do?"

"Selah, men are confusing creatures. They don't always say what they mean, particularly when they're in love."

"Love?" Selah scoffed. "One kiss doesn't mean love." She and Oliver had kissed many times, but she never loved him. Which was a good thing, considering how he had treated her when she needed him.

"It does when he's the *one*."

"Ruby, you're reading too much into this."

"Okay, maybe not love. But definitely like. Just because Oliver was an idiot doesn't mean all men are."

"I know," she said. "I just seem to fall for the wrong ones."

"How is Levi wrong?"

Selah opened her mouth to answer but then closed it. Other than what happened after their kiss, Levi had done everything right. He was always concerned with how she was going to get home. He was at her side when she had her panic attack. He made her laugh, he complimented her work, and he put up with her quirks. "He's not," she said, realizing her words were true. The walls around her heart started to quake, but she forced them to stand firm. "None of that matters. He made his feelings clear. He's not interested."

Ruby didn't say anything, which was unusual for her. After a few minutes she spoke. "Seems like you have *yer* mind made up."

"I do." Selah crossed her arms beneath the blanket.

As she rose from the chair, Ruby added, "Don't stay out here too long. You might catch cold."

"I won't." She turned and looked at Ruby. "*Danki* for listening. And for caring. And for the blanket."

Ruby bent down and gave her a quick hug. "Anytime."

Selah sat outside a little longer, trying to determine what she was going to do. She'd have to start her job hunt again, which she wasn't looking forward to. She would go back to making supper for Christian and Ruby instead of just helping every night when she got home from work. Life would go back to the way it was before she worked for the Stolls, just as if the time she spent with them never happened. Knowing she wouldn't see them every day depressed her, but she had to move on. She had no other choice.

Chapter 22

Delilah tried to focus on Freemont's sermon on Sunday. He was preaching for Timothy Glick, who was visiting his family in Lancaster with his wife and sons. The sermon focused on God's will, a topic she, and all Amish, was familiar with. Living according to the Lord's will and believing it was his will no matter what happened, good or bad, was the Amish way.

But this morning she was struggling to understand. She'd gone through worse in her life. The poverty of her childhood, which had been extreme because of the strict community she had grown up in. The death of her husband and leaving his grave behind when she moved from Wisconsin. Trying to be a mother to two stubborn grandchildren, who while growing into fine adults were hopeless when it came to finding spouses. Yet for some reason, Selah quitting had put her over the edge.

She couldn't stem her disappointment. She had known deep in her heart that Selah and Levi were meant for each other. She had also felt like Selah was already becoming a part of their family.

"For I know the thoughts that I think toward you, saith the Lord"—Freemont looked over the community members seated in Hezekiah Detweiler's barn—"Thoughts of peace, and not of evil, to give you an expected end."

I could use some peace too. She had been so sure about Levi and Selah, and she had followed Cevilla's advice about letting God oversee their relationship. The result? They were further apart than ever.

She didn't feel much like socializing after the service. Neither did Levi, apparently. He was standing just outside the barn but not engaging with anyone. She'd never seen him hold himself back during a social situation, which increased her worry. He was already quiet and sullen at home. Loren was subdued, too, and Delilah knew he was concerned about the bills and their lack of guests. Only Nina, who was talking to Ira near Hezekiah's optics shop, seemed to be behaving normally. But she was also overly quiet at home.

She saw Cevilla coming toward her, and she was tempted to pretend she didn't see her and go to the buggy. But when Cevilla waved at her, she tossed the idea aside.

"Delilah!" Cevilla was beaming. She also had a pep in her step Delilah certainly hadn't seen the day before. She smiled a little. She'd tired of waiting for Cevilla to return home and left, but forcing her to hash things out with Richard must have worked.

"*Mei* goodness," Cevilla said, sounding a little out of breath. "What are you doing all the way over here by *yerself*? Usually you're right in the middle of everything."

"We have a guest at home." Delilah hadn't planned to use Jackson as an excuse, especially since he wasn't at the inn right now. He'd left in his car right before they'd departed, not saying where he was going. Delilah got the impression that he didn't attend church. She wasn't sure he even believed in God. Perhaps she could have a discussion with him about that while he was staying at the inn. He was a nice young man, and he seemed interested in what she had to say— when it came to recipes, anyway.

"Oh? That's *gut* news."

She nodded her head and then said, "You look chipper."

"And you don't." Cevilla frowned. "What's wrong?"

"*Nix*. You and Richard worked things out?"

Smiling, she nodded. "We did. And I want to thank you. We'd probably still be giving each other the silent treatment instead of"—she leaned forward and whispered—"getting married!"

Delilah tried to show enthusiasm. She wasn't envious of her friend's happiness. She had loved Wayne deeply, and she'd never find another man like him. But although she was happy for Cevilla, it was difficult to show it. Cevilla didn't seem to notice, though. That was good, because she'd always been an open book when it came to her emotions.

"Please don't mention it to *yer familye* yet,"

Cevilla said. "We still have to tell Noah and Ivy. But I didn't want to miss telling you that we want our wedding to be at the inn."

That got Delilah's full attention. "You do?"

"*Ya*. Both our *hauses* are too small, and we think the inn will be the perfect place. We were thinking about late March or early April. And we'd like Selah to plan it."

"I don't think that's going to happen."

Cevilla lifted a brow. "You don't want us to get married at *yer* inn?"

"*Nee*, not that. Of course we'll host *yer* wedding. But Selah quit."

"*Nee*," Cevilla said.

"*Ya*. Out of the blue." Delilah patted Cevilla's arm. "But don't you worry, *mei familye* and I will make sure *yer* wedding is perfect."

"I'm not worried about that." She frowned. "Selah quit. I can't believe it. Did it have something to do with Levi?"

"I think so. She didn't say, and he's not talking." She glanced at him, seeing that he'd made his way to the buggy, just as eager to get home as she was.

"Humph." Cevilla tapped her cane on the grass. "We can't have that, can we?"

Delilah looked at her. "*Nee* interference, remember?"

"Oh. I did say that, didn't I?" She frowned. "Then we'll have to find a way to get them together without interfering."

"How?"

Cevilla grinned. "Leave that to me."

Levi picked up the last shovelful of manure and added it to the large pile behind the barn. Seth would pick it up later in his wagon to use as fertilizer on his family's farm. That was a good solution to one of their dilemmas. They couldn't have a smelly pile of manure within the proximity of the inn, especially during the summer.

He finished cleaning the barn and then took a shower. After getting dressed, he headed to the inn. There wasn't much else to do since Jackson was still their only guest, and it was already Wednesday. When he walked into the lobby, he saw Jackson sitting at one of the empty tables, his laptop open.

"How's it going?" Levi said.

"All right, I guess." He gestured for Levi to sit down. "Still looking for a job. There's a lot of part-time work out there, but I really need full-time."

"What about your business?"

"I have to set that aside for a while. I'm not making any money right now, and that's my priority."

Levi scratched his chin, an idea coming to him. "You said part-time jobs are available? What kind?"

Jackson listed a few jobs—convenience store clerk, fast-food worker, and delivery driver.

"There's also a job opening for a warehouse stocker at the discount department store in Barton."

"That might work," Levi said.

"Are you looking for a job?" Jackson looked surprised.

Levi nodded. "I've been thinking about it. There's not much maintenance to do here right now, and Dad's back managing the inn and doesn't need help." He didn't add that they could use the money Levi would bring in from an outside job, which was his primary reason for wanting to get one.

"You can apply online." Jackson turned the computer around so Levi could see the screen.

Levi looked at the unfamiliar machine. He'd used a computer exactly one time in his life, at the library to search for a book when the librarian was too busy to help him find the one he wanted. "Is this the only way to apply?"

"For this job, yes. Most places require online applications."

He pushed the computer back. "Then I can't apply."

"Is that a church rule?"

"You could say that." He frowned. Getting a job in the English world was more difficult than he thought. No wonder Selah had wanted to keep her job here. Had she found another one? He had no idea. He hadn't talked to her since she quit, and they had avoided each other at church.

"I have a way to get around that," Jackson said. "You give me the information for the application, and I'll type it in."

Levi thought for a minute. "I think that will work. Thanks."

They spent the next fifteen minutes filling out the application, which was surprisingly extensive. The inn's application for the maid job had been one handwritten page.

"Done," Jackson said, hitting a button. "And sent. Now you just have to wait until they call you for an interview."

Levi nodded as the front door opened and Cevilla walked in, Richard behind her. Levi got up from the table to greet them. "Hello," he said. "Nice to see you two smiling. I guess you worked things out."

"We did." Cevilla looked up at Richard, who was also grinning. Then she looked at Levi. "We would like to discuss a possible event at your inn."

He couldn't help but grin. "A wedding, perhaps?"

"Bingo," Richard said.

"Great. Dad's not here, though," he said, still speaking English for Richard's benefit as well as Jackson's. "He went to Barton this morning, but he should be back later this afternoon."

"Actually, we want to talk to you." Cevilla smiled, a twinkle in her blue eyes.

"I'll make myself scarce." Jackson shut the

laptop. "Lois has been asking me to stop by for a visit anyway." He put the computer in his bag and got up from the table.

"Cevilla and Richard, this is Jackson Talbot." Levi motioned for Jackson to come over. "He's a guest here, and he's also a friend."

Jackson grinned and held out his hand to both of them. "Pleased to meet you."

"Likewise," Richard said, shaking his hand. "Good strong grip. I like that."

"Thanks." He looked at Levi. "I'll be back later." He gave Cevilla and Richard a little wave and then walked out the front door.

Levi showed the couple to an empty table and then asked if they wanted any coffee or tea. "Not right now," Cevilla said. She pointed to the chair across from her. "Sit."

He complied, feeling a little intimidated by a woman who was half his height and close to four times his age. "You sure you don't want to talk to Dad? Or Grandmother?"

"We're sure, son." Richard turned to Cevilla. "My fiancée has some specific ideas about our wedding, and what she says goes."

That didn't surprise Levi one bit. "All right, Cevilla. What are your ideas?"

"First, we'd like to get married at the end of this month or in early April. A Tuesday, of course, and outside if the weather is nice."

This sounded typical to him. He'd never

planned a wedding, but he'd been to a few.

"Of course, we would rent the inn again," Richard said.

"That's not necessary. We wouldn't charge for your wedding."

"I insist, though. You'll be losing income because of us, and I can't in good conscience let that happen."

"Always a businessman." Cevilla patted his hand.

Levi started to protest, but he quickly realized that would be pointless. And they could use the money. "Thank you," he said.

"Here's the most important thing." Cevilla looked him directly in the eye. "We want Selah involved in the planning. Every detail of it."

Levi blanched. "I'm sorry," he said, feeling as though his stomach were sinking to his knees, "but she doesn't work here anymore."

"Your grandmother told me that on Sunday." A crafty grin stretched across her face. "I guess you'll have to convince her to come back."

Despair seeped through him. Having Cevilla and Richard's wedding here would not only help them financially but be good marketing. If the wedding went well, perhaps they could book other weddings here. But if Selah's involvement was the catch, there would be no wedding at Stoll Inn.

Levi turned to Richard, who was gazing intently

at the empty tabletop. He suspected something was going on here, but he didn't speak his thoughts. "I don't think that's going to happen."

"I'm sure you can persuade her, Levi." She smiled at him again. "Have a little faith." Cevilla clasped her hands together in a similar fashion to his grandmother, which raised Levi's suspicions again. Then she said, "You know, I think I do need to speak to Delilah," and then she slowly got up from the table. "Is she in the house?"

"Yes."

"I'll let you two talk for a bit, then." She touched Richard on the shoulder and then made her way toward the back of the inn.

"I hope she hasn't put you in too difficult of a position," Richard said.

Levi shook his head, even though he was telling a bald-faced lie. "If that's what makes her happy."

"Trust me, it does." He sat back in the chair. "I'd love to hear how you came to establish this inn. If you don't mind. Cevilla's right, I'm always the businessman."

"I don't mind at all." He was grateful for the diversion. But even he couldn't muster the optimism to believe that Selah would come back.

Delilah paced in the kitchen. Cevilla and Richard should be at the inn by now, talking with Levi about the wedding. She had no idea what the woman was up to, other than she was just as determined to get Selah and Levi together as Delilah was. She'd just decided to go to the inn herself when she heard someone come into the back of the house.

"Goodness, it's brisk outside." Cevilla shivered as she closed the mudroom door. "Spring is around the corner, but it still feels like winter."

"What happened?" Delilah gestured for her to come into the kitchen, uninterested in pleasantries.

"My, aren't we eager." Cevilla sat down, still wearing her coat. "I made it clear to Levi in no uncertain terms that Selah is to be involved in every aspect of our wedding."

Her mouth dropped open. "You're a genius."

Cevilla shrugged. "I have *mei* moments."

Delilah's grin faded. "But what if she refuses?"

"She won't. Trust me."

"I don't know how to thank you."

"You don't have to." Cevilla patted her arm. "I owed you one."

When Jackson arrived at the hotel, he didn't see his father's car in the parking lot, but inside he found Lois dusting the flat screen TV in the lobby. She turned when she heard him come in, and then she grinned and hurried over, waving her pink feather duster in the air. "Jackson! I've missed you!" She gave him a huge hug, enveloping him in a cloud of perfume.

336

"I haven't been gone that long."

"I know. I was just used to you being around. How are things at Stoll Inn?"

He gave her an update on his living arrangements, not worried that she would say anything to Dad about the inn. Not that there was anything to say. The place was homier than the apartment he'd shared with his father. "Haven't had much luck in the job department, though."

"There's a position available here."

"Yeah, but no thanks."

Lois frowned. "I didn't want to say anything, but . . ." She sighed. "I know you and your father have had problems. We've all had problems with him. But I'm worried about him. Did you know he has a new girlfriend?"

"I'm not surprised."

"She's younger than what's-her-face."

"Ashley."

"I think she's younger than you. He's not breaking the law, if you know what I mean. But still, it's unseemly. He's also been coming to work with alcohol on his breath. He never did that before you left."

A tiny sliver of guilt stabbed him, but he pushed it away. "I'm not my father's keeper," he muttered.

"I know. A child shouldn't parent their parent. But I'm concerned about him. I might fuss and complain, but your father has a good side under all the bad."

"I haven't seen it lately."

Lois put her arm around him. "He's in the office. Go talk to him."

He considered refusing her request, but then he rolled his eyes. "Fine. For you."

"Thank you, sweetie." She tapped him on the shoulder with her duster and then flounced back to the counter.

Jackson went to the office, stopping before the closed door. He thought about knocking, but then he just barged in. He was shocked by what he saw. His father, usually decently dressed, looked like he'd slept in his clothes. The manicured eyebrows had started to grow in, and Jackson could smell alcohol on him. Lois was right. He looked a mess.

"What are you doing here?" he snarled.

I have no idea. "I came to check on you."

He took a swig from his mug, and Jackson was sure it held more than coffee. "Go back to that Amish inn. Lois told me you were staying there, you traitor."

Jackson drew in a deep breath, ready to storm out again. But something held him back. Through the haze of his father's surly insult, Jackson felt compassion. The man was clearly miserable and determined to make everyone around him feel the same way. "You need help, Dad. Serious help. You can't keep hurting other people because you're hurting."

"I'm fine." His father started to take another drink.

Jackson grabbed the mug out of his hands. "You call getting sloshed before noon fine?"

"Mind your own business. Isn't that why you left? You don't want to be around me anymore?"

"Can you blame me?" Jackson stepped away from the desk.

His father stared at him, his body trembling. "Get out. Go back to those Amish people you like so much. I never want to see you again."

The compassion disappeared. Jackson threw the coffee mug in the trash can by the desk. He was so angry and hurt he couldn't say anything. He just rushed out the door and past the front desk.

"Jackson," Lois called out.

But he didn't stop. He got in his car and gasped for air. So his father didn't want to see him again? The feeling was mutual. He threw the car into reverse and squealed out of the parking lot.

He drove without thinking until he found himself back in Birch Creek, and pulled over to the side of the road. His father didn't want him, and his mother was too busy for him. He was an adult, though, so he shouldn't care. They lived their lives, and he lived his. "It's fine," he said out loud, his throat thick with emotion. "It's all fine."

Chapter 23

After Cevilla and Richard left, Levi sat on the couch and stared blankly at the empty woodstove. Maybe his family could cut their losses. Sell this place, go back to Wisconsin, tails tucked between their legs. Actually it wouldn't be embarrassing. People would understand a failed business. They happened all the time. They hadn't left Wisconsin on bad terms, and he and his father could go back to their jobs in construction as though their time in Birch Creek never happened. That was a more likely scenario than Selah agreeing to work with him again.

Or maybe he could just leave. His family was settled in this community. It wouldn't be fair for them to give up because of his mistakes. If he wasn't here, Selah would come back, and they could all move forward.

He looked around at the place he and his family had created. He loved the inn, and even though the work had been challenging and they had yet to see much success, being here felt right. He couldn't walk away from it. He was stupid and cowardly to think he could.

"Hey, Levi." His father walked into the lobby. He was still using his cane, but only when he was away from the inn or the house.

Levi straightened and managed a smile. "Back from Barton so soon?"

Daed looked confused as he sat down next to him. "Not really. I expected to be back by lunchtime."

It was already noon? He glanced at the clock. Twelve thirty. How long had he been moping about Selah? Then again, he still didn't understand why she believed he'd been telling his family there could be something between them. That's what she'd accused him of just before she quit. He'd avoided telling anyone how he felt about her, but he must have done something for her to believe he had.

"I think it was a good trip," *Daed* was saying. "I visited some of the businesses downtown, dropped off our business cards and brochures, and talked up the inn. Some folks hadn't even known we existed. I think word of mouth is going to work better for us than any advertising in the paper. We just have to get some more guests here and encourage them to spread the word."

Levi nodded, a knot forming in his stomach. He had to tell his father about the reviews. After he explained what happened and who was responsible, he added, "It's not Jackson's fault. He didn't know what his father was doing until he saw the reviews. He's been working to get them taken down."

His father stared straight ahead, rubbing his

healing leg. "Do you think the reviews are the reason we haven't had much business?"

"Besides it being the winter season, *ya*." He shook his head. "There are probably other reasons too."

"I agree." *Daed* clapped his hands on his legs and looked at Levi, his expression full of determination. "We don't need to worry about those reviews. We just have to do the work God has given us and do it honestly and diligently. That's our responsibility. God will see the rest through."

Levi nodded. "That leads me to something else." He explained Cevilla and Richard's visit. "*Daed*, it's *mei* fault Selah left. I'd rather not *geh* into details about that, but I'm not sure I can convince her to come back. Yet they said they wouldn't have the wedding here if she didn't participate. That's their condition."

"I see." *Daed* pressed his lips together. "Does *yer grossmutter* have anything to do with this?"

"I don't think so. She hasn't said anything about Selah since she left."

Daed paused again. "I don't like conditions," he said. "This seems a bit manipulative."

"They're right about Selah, though. She planned Richard's surprise supper mostly herself. *Grossmutter*, Nina, and I just executed her plan. She's really *gut* at making an event special."

"She also seemed to enjoy it, from what little I saw." *Daed* sighed. "I'm going to leave this up to you, *sohn*. If you feel pressured to talk to Selah, then I'll have a word with Cevilla."

That would be the easy way out. But Levi couldn't allow his father to get him off the hook. And he did owe Selah a huge apology. More than one. "I'll *geh* see Selah. I just can't promise she'll agree to come back."

"If she doesn't, we'll figure out something else. I can't believe Cevilla and Richard will find another place for their wedding if Selah isn't involved. After all, it's her choice whether or not to work at the inn." *Daed* looked at him. "Levi, if you ever need to talk about what happened with her, I'm here. Women are hard to figure out."

"Even *Mamm*?"

"She had her moments." His eyes grew wistful. "So did I. But she accepted me for who I am, warts and all, and I accepted her." He smiled. "That's what you do when you love someone." He got up from the couch. "I'm ready for lunch. See you back at the *haus*?"

Levi nodded, but he held back for a minute. He'd go see Selah this afternoon, hoping she'd be home. And he prayed that she would at least be open to listening to him. If not, then at least he would have tried.

Selah waved to Cevilla and Richard as he pulled his car out of her driveway, a big smile on her face. They had worked things out, and now they

343

were getting married. Richard had even said he was going to get rid of his car by the end of the week. "I'm ready to start my new life," he said, looking at Cevilla with love in his eyes.

"We both are." She patted his knee and then looked at Selah. "We wanted to tell you about the wedding in person. You put so much thought and care into our Valentine's Day supper—"

"We're sorry about what happened," Richard added. "That wasn't our best evening together."

Cevilla gave him a curt look and then continued. "*Anyway,* because of that we wanted you to be among the first people to know." She glanced up at the clock on the wall. "Oh, Richard, look at the time. I didn't realize how late it was. We must be going, Selah. Sorry for the short visit." They both slowly got to their feet.

"I'm happy for you," Selah said.

"Thank you." Cevilla smiled. "Love is in the air, Selah Ropp." She winked at her, and then she and Richard left.

Selah wasn't sure what Cevilla meant. Both she and Richard could be a bit perplexing. She went back into the house and slipped on her coat, bonnet, and boots, intending to take a long walk.

The ground outside was dry, but the overcast sky seemed to threaten rain or even snow. She wouldn't let that stop her, though. She couldn't spend another minute in the house, her thoughts bouncing back and forth, trying to figure out what she was going to do about getting a new job. She stepped outside, but then she halted. Levi was walking up the driveway. What was he doing here? What was she going to do? Go back inside? Wait on him? She closed her eyes and took a deep breath. No need to get worked up—yet. But lately Levi gave her plenty of reason to. She would wait on him, but she wouldn't go meet him.

"Hey," he said as he stopped in front of her. He looked down and pressed his toe against the grass in the yard. "Looks like you're going somewhere."

"I am." No need to tell him she was still at loose ends.

"Guess *mei* timing isn't that great. I won't keep you." He finally met her gaze.

Her heart seemed to flip in her chest. He was still so attractive to her that her knees almost buckled. She'd never had such a strong reaction to a man—ever. Her attraction to him cut through her anger and disappointment. She lifted her chin, determined to keep the lid on her emotions tight. "How can I help you?"

"By coming back to work at the inn," he blurted. "I'm not going to beat around the bush, Selah. I don't know if you've heard yet, but Cevilla and Richard are getting married. They want to have their wedding at the inn, and they also want you to plan it. In fact, they insist on it." He paused, still looking at her. "I know you're upset with me enough to have quit, but I'm asking you to look past that and work for us again, at least until after this wedding. I won't be involved in the planning, if that helps you make a decision. You'll be working with Nina and *Grossmutter*. And I'll stay out of *yer* way."

She frowned. "Cevilla and Richard stopped by earlier to tell me they were engaged, but they didn't say anything about wanting me to help with their wedding."

Levi shrugged. "You never know with those two." He met her gaze. "I'll give you some time to think about it."

"I don't have to." She wasn't going to let her personal problems get in the way of her friends' happiness—and she still needed a job. She'd make this work. "I'd be honored to help make the plans for Richard and Cevilla. So I'll come back at least until after the wedding, as long as it's okay with you—I mean with *yer familye*."

"Of course it's okay." Sincerity radiated from his eyes and words. Then his expression grew impassive again. "We appreciate it. This event will help the business."

Business. It was always about business with him—except when it wasn't. "I understand. When do you want me to start?"

"Tomorrow. I'll let the *familye* know. You can resume *yer* regular hours."

"All right."

He looked at her again, and she thought she saw his stone-faced expression slip. But it must have been her imagination, because he turned on his heel and left.

She sat down on the front stoop, the cold concrete seeping through her coat and dress, her walk forgotten. She had her job back, at least temporarily, and she would be working solely with Nina and Delilah on the wedding plans, which was great. She did enjoy planning the Valentine's Day supper, and she already had a couple of ideas about the wedding.

She should be happy that this had all fallen into place. But she wasn't.

Jackson returned to Stoll Inn right before supper. He wasn't in the mood for company, having driven all over Amish Country that afternoon, trying to squash his anger. He'd stopped on one of the back roads in Holmes County, pulled over to the side, and stepped out of the car. On both sides of the road were rolling farms, waiting for the weather and ground to warm up enough for planting. He saw Amish homes in the distance, all similar to the Stoll family's house and other homes he'd seen in Birch Creek.

He breathed in the crisp air, and although he was still hurt and upset, he felt some of the tension release from his shoulders. Growing up in northeast Ohio, he had always taken Amish

Country for granted and never been interested in visiting here or taking stock of the slower pace of life. But that had changed. Being here didn't make his relationship with his father better, but getting away from the noise and stress of his life did ease the strain, if only temporarily.

While he was on the road, he'd even given a fleeting thought to trying church. Not an Amish church, of course, but maybe a regular one. *The Stolls must be rubbing off on me.* But religion had never been a part of his life, and he wasn't sure it mattered anyway. One thing for sure, though, it mattered to the Stolls. He'd had a good view of how they lived, and the image they presented to him the first day he'd stepped foot into the inn wasn't any different from the one he saw when he was in their home. None of them had ranted and raved about the fact that guests had been nearly nonexistent, and he knew they had to have extra bills because of Loren's surgery. Yet they went about their lives with patient faith. Maybe there was something to this God thing after all, at least for them.

When he walked into the inn, Loren was just coming out of the office. "How was your day?" he asked, genuine interest in his eyes.

What a difference from how his father talked to him. "Okay. I got some job leads to pursue tomorrow." He wasn't about to reveal the disaster of a relationship he had with his dad.

What relationship? He was pretty sure it was nonexistent now.

"Excellent. Will you join us for supper tonight? Or did you already eat?"

A little while ago he hadn't wanted company. Now he realized he didn't want to be alone. "I haven't eaten, so yeah, I'd like that. Thanks."

He walked with Loren to the house and listened as he told him about the wedding for that elderly couple Levi had introduced him to that morning. "They're over eighty years old," he said. "They have more energy than I do some days, though."

As they entered the kitchen, the delicious aroma of freshly baked bread hit him. His stomach growled, and he realized he hadn't eaten lunch.

Loren went to the stove and peeked into the stewpot on one of the gas burners. "Jackson's joining us. What's for supper?"

"Vegetable beef stew and the bread I just made," Delilah said, tapping him on the arm. "Now put that lid back on."

The back door to the kitchen opened, and Levi walked in from the mudroom. The bustling in the kitchen stopped as Loren, Nina, and Delilah looked at him.

"You've been gone a long time," Loren said.

"I had some thinking to do."

"Did that thinking include Selah?"

Jackson frowned. He knew Selah had quit—rather angrily. He'd been right there when it happened, and Levi had seemed stunned. Whatever was going on was none of his business, so Jackson had just left, no questions asked. But that was days ago. Had something else happened while he was gone today? Everyone suddenly seemed on edge.

"I saw her." Levi sat down at the table. He looked tired and downtrodden. Very much unlike himself.

Nina sat next to him. "What did she say?"

Loren must have filled everyone in on Cevilla's request. "I told her Cevilla wants her to plan her wedding here at the inn, and she agreed to come back to work for us so she can. She'll be here in the morning."

"That's wonderful." Nina grinned, but she looked a little confused. "Then what's got you looking like you just lost your best friend?"

"Nina," Loren said. "I think the rolls are done."

"They've got two more minutes, Dad."

"Nina." Delilah picked up her spoon and stirred the stew again. "Get the butter out of the pantry."

"I'll go wash up." Levi got up from the table and left.

Jackson watched him leave. Something was definitely going on with him and Selah. "I should probably do the same," he said, following Levi out of the kitchen. He hurried to catch up to him before he went into the downstairs bathroom. "Hey," he said. "Everything all right?"

"Yep." His smile was less than halfhearted. "It's all great."

"Are all you Amish bad at lying?"

Levi let out a bitter laugh. "I hope so, since we're supposed to be honest." He glanced down at the floor. "I've just got a lot on my mind."

"About Selah."

He looked at Jackson. "It's that obvious, huh?"

"Kind of. Plus, I was there when she quit, remember? Whatever's going on, have you thought about talking it out with her?"

"It's complicated."

"What relationship isn't?"

Levi shook his head. "We don't have a relationship."

"And that's where I think you have a problem." He clapped the man on the shoulder. "I'm not an expert on women or anything, but if you need to talk about it, I'm here."

Levi nodded. "I appreciate that. I'll wash up upstairs."

As Jackson watched him go, he tried to figure out what had possessed him to be Levi's listening ear. Levi had called him a friend when he introduced him to that older couple, and the family did treat him like a friend, but Jackson didn't do friendship. He was a loner, some of it forced on him because of family, the rest because he chose to be. But for some reason he'd been compelled to reach out to Levi. He just hoped the guy didn't think he was a weirdo for doing so.

After supper, Jackson was invited to join Loren, Nina, and Delilah in their living room, but Levi went upstairs for the night. Loren read the paper, Delilah sewed, and Nina looked through a magazine. Normally Jackson would pull out his phone and surf social media, but he kept it in his pocket and picked up a newspaper from the basket by the coffee table. *The Budget.* He started to read, soon engrossed in the comings and goings of the Amish from all over the nation. It was like a paper version of social media for the Amish.

There was a knock on the front door, and Loren went to answer it.

"Is Jackson here?"

Jackson's head jerked up at the sound of his father's voice. *Oh no.* He shot up from the chair and rushed to the door. "Loren, this is my father, Trevor Talbot," he said quickly. "Dad, what are you doing here?"

His father looked even worse than he had earlier in the day, if that was possible. He nodded at Loren and then said to Jackson, "Can we talk? Outside?"

His guard up, Jackson moved out to the small front porch, which was much like the larger porch in front of the inn. Loren closed the door behind them, and Jackson and his father walked away from the house. With spring's arrival came more evening daylight, and he searched his father's eyes, looking for signs that he'd been drinking and driving. But although he looked wrung out, he wasn't wild-eyed, and Jackson couldn't smell any alcohol. *Thank God.* That still didn't mean he wasn't here to make trouble. "What do you want?"

"Lois quit."

"She did?" Jackson said, surprised.

"She's been threatening to for years. I guess our fight today was the last straw."

"So you want me to convince her to come back to the hotel? To tell her everything's all right and she doesn't have to quit?" He shook his head. "Forget it. I'm not lying on your behalf. You want her back, you convince her."

"I will." His father grew quiet and averted his gaze. "She really cares about you. I didn't realize that until today."

"She's a good woman." A lump formed in Jackson's throat. Over the years Lois had been a bigger presence in his life than his own mother. "You don't treat her right."

"She made that clear. She also made it clear that I don't treat you the way I should." He paused. "She's right about that too."

Jackson thought he must have landed in some sort of alternative universe where his father actually admitted to his faults. "Have you been drinking?"

"Not since this morning." He slipped his hand into the inside pocket of his coat and handed Jackson a piece of paper folded in half lengthwise. "This is for you."

Jackson took the paper and opened it. When he read the words, his mouth dropped open. "You paid off my loans?" After the initial shock he thrust the receipt back at him. "I can't let you do this. It's going to cost me too much."

Dad shook his head. "Not this time, and it's too late. I've done it. I should have paid these off a long time ago. Maybe that's why all this time I hung on to the information I'd need to do it." He sighed. "You're right, Jackson. I need help. I have for a long time. I can't explain it, but when you left my office this morning, something finally clicked in here." He tapped his head. "Ashley dumped me because of my drinking. I don't want to keep hurting people because of that— especially you." He finally looked at Jackson. "I'm going to start going to some meetings, and I have a doctor's appointment tomorrow to figure out what else I can do to get my life together."

"What about the hotel?"

"I'm going to see Lois after I finish here. I'll get down on hand and knee if that's what it takes to get her to come back."

"You might have to give her a raise. A big one."

"Whatever it takes." He paused again. "I'm not asking you to come home. I don't think that would be a good idea for either of us until I get back on the right track. I was on the right track . . . once. When I met your mother. We had a few good years, she and I." His lower lip quivered. "The best thing about them was you, but I let my resentment over the divorce eat me alive. I'm sorry, son. For everything." Before Jackson could react, his father gave him a quick, hard hug and then walked away.

Jackson couldn't move. When was the last time his father hugged him? Tears came even though he tried to fight them off, and he watched his father's car pull out of the driveway. He looked at the loan payoff. If he didn't have the proof right here in his hands, he wouldn't believe what had just happened. *A miracle, that's what.* He looked up at the sky.

Chapter 24

The next day, Selah went to work, her nerves in overdrive. She kept telling herself that the family wanted her there, but she wasn't sure they wouldn't be angry with her for quitting. When she arrived, though, Nina gave her a hug, Delilah gave her a cinnamon roll, and Loren said, "Welcome back." Levi was nowhere to be found.

The women spent some time at the kitchen table discussing plans for the wedding—the food, the guests, the set up in the area along the side of the inn. The latter hadn't been fully landscaped yet, and probably wouldn't be by the time of the wedding, but they could do some things to the yard to make it look special.

Right before lunch, Nina jumped up from her chair. "The laundry! I forgot all about it."

Delilah frowned. "The clothes will all be wrinkled by now."

"I'll iron them, *Grossmutter*. Don't worry. But I better get them out on the line." She dashed out of the kitchen.

"Sometimes that *maedel* would forget her feet if they weren't attached to her body." Delilah turned to Selah. "I'm glad you decided to come back."

"I'm sorry I quit on short notice." She looked down at the table. "That wasn't right of me."

"Well, it all worked out for the best, didn't it?" She patted Selah's hand. "Now, we have some extra chairs in the shed behind the *haus*. I can't remember how many, though. Would you mind counting them? Then we can determine how many we still need for the guests. I also need to get with Cevilla and find out how many people from Richard's side will attend." She shook her head. "Never in *mei* life would I have thought I'd be planning a wedding for Cevilla Schlabach. God has a sense of humor."

Selah smiled, but she'd have to take Delilah's word for that. Nothing about her own life had been funny lately.

She went out to the backyard and found the shed. It was small, and she wondered how many chairs would fit in there along with the yard tools usually kept in a shed. Enough apparently for Delilah not to remember, but then the woman was in her seventies.

Selah opened the door to the shed and had walked inside before she realized Levi was there. She froze a few steps from the doorway as he turned a metal bracket in his hand, the kind used for wall shelving. As he looked up, the shed door closed behind her, leaving the two of them in the small room, the only light available streaming from the window near Levi.

"I'm sorry," she said, taking a step back. "I didn't know you were in here."

He quickly turned from her. "*Grossmutter* wanted me to clean up a little in here. Hang the rakes and shovels on the wall, put up some shelves, that kind of stuff."

"I'll come back later, then." She started to leave.

"What were you looking for?"

She turned. Hammer now in hand, he was positioning the bracket on the wall, not looking at her. "Chairs. Delilah said you have some in here, and she wanted me to see how many."

He frowned. "We keep the chairs in the basement." Levi gestured around the space. "We don't have room for them here, plus we have a lot. We bought some extra ones when we started renovating the inn."

"But I'm sure she said to check the shed." Unless she'd heard her wrong.

A click sounded behind her, and she turned toward the door. Levi moved past her and turned the knob. The door wouldn't budge. He tried again. "It can't be locked," he muttered. But when he tried to open the door once more, he still couldn't.

"We're locked in here?" Selah said.

"*Nee.*" He pushed on the door again. "The only way to lock this door is with a key, and I have the only one. Plus it has to be locked from the outside . . ." He smacked his forehead with the palm of his hand. "They didn't."

"Who didn't? What's going on, Levi?"

He turned to her. "I think Nina and *Grossmutter* locked us in here."

Levi pushed against the door again and then pounded his fist against it. Unbelievable. How could his sister and grandmother be so devious? Nina had to be the one to lock the door. Grandmother moved fast, but not that fast. Before he went into the shed, he saw his sister hanging clothes on the line, which was a fair distance from the shed. He'd thought it was odd that his grandmother had a list of chores for him to do this morning. "Make sure to do these in order," she'd insisted, giving him the *look,* which meant she would shut down any contrary discussion. He'd perused her instructions—clean the windows and screens, then the gutters, and then the shed, making sure to hang the garden tools on the walls.

And now Selah was here, looking for nonexistent chairs on his grandmother's orders. "Something fishy is going on here."

"Can we get out through the window?" Selah asked, her hands clasped together.

He shook his head. "It doesn't open. There's no sash or lock on it."

Her eyes widened. "Then how are we going to get out of here?"

"Hey." He went to her, stopping short of putting his arms around her—the worst possible thing he could do. "It's okay. I'm sure Nina will let us out in a few minutes."

"Why would she lock us in here?" Selah looked around the shed.

"Because *mei grossmutter* told her to." He knew he shouldn't have trusted *Grossmutter* to keep her promise not to meddle. Interfering was in her bones, and now she had gone over the top and dragged Nina with her. Then again, he had a feeling she didn't have to twist his sister's arm to get her to agree to this scheme. "I'm sorry."

"They want us in here together." She scowled. "Why?"

"Why do you think?" He crossed his arms over his chest. "So we'll work things out."

She walked to the back of the shed, which was only a few feet from where he was standing. "There's *nix* to work out."

"You and I know that. But they don't."

Selah turned around and put her hands behind her back. "What are we supposed to do while we wait?"

He rubbed the back of his neck. "We could yell and scream until *mei daed* hears us. Or Jackson." He was sure the two of them had no idea what *Grossmutter* and Nina were up to.

"And if they don't?" She bit her bottom lip.

"Are you claustrophobic?" The shed wasn't

that small, but considering she'd had a panic attack before . . .

"I'm not going to flip out, if that's what you mean," she snapped. Then she cleared her throat. "I'm not going to panic. I promise."

"I wouldn't judge you if you did," he said softly. "You're not the only person in the world to have a panic attack."

"You think I don't know that?" She blew out a breath. "This is so stupid. I can't believe we're stuck here like this." She leveled her gaze at him. "Together."

"Look, I'm not happy about it, either." Her little dig didn't get past him. "You can be crabby about it, or you can make *yerself* useful and help me hang some tools."

"That's *yer* job, not mine." She crossed her arms and didn't look at him.

He ground his back teeth. "It's not *mei* fault this happened. When we get out of here, you can give *mei familye* a piece of *yer* mind, but I'm not going to listen to you snap at me for the next hour or two or however long we're stuck in here."

"Hours?" She looked like a deflated swim raft. "I can't spend hours in here with you."

"The feeling's mutual, trust me."

"Ooh." Her fists clenched at her sides.

Levi wasn't going to put up with this. He grabbed his hammer, the bracket he'd been examining when Selah came in, and some nails.

Then he stood on a stool, almost pushing Selah out of the way. "What did I ever see in her?" he mumbled.

"I heard that."

He froze. He hadn't meant to say those words out loud. He slammed the hammer as hard as he could, ready to drive the nail—and his frustration—into the wall. He missed.

"Ahh!" he yelled. Then he wavered on the stool, losing his balance and dropping the hammer. He fell against Selah, and they both tumbled to the floor.

The wind blew out of Selah's chest when Levi fell on her. But he immediately rolled off her, and when she caught her breath, she sat up. He was curled in a lump on the floor, groaning.

"Levi?" She scrambled to him and put her hand on his shoulder. "Are you okay?"

"Barely," he croaked. "Are you?"

"*Ya.* Can you move? Did you break anything?" She moved closer to him, peering at his face over his shoulder. His eyes were shut, and he was holding his hand. "Levi, talk to me."

"I'm all right." He rolled toward her a little bit, and she moved away until he was flat on his back. "Good grief, that smarts."

"What hurts?"

"*Mei* thumb. I hit it with the hammer." The color drained from his face as he held up his hand. His thumb was already red and swollen, and there was no way to get any ice. Her anger toward Delilah and Nina grew. Locking the two of them together might have seemed like a joke to them, or even like they were doing a favor for her and Levi, but nothing could be further from the truth. Now Levi was injured. Now on her knees, she put her arm around his shoulders and tried to lift him to a seated position, which was difficult in the confined space.

"What are you doing?" he asked, giving her an odd look.

"Trying to help you sit up."

"I can do that myself." But he winced as he sat up and leaned his back against the shed wall. He held his hand in his lap, not looking at her. She scooted away from him, staring at the wood floor, which was covered in dirt and dust. Guilt and concern slammed into her. This was her fault—at least his thumb injury. She had been pushing his buttons on purpose, out of her own frustration. Would she ever stop dragging other people into her emotional issues?

After a few moments she couldn't take her conscience anymore. "I'm sorry," she said, her voice low.

"It's not *yer* fault." He leaned his head against the wall.

"Don't let me off the hook that easily. I was trying to get a rise out of you." She sat back, her legs tucked to the side, and stared at her lap, embarrassed.

"It's not like I didn't deserve it." He wiggled his thumb, wincing again. "I think I might have broken it."

She got up from the floor and looked around the shed, finding some pruning shears. She picked them up and cut a jagged piece of cloth from her apron.

"What are you doing now?" he asked, his brow lifted.

"Stabilizing *yer* thumb." She knelt next to him and wrapped his thumb the best she could. When he flinched as she tied the scrap of cloth together, she loosened the knot.

"*Danki*," he said.

"Does it feel better?" When she looked at him, he was staring at her, his green eyes not moving from her face.

"Some," he said, still gazing at her.

Her heart somersaulted, and as she usually did when her attraction to him overwhelmed her, she started to move away. But he touched her forearm with his good hand.

"Don't, Selah. You don't have to run from me."

"I'm . . . I'm not."

Levi gently squeezed her forearm. "You are. You have been since the first time we met."

"That's because you're *mei* boss."

He shook his head. "I'm not talking about that.

That first day, at Martha and Seth's wedding. You couldn't get away from me fast enough."

She saw the flash of hurt in his eyes. "That wasn't because of you."

"You could have fooled me." He released her arm. "Now it's *mei* turn to apologize. I always seem to cross the line when it comes to you. I can't help it. But I don't want you to be afraid of me. I don't want to be the reason you can't work here or that you feel uncomfortable around me."

"You're not," she whispered, sitting back on her heels. "I'm the problem."

"I'm the one who kissed you."

Selah met his gaze again. "I didn't exactly stop you, did I?"

His eyes darkened. "*Nee.* You didn't."

"But then you said the kiss didn't matter."

"That's because I'm an idiot." He moved until he was sitting directly in front of her. "Selah, when I'm around you, *mei* brain takes a vacation. I can't help it. You're beautiful and kind and smart, not to mention a little mysterious."

"And more than a little messed up." Her heart was warmed by his words, but she couldn't accept them entirely.

"Who isn't messed up?" He gave her a half-smile. "We all have our stuff, Selah."

"Not you, Levi."

"I just smashed *mei* thumb with a hammer and fell off a stool."

She shook her head. "That doesn't compare to . . ."

"I know." He took her hand and then looked into her eyes.

When she saw the questioning there, she nodded and squeezed his hand. "But you don't know. I haven't told you anything about *mei* problems . . . *mei* past."

"You don't have to. Selah, even though *mei* actions lately haven't shown it, I care about you. *Nix* you could tell me would change that."

"I have clinical depression." There. It was out now, like an open wound. And now that it was, she couldn't stop there. "Before I left Birch Creek, I ran away from Christian to be with *mei* English boyfriend. I thought he was the answer to all *mei* problems." She swallowed. "But he said I had to prove that I loved him. He wanted to . . ." She couldn't face Levi. "He wanted . . ."

Levi squeezed her hand. "I get it."

"When I wouldn't, he dumped me. I had nowhere to *geh* but back to *mei bruder*. I knew something was wrong with me—and not because he rejected me. He was a jerk, but I had *mei* own problems."

Levi's voice was low. "Sounds like you were better off without him."

"That was *mei* wake-up call to get help. I've been in therapy ever since. I take medication too. I didn't have it with me the night of the blizzard, and that's why I panicked. Now I have it with me at all times."

"Do you have it on you now?"

She shook her head. "It's in *mei* purse."

"Are you feeling panicked?"

Selah held on to his hand. "*Nee*. Not when I'm with you." She looked down at their hands clasped together. "Can you see why I keep *mei* distance? I don't make *gut* decisions when it comes to men. I get rattled sometimes. I can be mean when I'm angry, as you found out."

"And I'm dim-witted when it comes to women. I've made that painfully obvious. Although in *mei* defense, until you, I'd never met one who was worth getting dim-witted about. And I'll state it again—*nix* you can tell me could change *mei* feelings about you. Whatever problems we have, whether separate or together, we can work it out."

"We have to. We're coworkers."

Levi looked at her for a long moment and then pulled his hand away. "I guess I made another mistake." He sat back from her, pain in his eyes, and she knew it wasn't from his sore thumb. "I thought you felt something for me too."

Levi's heart ached more than his thumb, which was saying a lot, because his thumb was throbbing. How could he have been so wrong about Selah's feelings for him? Or lack of, apparently. He usually could read people well, but when it came to her, he failed time and time again.

Trying to gather his composure, he shrugged. Better to make light of things than to get into another argument. "But hey, I'm glad we cleared the air. Because you're right, we'll be working together, and we have to keep things professional between us—"

"Would you stop saying that?" She leaned toward him. "If I hear the word *professional* come out of *yer* mouth one more time, I might just . . ."

His heart hammered in his chest. "Might what?"

Her lips lifted in a saucy smile. "I might have to kiss you."

Now his heart was beating at light speed. "What?"

"You heard me." She moved closer, until they were nearly nose to nose. "Levi, you didn't make a mistake. Which annoys me a little since I make so many, but I think I can overlook that. I care about you. A lot."

"You do?"

"*Ya*," she said, sounding a bit breathless. Then she pulled back a little.

"What?" he said softly.

"I'm scared, Levi. Of what I feel for you. I'm not an easy person to deal with sometimes."

"That's not a problem. Easygoing is *mei* middle name. Sometimes I can be too easygoing, so it's good to have a *schee*, smart *maedel* to keep me on *mei* toes."

Her expression grew serious. "You really mean that?"

"I do." He leaned his head toward her. "I really, really do—"

A click sounded, and the door swung open. He and Selah scrambled away from each other so fast that a plastic flowerpot fell off the shelf above him and knocked him on the head.

"Are you okay?" Selah asked, and then she put her hand over her mouth. A giggle escaped, and she tried to keep a straight face. "You aren't hurt again, are you?"

"*Nee. Gut* thing that pot wasn't heavier."

"Levi? Selah?"

They both turned to see Nina walking into the shed, tentatively.

Levi scrambled to his feet. *"You,"* he said, marching toward her. He wasn't mad at her and *Grossmutter* anymore, but it wouldn't hurt for them to believe he was for at least a little while. It served them right. What if he and Selah were still fighting? What if they hadn't come close to kissing . . . Well, maybe it was a good thing Nina opened the door when she did.

"You're mad, aren't you?" Nina said, backing away. When he followed her out of the shed, she said, "I told *Grossmutter* and Cevilla this was a terrible idea."

"Then why did you *geh* along with it?" Selah moved to stand by Levi. Close by him, he noted with satisfaction.

"They said that was the only way to get you two to talk things out. Cevilla also said it worked for her and Richard."

"Someone locked them in together?"

"Not exactly." Nina looked from Levi to Selah. "You did talk things out, didn't you?" she said in a small voice.

"That's none of *yer* business." He took a step toward her, mustering a menacing look.

Nina sprinted away toward the house.

"Coward," he said, and then he laughed.

"You're being a little cruel, don't you think?"

He turned to Selah. "She's getting off lightly. Remind me to tell you about the time she put worms and frogs in *mei* bed. She was grounded for a week, while I got to eat all the rhubarb pie I wanted. Ah, good memories."

She smiled a little. "I don't have too many of those to look back on," she said. "You have a wonderful *familye*, you know that?"

He nodded and glanced back at the house. "*Ya*," he said. "I definitely do."

Over the next three weeks, the inn had a sudden influx of bookings, and so in addition to planning the wedding, Selah kept busy cleaning, doing laundry, and helping Nina and Delilah with the guests. After their encounter in the shed, Levi admitted that he'd applied for another job. But he gave up on that as April arrived. He had plenty of maintenance work around the inn and on the grounds.

Jackson had offered to leave the inn and find another place to stay, but Loren, who was now back to working full-time, and Delilah wouldn't hear of it. "Not until you can find a place that's decent," Delilah said. By the week before the wedding, he had not only found a nice apartment but had started working for a company in Barton as their IT person. "It's not my own business," he said, "but I can work at that on the side."

Although they were busy, Selah and Levi did find time to spend together, and she treasured every minute.

The Saturday before the wedding, Selah did some weeding and put some finishing touches on the landscaping. The weather was too cool and unpredictable to put out hanging flower baskets, but the daffodils and tulips were coming up, and the bushes needed some trimming. Levi had joined her, and while she pulled weeds, he added mulch on top of the dirt. He worked faster than she did, and eventually he was crouched next to her, helping her pull some particularly stubborn weeds. He leaned over to grab one, lost his balance, and knocked both of them over.

"Sorry," he said as she lay sprawled on the

ground, half in the grass and half in the flower bed.

"You did that on purpose!" she said, laughing.

He put his hands on both of her shoulders, hovering over her, and grinned. "Did not."

"I don't believe you."

"Have I ever lied to you?"

She stopped giggling, her expression growing serious, her eyes growing dark. "*Nee.* You haven't." She froze, unable to take her eyes off his. He was covered in dirt and mulch, and she imagined she didn't look much better. But that didn't matter. Nothing at that moment mattered but each other.

"I love you," he said.

"What?"

He frowned. "I . . . love you."

Selah froze again, unsure what to do but sure she was messing this up. Levi had just said he loved her, something she had dreamed about more than once lately, and all she could do was clam up.

Hurt crossed his face as he scrambled away from her. "Sorry," he mumbled. He turned and started yanking on the weeds, pulling out the stubborn things as though they were barely connected to the ground. "We should finish this up," he said, his tone brusque, his back still turned.

She couldn't let him continue to feel like he'd made a mistake or had misread her feelings. He knew and understood more about her than anyone she'd ever met, and the last thing she wanted was to hurt him.

Selah went to him and reached for his hand. She tugged on it, and they both got to their feet. Without a word she led him to the back of the yard, off to the side, which was going to be a private prayer garden for their guests—another one of her ideas. Right now it was a patch of tall grasses and weeds that would have to be mowed before the wedding.

She stopped when they were out of sight of the inn and the house. Her mouth was as dry as a desert as she looked up at him. "I'm not an easy person to live with," she said, her voice turning thick. "I've been cruel to others, Ruby and Christian in particular. But with God's help, I'm trying to do better." Tears ran down her face. "I wish I wasn't like this, Levi. I wish I could be happy and optimistic all the time like you are. I wish I could say I won't have periods when I'm down, when I'll fight the depression. I wish—"

"You don't have to be afraid." He kissed the top of her forehead.

She frowned. "I didn't say I was afraid."

"Then tell me you aren't."

She couldn't.

He took a step back. "Selah, you know how I feel about you. What I don't know for sure is how you feel about me. *Nee* excuses, *nee* sidetracking. Just honesty."

373

Selah touched the side of his face, running her thumb across the side of his jaw. "I think you already know."

"I want to hear the words."

Her fingers began to tremble. She had spent years stifling her feelings, banking the fortress around her heart. To tell Levi how she felt about him would bring the last of that stronghold down. There would be no turning back. She looked up into his eyes, the love she saw there washing over her like a soft ray of sunlight. How could she not tell him the truth?

"I love you, Levi." She moved close to him and put her arms around his neck. "I one hundred percent without a doubt love you."

He grinned, his hands touching the sides of her waist. "I knew it." Then he took her in his arms. "I've said this before," he murmured near her ear, "but whatever happens, we'll face it together."

"The eternal optimist," she said, leaning her cheek against his shoulder.

"*Nee*. A man who has faith."

Epilogue

"She's a *schee* bride, don't you think?"

Selah looked at Levi as he handed her a cup of cider. "The prettiest," she said. She sipped the drink as Levi winked at her before wandering off, always playing the gracious host. The scent of flowers wafted through the air, and it was a perfect day for a wedding. The ceremony had been held in the inn's lobby, cramped with guests, but no one minded. Richard's granddaughter, Meghan, had arrived two days earlier and helped with the last-minute preparations. Now she was talking with Jackson, which made sense. They were the only English people there.

Cevilla had told her Richard's daughter declined to attend. Selah hoped that whatever strife was going on between father and daughter would be patched up soon. She had seen a lot of miracles lately, and she had faith that God would work out their relationship for good.

The reception was outside on the lawn, which looked beautiful and perfect. Selah, Levi, and Nina, with some help from Meghan and Jackson, had worked overtime to get the grounds ready, and although the prayer garden still needed work, they had a good start on it. But the best news was that the inn was booked solid for the next three months—another miracle after so many challenges.

Not wanting to spend so much time on the sidelines, she mingled with the guests, spending extra time visiting with Martha. The two of them, while still close, hadn't spent much time together since Martha's wedding. Selah planned to rectify that. A few months ago, she'd felt like an outsider in Birch Creek. Now she was part of the community.

When the festivities were over, she helped with the cleanup. It was nearly dark, and she was tired but happy. Seeing Cevilla and Richard's joy was contagious.

"You look happy," Levi said, coming up to her as she folded a tablecloth.

"I am. Turns out I like putting on weddings."

"Oh, you do?" Levi grinned and put his arms around her waist.

"Levi, what if someone sees?"

"Everyone's gone home, except for *familye*. And it's not like they haven't figured out what's going on. Although to *Grossmammi*'s credit, she hasn't said a word."

"I think she learned her lesson."

"Not to interfere? That's a miracle in itself."

"One of many."

He grew serious. "*Ya*. One of many." He gave her a quick hug and then let her go. "So you like planning weddings, *ya*?"

"I do." She picked up another tablecloth. "Maybe we can start hosting more, like we talked about."

"Richard, Jackson, and Meghan already said they would spread the word. We just have to make sure we don't book one the second week of May."

"Why? Do we have an event I don't know about?"

"*Ya.*" He took her hand, his heart in his eyes. "Our wedding."

She dropped the tablecloth, not caring if it landed on the ground.

"What do you say, Selah? Will you marry me?"

She thought about her plan—living on her own, being single for the rest of her life. That had been all she'd wanted a few months ago. Now all she wanted was standing right in front of her, waiting for her answer.

Selah kissed him. "*Ya*, Levi. I'll marry you."

"I think we should add a condition to that," he said.

"What?"

"Cevilla, Delilah, and Nina have to organize the wedding." He winked.

She nodded and hugged him. *Serves them right.* Although they both knew the three of them wouldn't mind doing that one bit. "Sounds like a plan to me."

Acknowledgments

I always thank my fabulous editors, Becky Monds and Jean Bloom, for their invaluable help when I write a book. But in the case of *The Innkeeper's Bride*, they need a double portion. Thank you both for putting up with changing deadlines and heavy edits. I've also learned not to try to write a book so soon after shoulder surgery. ☺

Thank you to my agent Natasha Kern for checking in with me during my recovery and giving me support. Thank you for always being in my corner.

Another big thanks to Cheryl Connors for sharing with me all of her innkeeping expertise. Who knew I would have so much fun writing about an inn? (She probably did!)

And as always, thank you dear reader. I hope you enjoy Levi and Selah's story, and that your heart is warmed that Cevilla found her happy ending.

Discussion Questions

1. Selah tends to catastrophize things—she makes them bigger and more dramatic than they really are. What advice would you give her to curb this behavior?

2. The Amish are known for their hospitality, even when they aren't running an inn. What are some ways you show hospitality to others?

3. Has anyone ever pressured you to do something against your values, the way Jackson's father pressured him? How did you handle it?

4. When Jackson stays at the inn, he talks to the Stolls about "unplugging." What is your opinion about the technology that fills our lives? Are we too connected or not?

5. In what ways do you think technology makes our lives harder rather than easier?

6. Selah realized she had to turn her fears over to God. Discuss a time when you found yourself having to do the same thing.

7. Both Cevilla and Delilah were impatient when it came to their loved ones. What do you do when you become impatient about something important to you?

8. Do you agree with Levi when he tells Jackson that "We must always forgive"? Explain your answer.

About the Author

With over a million copies sold, Kathleen Fuller is the author of several bestselling novels, including the Hearts of Middlefield novels, the Middlefield Family novels, the Amish of Birch Creek series, and the Amish Letters series as well as a middle-grade Amish series, the Mysteries of Middlefield.

Visit her online at KathleenFuller.com
Instagram: kf_booksandhooks
Facebook: WriterKathleenFuller
Twitter: @TheKatJam

Books are produced in the United States using U.S.-based materials

Books are printed using a revolutionary new process called THINKtech™ that lowers energy usage by 70% and increases overall quality

Books are durable and flexible because of Smyth-sewing

Paper is sourced using environmentally responsible foresting methods and the paper is acid-free

Center Point Large Print
600 Brooks Road / PO Box 1
Thorndike, ME 04986-0001 USA

(207) 568-3717

US & Canada:
1 800 929-9108
www.centerpointlargeprint.com